I0748056

WOLF'S FATE

USA TODAY BESTSELLING AUTHOR

EVE L. MITCHELL

COPYRIGHT @ EVE L. MITCHELL 2024
WOLF'S FATE
by Eve L. Mitchell

All Rights Reserved

This book is intended for the purchaser of this book ONLY. No part of this book may be reproduced, distributed, or transmitted in any form or by any electronic or mechanical means, including photocopying, recording, information storage, and retrieval systems, without prior written permission from the author, except for the use of brief quotations in a book review.

Copyright infringement is against the law, please do not abuse the hard work of the author.

This book is a work of fiction. Any references to real events, people, and places are used fictiously. Any resemblance to any person, living or dead, or events or occurrences, is purely coincidental. The characters and storylines within this book are created by the author's imagination and are used fictitiously.

Cover design provided by Anna Spies @ Atra Luna Graphic Design.

Editorial services provided by Helayna Trask with Polished Perfection.

WOLF'S FATE

Willow Harper thought she was finally beginning to understand the world she'd been thrust into—a world where she's connected to the enigmatic shifter Caleb Foster. But Caleb has vanished, leaving Willow vulnerable and alone.

The longer Caleb stays away, the more dangerous his absence becomes—not just for him, but for *her*. Other shifters, drawn to her for reasons she can't explain, are closing in.

She knows severing their bond may be her only hope, yet the deeper their connection grows, the harder it becomes to let go— especially when her feelings for him are anything but simple.

Hunted by dangerous enemies and haunted by the lingering bond to a man who's no longer there to protect her, Willow must find Caleb before it's too late. Together, they'll have to face the threat to her and, perhaps, confront the darkest parts of Caleb's past.

But with each day that Caleb stays away, they risk not only losing each other—but everything they're fighting for.

ONE

Willow

"I THINK I NEED TO HAVE SEX WITH MY HUSBAND."

Coughing on my water, I sprayed my canvas as I choked out a laugh. "Lorna!" I looked at the older woman, who was frowning at the canvas in front of her. I quickly dabbed at my canvas before the water did too much damage.

Lorna glanced up at me and then at Peter, who seemed to be eager for an explanation. I saw her blush and then, with a slight shrug of her shoulders, I watched her shake off her doubts.

"What do you see on the table?" she demanded of Peter, my other art student.

"Um..." He cast a quick look at me before he answered. "Fruit."

Lorna nodded triumphantly, her expression one of someone who just won a major argument. "Fruit. *Exactly*." She frowned at me. Motioning for me to come over, she pointed at her canvas in accusation. "I painted a cock and balls."

Peter got off his stool, and the three of us gathered around

1

her easel. I tried to hold back my laughter because I was her teacher, not her humiliator, but it was very hard because she had indeed painted something very close to resembling male genitalia.

Moving closer, I looked around her easel to the small table with the offending fruit in the center—some apples, a couple of bananas, and an orange. They were arranged innocuously. Standing back, I met her expectant look. "Well...it seems that your subconscious is telling you something."

Lorna's hands flew to her cheeks, and Peter narrowly missed getting her paintbrush in his eye. Seeing his overly dramatic jerk of his head away from her, I started giggling.

"Oh my," Lorna murmured, her eyes still glued to her artistic offering. Leaning forward, she let out a grunt of dissatisfaction. "I didn't even use artistic license," she grumbled. "That looks to scale."

I automatically looked again, and then I cracked up when I saw her impish smile.

My watch vibrated against my wrist, and I lost my smile a little. "Okay, you two, lesson's over." With a mock scowl at Lorna, I shook my finger. "You're lucky I don't give out detention."

Lorna huffed as she got off her stool. "I'm old enough to be your mother," she reminded me.

"Who paints pornography." Peter chuckled, packing his paints away.

Lorna, who was on her way to the sink to wash her brushes, gave a small curtsy in acknowledgement. "I didn't get two boys delivered from the stork, you know."

The petite mother of two and Peter fell into easy, familiar

banter as they tidied up their workstations. I half listened to them as I covered my own easel and watched the seconds tick past on my watch.

After a few more minutes, they both hugged me—Peter's lasting a bit longer than it should, as usual—and left with a promise to see me on Thursday. Once they were gone, I tidied up their tidying up, a small smile on my face as I did so.

When I checked my watch again, I lost any humor I may have had. Walking over to the small sales counter, I waited.

Right on time, they both walked into my store. One russet-haired and brawny, the other leaner but just as fierce.

"Willow," Royce greeted me with a warm smile. "How are you?" His gaze darted over my face, seeing things that makeup failed to hide from someone like him. "You look tired," he added sympathetically.

"Hi, Royce. Hi, Ned." Ned gave me a simple nod. He was usually quiet, although today I saw his attention land on Lorna's piece, and his lips twitched.

That small smile relaxed me, even if it wasn't for me. It reinforced my belief that Ned was just stern and I shouldn't take his grim demeanor personally. He saw me watching him, and I tried not to bristle as his gaze swept over me, his frown returning.

"You look like shit."

My smile was as brittle as I felt. "It's always a pleasure to see you."

I heard Royce's huff of laughter from the other side of the room, where he was admiring the new art on my walls.

"My wife would love that," he told me, pointing to the painting. It was of a messy coffee table, littered with an open journal, a coffee mug, and some fresh-cut flowers lying beside them waiting for a vase, or maybe waiting to be hand-tied with the length of pink ribbon lying over the table, twisting and turning as it lay strewn across the contents and the lightly checked tablecloth. A simple wooden spindle-backed chair sat half pulled away from the table, giving the impression that the person dealing with the flowers had just left their seat.

"You like it?" I asked him, walking to stand beside him.

"I like the way you use light," Royce told me, and I could hear the sincerity of his words. "It's clever. It's more than just adding shadow or using light to draw the eye to the main focus; it's the way you add depth and emotion to your work." He pointed at one of the fatter curls of the ribbon. "See, here, the light is skimming along the edge. The source of the light is directional, but if you don't look closer, you won't see the shadow on the same piece where the edge is frayed and worn. You highlight the superficial but see the depth when you look closer." He gave me an appreciative glance. "As I said, clever. You tell a story with it and what the overall piece is."

Wow. I had expected a "yes," maybe a follow-up, generic comment. Instead, I got an in-depth compliment, which I hadn't been expecting.

"Thank you," I told him honestly. "That means a lot." I knew I was blushing furiously, and Royce patted my shoulder as he saw my struggle to accept the compliment.

"We done bonding?" Ned asked from behind us.

I probably wouldn't have heard the low huff of displeasure if I hadn't been beside Royce.

"Don't be an ass," Royce said with a hard look. He turned

to me once more. "But he is right, we should move." His eyes flicked to the storage cupboard. "Anything new?"

I almost laughed. Instead, I went and opened the door. I heard someone's mutter, but it was too low to make out.

"All of this?" Ned asked doubtfully.

"Yup." I stepped back as Ned moved in front to start lifting out the artwork.

"You've been busy," he told me, and had I not gotten accustomed to him over these last weeks, I may have said his look was one of concern.

"Willow?" Royce, on the other hand, was looking at me with concern. "This is too much." His hand gestured to the pile. "You need to rest. Your illness..."

"Is *my* illness," I spoke quickly. "I'm fine." I watched Ned flicking through my work. They would check whatever I had created and then filter through the ones that had anything related to their world. They'd been doing this every week since I met them, and so far, they'd only ever handed me one sketch back. Everything else, they took, their frowns becoming deeper every visit.

It had been three weeks since that day Caleb walked away and never looked back. I'd been left in the town on Blackridge Peak with a pissed-off alpha, a shaman, and a doctor who was more interested in studying *me* than the fact that Caleb had vanished off the face of the earth...mountain...whatever.

"Thirty," Ned said with a grunt, his look assessing. "I think you need to rethink the offer of being with us."

I was already shaking my head. "No, I don't need to move to your *pack*." I saw the flat look. "I'm not part of your...community. I already put you at risk by this." I waved my hand over the pile. "I think that's enough. I don't need to be closer to you." I gave them both a self-deprecating look. "I still need to sleep *sometime* after all."

"You think you would see more if you were amongst us?" Royce said with understanding.

"I do." I saw their looks and felt the panic building. "Please don't tell Cannon this," I asked them both. I saw the look they shared, but they both nodded their agreement. However, I only believed Royce would keep quiet. Ned would tell Cannon. I also saw the younger man knew exactly what I was thinking, and for the first time, I saw *him* break our stare as he looked away with, if I didn't know better, what would've appeared to be guilt.

"This is..."

I looked over at Royce, and I knew which sketch he was focused on. Walking over, I looked at what he was holding.

"I wish I knew what caused him this pain," I admitted quietly. The sketch was of Caleb—when was it not?—sitting in front of that large log cabin I'd drawn months ago, a place now as familiar to me as my own home. He was looking to the left, his chin in his hand as he stared at some point in the landscape beyond my vision.

What caught our attention wasn't where he was or what he was looking at, but how he looked. His jeans were ripped and torn, his chest bare, with three long scratches barely visible— just enough to leave us wondering how bad they were. His hair was longer, unkept, strands falling over his face and obscuring his features, though bruises and scratches still peeked through. And yet, despite the clear signs of violence on his body, the overall impression of him could only be described as tortured.

I felt Ned as he looked over my shoulder. "Looks like he fought a bear," he said with interest.

"A bear?" I asked with alarm.

"It's not the bear he's fighting," Royce said with a sad shake of his head. He exchanged a look with Ned. "Cannon needs to try again."

Ned snorted. "He would if he could find him."

"Find him?" I looked between them both. "He's right there." I pointed at the cabin. "He's always there," I added softly.

"Until a shifter takes a step onto Shadowridge Peak," Ned corrected me gruffly. "Then he's gone."

"Then *find* him," I demanded, my exasperation seeping through. "You are supposed to be hunters. Go hunt."

Royce gave a low chuckle. "We *are* hunters, but it's a different game when the prey knows how to hunt as well."

"Or better," Ned conceded.

"So what you're saying is...you can't find him because he's hiding from you too well?" I asked incredulously.

Royce gave me an indecipherable look. "I don't think he's hiding," he told me. "He's just not ready to be found."

Which sounded like hiding to me. I returned my attention to the picture of Caleb. "Stalk his ass until you get him," I demanded. Reaching for my artwork, I flipped through them. "You have *all* the locations—stake him out."

"Stake?" Royce asked curiously. He made a stabbing motion with his hand. "Stake him with a knife or with binoculars like a spy?"

"Yes! Have someone there until the stubborn bastard turns up."

They both looked at me with sympathy. "It's not that easy," Royce reminded me, for what felt like the ten thousandth time.

"He's dangerous," Ned added, as if I needed reminding—which I didn't. I just had a hard time believing it.

Or if I was honest with myself, it wasn't that I didn't believe it, it was that I didn't *accept* it.

"I think you both underestimate him," I grumbled, busying myself with bundling up my work.

"And I think you should trust our judgment on this," Ned snapped back. "You're seeing it through emotion, and we're seeing it through experience."

I clenched my jaw to stop myself from having the same old argument. The fact that I was used to arguing with this man should have been a sharp reminder of how bizarre my life had become.

Royce was also used to us and had already taken the bundled items off me. "Ned, get the truck," he ordered, and I saw the conspiratorial wink he gave me. When Ned left, I mumbled my thanks, which Royce waved off. "Got two kids at home; I'm used to the squabbling." He looked around my store, checking he hadn't missed anything. "I'd prefer it if I only heard the squabbling at home."

"Then stop bringing Ned," I suggested without thinking and was grateful when Royce laughed. "Sorry." Pushing my hair behind my ear, I looked away from Royce as I struggled to try to find words. "He doesn't know him. He's not the person Ned thinks he is."

Royce said nothing, but the sympathy in his eyes told me he was on the same page as Ned—just not as vocal about it. He left soon after, and once again, I was alone in my shop with the familiar feeling of frustration that surfaced every time they came.

With a sigh, I forced myself to resume cleaning up. I could dwell or I could try to be productive. Easier said than done. Several times, I caught myself motionless as I stared into nothing, thinking about the last few months.

Nothing was the same after Caleb came into my life, yet as I looked around my gallery and teaching area of my store, somehow everything was the same.

Except me.

And possibly my friendship with Lily. She was still unforgiving in my "vanishing act" as she called it. It didn't help that when I returned, I was reluctant to talk about where I had been or what had happened. I refused to discuss Caleb, so Lily, being Lily, had firmly settled on the incorrect assumption that he had his wicked way with me, and then once he got what he wanted, he left.

Lily and I were still close, but the speculative look in her eye when she thought I wasn't looking was an unwelcome one. We'd agreed to not talk about it, which is where the crack between us was slowly widening into a wedge, and I feared it may grow bigger still as we drifted apart.

She knew nothing about my visits from Royce or the others. Now that she worked out at her dad's lumber mill, the only time I would see her through the day was the occasional lunch hour. Those that we could work around, and by we, I meant me and the shifters who frequented my store to remove the paintings or drawings that I had created of Caleb or their world.

Their world.

The world where men and women *shifted* into wolves. Into

animals. Animals that hunted like the wolves in nature, only there was nothing *natural* about shifters. Supernatural beings that were infused with magic from their Goddess Luna.

I still felt guilty when I thought of another *being* that wasn't God. It could be the Catholic in me, or it could be the fact that my human brain wasn't equipped to deal with the whole theological argument. How was Luna any different from Buddha, or the teachings of Hinduism or Jainism? Their religion wasn't the religion that my foster parents had instilled in me, but who was I to say it was wrong?

"They change into animals," I grumbled to myself. "So?" It was the same old argument I kept replaying, and the fact that it was always with myself didn't make it any easier. "You change into a zombie when the ME is bad."

Yeah, it wasn't the same and I knew it. While I may feel like death during an ME episode, I wasn't an *actual* animated corpse. I thought about when Caleb had to carry me up the mountain. Perhaps the jury was still out on that, I joked to myself, but no matter how much I tried to lighten my thoughts, the fact was that I was human.

And Caleb was not.

Caleb... It all came back to Caleb. *I* kept going back to Caleb, only I hadn't seen him since he walked out on all of us. I hadn't heard a word from him. All I had was the gnawing feeling of doubt and failure.

The feeling that *I* had somehow failed *him*.

TWO

Willow

AFTER LOCKING UP THE STORE AROUND FOUR, I BEGAN THE walk home. I'd always managed my illness well, or so I thought. But since meeting Caleb and being introduced to Doc, I'd adopted a more, shall we say, structured approach to my health.

Doc had more or less replaced my physician, which was great on one hand for costs, but on the other, he was *way* more involved than what I was used to. I had meal plans, workout regimes, including minimum exercise minutes per day, a sleep journal... It was a lot.

I couldn't really complain—though clearly I was since I was complaining right now—because, in truth, I did feel better. Doc wasn't an imposing man. He was almost fully human; he didn't have the bulging muscles or the *solid* look about him like the others. He was lean, average height, and could blend easily in a crowd. However, when the crowd was one of shifters, I bet he stood out.

No, Doc wasn't like them—and yet somehow, I followed his health plan religiously. He didn't scare me. I didn't know him

11

well enough to disappoint him. Yet, I couldn't shake the feeling that I would get punishment if I didn't stick to his plan. He reminded me of a stern headmaster. Content when I was compliant, but one foot wrong and I would be writing lines until the end of time.

Lily had taken note of the change in my health plan, and while she hadn't said much, she obviously approved.

In truth, so did I. I noticed a difference in my energy levels. I had an appetite, and with the exercise and calorie management, I was actually gaining some weight and strength. My normal walk home, which used to take about thirty minutes, was now carried out in twenty. More importantly, I could walk home and back without overdoing it.

I'd had a few spells of ME since my return because, while Doc could tell me what to do and when to eat, he couldn't control my sleep pattern. He couldn't stop me from seeing what I saw when I closed my eyes.

He couldn't put an end to the insights I had into his world.

Once more, my mind had come back to Caleb.

Always, always Caleb.

He wasn't even that good-looking. *Liar.*

He was grumpy. *True.*

He was a terrible conversationalist. *Not true, he just kept certain things from you.*

He was a liar.

That one I didn't need my internal monologue to repeat, which I already knew. Caleb had told me himself that he lied. He'd warned me. Repeated it several times throughout our time traveling to meet Cannon and the others.

Our short time together had been fraught with nothing but

adversity, with a few scatterings of amicable times. Caleb Foster was not someone I *should* miss, but I did.

A lot.

I also worried about him, because although Cannon or the shaman would tell me *where* he had gone, they didn't tell me *why*. I knew that they knew. I knew it was bad. I knew that his being alone was not good for him. They hadn't needed to tell me that—I drew it every day, sometimes more than once, just like I had the afternoon that Doc put the sketchbook in my hands and told me to show them.

He was on a mountain. I didn't know which one that was called Shadowridge Peak. I had googled it, but I wasn't surprised to find no search results. I assumed it was a mountain with a peak. Didn't all mountains have peaks? I knew it wasn't near them, but I thought it was still in Colorado. Maybe. Or Wyoming, or Idaho, or Montana...or any of the states that housed the Rockies.

If he was even still in the Rockies. Or in America.

My head hurt thinking about it. About him. But how could I not? The need to draw him, to catch glimpses of him, to know that he was safe, it was constant.

The other constant thing was the darkness descending on him.

Don't get me wrong. No one would ever describe Caleb as fluffy or light—the thought alone made me giggle—but he wasn't exactly *dark* either. He was still approachable. Kind of. He wouldn't hurt you. Much. Chewing my lip, I tried to stop my negativity. But it was so hard because I was severely pissed off with him.

I could still see him walking away and *never looking back.*

I wanted to lie, even to myself, and say that I didn't remember everything in the chaos that ensued, but I did. I remembered it all. Running to the door, screaming into the emptiness for him, and silence was my only answer. After I went back into the room, a sketchbook was thrust into my hands, and I was told to draw.

And I had.

I had drawn it all.

"Show us, Willow," Doc told me. "Show us what we've done."

I hadn't been able to keep hold of the pen. I'd dropped it, and then after the second or third sketch, I wished I'd been able to drop it again, but my grip had been firm, and there was a better chance of Caleb coming back than me letting go of that pen.

The sketches were full of pain. Brimming with anger. Saturated in hate.

Scenes of death, human and wolf alike. Caleb was featured in them all, appearing as I had never seen him.

Savage and brutal.

In others, he was a wolf. I had never seen him when he was shifted, but as I sketched, I knew the gray wolf was him. Blood dripped from his maw, his eyes narrowed in a mix of anger and loathing.

Was it self-loathing? Had he been attacked? The casualties were high, and though I knew little of their world, I doubted it was so densely populated that they could afford such losses.

The men who witnessed my drawing were silent as Doc took scene after scene off me. The shaman had seen as much as he could, and once during my frenzied production, he had requested to taste my blood. He'd asked again before he left, and by then, I was too spent to protest.

Or ask what my blood told him that my sketches could not.

No one answered that question when I asked it the next day. There was a lot that Cannon and his men didn't say.

Maybe they couldn't? Maybe they didn't know? But I didn't believe that. The alpha, Cannon, knew. I saw the truth in his eyes, and I was certain he knew everything—he just chose not to tell me.

Which left me with notebooks, sketch pads, canvases—anything I could draw on—filled with scenes that offered no answers, only adding to my growing list of unanswered questions.

I'd also learned not to ask. I wasn't scared of them. I thought of the large alpha, who had stepped in front of me and told Caleb to go. Cannon was definitely intimidating. Like I had with the shaman, once I opened my eyes and paid attention to what was in front of me, I could sense the power of the alpha.

Doc had told me it was something they called Will. Apparently, an alpha could use their Will and make a shifter do something. Like compulsion but without the brainwashing, although they did remove the element of free will. Which was kind of freaking terrifying, but I'd kept my thoughts to myself on that one.

Despite that though, I didn't feel fear with them. I was slightly uncomfortable, I wouldn't lie, but I wasn't there against my will.

I'd reached home, and checking my watch, I grinned at my straight-up twenty minutes. Yeah, I could say what I wanted about the shifters or Doc, but without him, I wouldn't have been walking home in twenty minutes *and* still feel fresh and fit enough to turn right around and walk back.

As I opened my front door, the thought of turning around and walking back was exactly what I wanted to do. Instead, I took a step into the chaos that used to be my home.

The sound of the door snicking on the latch made me jump, but it didn't have the power to tear my eyes from the broken and torn furniture in my living room.

Walking a few steps broke my trance, and I pulled my phone from the back pocket of my jeans. Unwrapping my scarf from around my neck, I dialed 9-1-1 and immediately hung up. I didn't know anyone who would do this. I knew that wasn't the point, but given what I had been drawing recently, I was already picking my way carefully over the mess to my studio.

A part of me wished I hadn't. Everything was destroyed. Sketchbooks were ripped and torn, and canvases had been sliced viciously with knives.

Or claws.

With trembling fingers, I pressed the contact button on Royce's name.

"Willow?"

"My house has been broken into." Saying it out loud made it real, and I felt the tears spill over. "Everything"—my breath hitched—"everything is ripped, torn or broken. I haven't been into my bedroom," I admitted in a whisper.

"You haven't checked every room?" he demanded roughly, and I understood what he had just implied—they could still be here. I heard him speak to someone else, Ned probably. They wouldn't be home yet. I couldn't hear what he said over the thudding in my ears. My heart was close to bursting with fear.

"My bedroom and the bathrooms," I suddenly remembered to speak. I was pretty sure Royce asked me what rooms I hadn't been in.

"Luna, Willow!" he scolded. "That's half your house!"

I was nodding in agreement, pointless because he couldn't see me, but I was completely numb. "I'm calling Caleb."

"Will—"

I cut him off when I hung up. Still unmoving, I searched for his name and pressed the call button.

When the automated voice told me the number was no longer in service, I hung up and dialed again. I did it three more times before my brain finally sent the message to my fingers to stop wasting my time.

Part of me knew I needed to open the bedroom door and see what they had done to it. Part of me knew that I would never unsee it, and I wasn't sure that I could handle it.

So I checked the bathroom first. Thankfully, my cabinet and my shower curtain were the only things damaged. The cabinet wasn't even damaged, it was only my guest towels and toilet paper that were strewn about.

Closing the mirrored cabinet door, I caught sight of my reflection. What a difference a home invasion made. I'd been smiling, confident, *happy* with myself when I walked home. Now I looked haggard. My eyes were wide with fear, my skin whiter than pale.

The sudden ringing of my phone made me scream in fright, and it clattered into the sink as I dropped it. Scooping it back out, it took me two attempts to answer it.

"Royce?" I stared at my reflection as I answered the call.

I heard his huff of relief. "Is the house clear?" he demanded.

"I haven't gone into my bedroom."

"Why hav—" I heard him cut himself off as he took a deep breath. "Willow, are you armed?"

I saw the surprise on my face as he asked the question. If I'd ever wondered in the past how I would react in a stressful situation, the answer seemed to be *stares at herself in the mirror.*

"Willow?"

His sharp voice brought me back to the present. Again. "No!" I lowered my voice. Stupid really. If they were still here, they heard me the moment I came home. "I don't...don't have a gun."

"That's fine. I wouldn't expect you to. Get a knife."

A knife? That meant I would need to be close to them. Suddenly a gun seemed more appealing, and now I knew I had lost any sense of normality because I was considering the benefits of buying a gun.

"Willow, go to the kitchen and pick up the biggest knife you can." His tone was calm and patient. It made me feel normal. Caleb would have shouted, which would have also been welcome.

"Okay."

Once I was armed, Royce asked me if the back door was broken or damaged, and when I told him no, I could almost *hear* the look he would have shared with Ned.

"This wasn't Caleb," I told them, walking to my bedroom door.

"Willow—"

"I know him." It was my turn to talk over Royce. "I know when he's been here. This isn't him. I'd feel it."

"Or she's delusional because she's in love with him." Ned's snort of contempt and low murmur probably wasn't meant for me to hear, but that didn't mean I didn't.

"I'm not in love with him." I was outside my closed bedroom door. "Do I open it?"

"Yes." Royce hadn't become distracted from the situation at hand. "Don't be a hero," he added.

If that was his advice, I should have gone back outside and called the police. Not gone and got a knife and then lingered in my hallway, bracing myself for whatever, or *whoever*, was inside my bedroom.

"I'll never be the hero," I whispered, realizing I needed a hand to open the door, and my options were to let go of either the phone or the knife. I stared at the chef's blade in my hand and could hear Caleb in my head, telling me that I was more likely to cut myself with it than anyone else.

Bending low, I placed the knife on the floor.

Straightening, I put my phone in my back pocket, still on the call to Royce. My door swung open slowly, and had I not been in this moment, I would have remarked on the added dramatic effect. However, right now, it only added to the building anticipation that there was someone in my house waiting to kill me behind this door.

There wasn't.

There was, however, a clear indication of how they had gained access to my house, because my bedroom window was open as far as it would go. Like my studio, everything was shredded. Literally shredded in this room. Feathers from my duvet still floated in the air, and I knew that it was because I'd just opened the door.

I didn't check my bathroom because I knew I was alone. I wished I'd known that before I called for help. I would have still called, but I wouldn't have had to admit I hadn't checked my house first. But then curiosity got the better of me to see if they had done anything in here. The bathroom cabinet hung off the wall, it had my hygiene products in it. Tylenol and tampons covered the floor I wasn't sure what my sanitary products could have possibly been hiding, but I stooped to pick up the discarded tampons from the floor.

Remembering they were waiting for me to confirm my situation, I fished the phone out of my pocket. "There's no one here."

"You need to call the police."

"You don't want to come here? See it?" I felt weirdly disappointed.

"We're coming," Royce confirmed. "But you need to call the police and report this." He let that sink in. "Have they taken anything?"

The only thing I had of value was my laptop, and it was with me, as it was the one I used for work. The only other thing of value that I owned that had a monetary worth was the paintings they'd destroyed.

"I don't think so."

"Okay. Call the police. Then wait for us. We're on our way back."

"Okay."

I don't remember much of my phone call with the police. Whispering Pines had a small police department. I wouldn't even have been able to say which officer I spoke to, but I didn't think they asked me anything too strenuous.

They told me not to touch anything, and despite knowing better because I lived in this town, I felt a pang of disappointment when no CSI arrived at the crime scene.

Royce and Ned arrived just before the cops were leaving, and I sighed with relief when I saw them. They didn't stop, merely circled my block. When the police were gone, I opened the back door to my two visitors.

Royce walked past me, Ned close on his heels, and I dutifully followed them to the studio.

"I'd taken everything to the store," I informed them. "There was nothing of danger here."

Royce looked relieved, but Ned was still watching me. "*All* your drawings of Caleb were at the store?"

It's amazing how quickly you could go off someone. "No." There was no point in lying.

Ned nodded, brushing past me on his way to my bedroom. He saw the knife on the floor, but despite the look that told me he knew *exactly* what I had done, he didn't comment.

He took one look at the bedroom and turned to ask me a question that I hadn't even thought of.

"Have you checked the store?"

THREE

Willow

WE RODE IN SILENCE TO THE STORE. ROYCE KEPT checking on me in the rearview on the short drive, but I didn't meet his look. I didn't know what to do. This was my life. Whoever had done this was messing with all I had.

I was no one. *No one.*

At the store, I saw the door was intact, but still, I held my breath as I pushed the door tentatively open. Ned gave a huff of impatience, picking me up and moving me out of the way, ignoring my squawk of complaint. He and Royce walked in ahead of me, and my indignant protest faded on my lips as my eyes darted around my store.

Papers were scattered, and the easels with Lorna's and Peter's works in progress were knocked over and looked like someone, or someones, had walked over them. The small sales counter I had, with one drawer, was knocked over completely, and one of the doors to the inner shelves was hanging off broken.

I was aware Royce was talking to Ned, but I couldn't hear

them. My attention was on the artwork that was on display to sell.

Each piece had been ravaged, four deep tears ran from left to right on each piece. I had a wild flashback to the film franchise with Freddy Krueger, and I couldn't shake the image from my head as I imagined the shifter who had been here, ripping their claws into the art as they walked in a slow and steady prowl from one end of my display wall to the other.

Deliberately.

Because that was what this was—a *deliberate* warning to me. There was no art here that showed their world; Royce and Ned had already removed it.

Had they known that? Had they known that it was gone?

I didn't know what to do. Ned was in my storage closet, which was as empty as they'd left it this morning. Royce was on the phone, his voice too low for me to hear. My hands were shaking as I tried to tidy up, reaching for one of the easels and lifting it to set it right, but the legs were broken, and it had no stability.

I let it fall again, jumping at the sound of the impact as it fell back to the floor. Looking around my store, I felt disconnected. Here was a mess, and my house was worse. What had they been looking for? What had they hoped to achieve by leaving this obvious mark that they'd been here?

Was it simply to instill fear? If it was, it was working.

Royce was speaking to me, but I couldn't hear what he was saying. His voice was distorted. I felt like I was underwater, and I couldn't breathe. My movements felt sluggish. My mind was swirling as I thought of too many scenarios of "what-ifs."

I was against the wall, but my knees were weak, and I slid

down to the floor, pulling my knees to my chest, trying to make myself as small as possible. My left hand clutched my phone, and I just wanted to call Lily. I wanted someone I trusted to sit beside me and tell me it was going to be okay.

I wanted Caleb.

The urge to call him was as strong as it was useless. His phone was disconnected. *He* was disconnected. From me. From the world. He wasn't the person who was going to be here for me. Even though he had dragged me into his world, he'd left me in it.

Tears burned my eyes, and I rubbed my eyes furiously. I would *not* cry. I was *not* weak. I needed to take a moment, and with a deep breath, I pushed myself to my feet.

"You okay?"

Turning my head, I saw Ned in front of me. He looked concerned. "No." The answer was honest, and I saw his understanding. "But I won't fall apart."

"You just had a panic attack."

"Sue me." I looked over at Royce, who was still on the phone. "Cannon?"

"Yeah, he wants you on Blackridge Peak."

I snorted. "No, he doesn't," I told him, my voice sounding harsh, my shock probably still overriding my normal manners. "He wants me as far from shifters as possible." Looking around, I let out a deep sigh. "I don't want that either."

"You don't understand," Ned's voice was tight. "Caleb is—"

"Not responsible for this." My voice was just as hard as Ned's. "You don't *know* him."

Ned folded his arms across his chest and watched me. "And you do?"

"Do I?" I took a long inhale again. Deep breathing calmed you, right? I needed it to, because I was about to lose my shit completely. "No. I don't. I know very little about him. His past? Not a clue other than what I draw. I know he's a loner. I know he has really bad skills at small talk. I know he resents my paintings and drawings as much as you do. No, *more* than you do. Because they may be about *your* world, but they're about *him*. And he hates it. But he wouldn't do this. He's always protected me. This"—I gestured to the ransacked room, my voice trembling—"he would never do this."

Ned was shaking his head in disagreement, his frustration seeping through. "You don't know *what* he is!"

I felt a sliver of doubt at Ned's reaction. "A shifter?"

"A rogue," Royce told me, putting his phone in his pocket. "Caleb is not the man you thought you knew."

"Yes, he is."

Both of them looked at me with sympathy. "No." Royce's voice was gentle. "A rogue is dangerous. Wild." His gaze flitted over the room, taking in the carnage. "Caleb's lost. The man you thought you knew, he's gone. Only the beast remains."

"Beast?" I heard my fear.

Ned winced a little. "Animal," he corrected Royce. "Beast is misleading," he muttered.

Royce gave a non-committal shrug as he watched me. "For what it's worth, Willow, I don't think this was him. But you need to understand what he is now."

"I understand he's gone." I tried to sound patient. "I understand I don't know as much about him or much about his past. But if he's lost?" Royce gave a slight dip of his head. "Then why aren't you trying to find him?"

"We are. But the circumstances and how we deal with him are different from before."

Deal with him? That didn't sound good.

"And while you do that..." I looked at my store, knowing that my home looked in the same state of mayhem. "How do I deal with this?" I knew what Royce was going to say, so I stopped him before he suggested it again. "I will not leave my home."

He had no idea how much I'd endured to get here. Losing my foster parents, battling a debilitating illness, and fighting through a legal struggle over what John and Jan had unexpectedly left me. Even after it was settled, I could hardly believe any of it was really mine. When I moved to Whispering Pines, it was for a fresh start. Again. As a foster kid, starting over was a way of life, but this move, *this* time, was supposed to be different. It was supposed to be my last move. I refused to give that up and run away.

"We can't protect you here," he told me gruffly.

"Shouldn't we be focusing on *why* I need protecting? Who else would do this?" I asked.

"I don't know," Royce admitted, sharing a look with Ned. "I don't even know where to start."

"Fantastic." I could hear my sarcasm, and they didn't call me on it. I knew we were all struggling with this. "Maybe they're watching you?" I spoke suddenly. Both men stared at me. "Think about it. No one knows me. I'm literally not even a blip on a shifter's radar. I have this weird link or whatever with Caleb, and I paint some pretty landscapes I've never seen. But think about it, if you *didn't* know I knew Caleb or that some of my art was of him, would my landscapes *really* stick out? Or, are you seeing the link because you have the information any other shifter wouldn't?"

"Some are quite obvious," Ned grumbled.

"Obvious to who? You? Your pack?"

Again they shared that look. "It's not our packlands," Royce grudgingly told me. "They're Caleb's."

I hadn't known that, and I thought about it. About him. "I know I may be speaking out of turn," I said hedgingly, "but I can't think his home is well known."

Royce smiled briefly. "I don't know him, you're right," he started, "but I knew of his pack. His old pack, they were… friendly. Welcoming."

Two words I would never have associated with the man I'd come to know over these last few months.

"It's possible that the scenes you paint are known to others who knew the old pack."

"Old pack," I mused. "Where's the new pack?"

"Only Caleb is left." Royce's emotions were closed off, but I didn't need him to draw me a picture. This is why they thought he'd gone off the rails. He had no one to rein him in.

Which wasn't true. He had me. Kind of. And them, if he wanted it, I guess.

"What do we do with this?" Ned changed the subject, which I was relieved about.

"You go and tell Cannon. Maybe ask the shaman if he can speak to your Luna and tell her to ease up a little on me?" Pushing my hair back, I let out a sigh. "And I'll clean up."

"That's it?" Ned asked me dubiously.

"I'm tougher than I look," I told him with another small

sigh. "I've handled worse. I just need you to find out if I'm in danger."

Ned circled his finger around in the air as he gave me a look of skepticism. "Did you miss this?"

"I was here all day." I thought about it. "This could have happened at any time, but they waited until I was gone." Turning in a small circle, I considered my line of thinking. "Yeah, this is to scare me, but I don't think the message is for me."

Royce was frowning as he considered my argument. "We'll look into it," he told me. "I'm not so sure about you being left alone."

I made the decision. "I won't be, I'm telling my friend Lily everything."

"Willow, you—"

"I didn't ask for this," I cut Ned off. "This is my life, my livelihood. I am not part of your world. I left your...home on the promise we'd figure out how to fix this. Once we did, I would return to the reality where people who become wolves aren't part of that." I looked between them. "That's what the plan was before this, right? Sever the tie I have and go back to my life. Lily is part of my life."

"You can't tell her we're shifters," Royce said firmly. "I agree, bring her in, but I would ask that you keep that part to yourself." He held my stare. "Please."

It was the *please* that did it. I nodded once and I felt the tension ease. "You should go," I told them both. "Thank you for coming back." I suddenly had a thought. "Where are the ones you took this morning?"

"We burned them already," Ned said nonchalantly as he

walked the store one more time. Not realizing his casualness was as hurtful as their actions.

"Then I'll do that going forward," I offered bravely. "You don't need to come and get them. Until this is over, anything that isn't like that"—I pointed to the destroyed picture Royce had admired earlier—"I'll destroy." I saw Ned's doubt. "Trust me, okay. You think I want more of this?" I pointed at my broken store.

"Anything that you doubt…" Royce began.

"I'll email." I held my phone out. "I need an email to send it to." It didn't surprise me that it was Ned who took my phone. "Who knows, maybe with fewer shifters visiting me, I'll become as uninteresting as I was before." Ned's lips twitched, but he didn't laugh.

They offered to stay and help, but now that I had decided my plan going forward, I wanted them gone. It wasn't personal. I was just ready to move on with my life. I needed to fix my store and my house, and I didn't want to do it with them, but I also didn't want to do it alone.

When they had left, I resumed my spot on the floor, back against the wall, knees drawn up, chin on my knees. I hit dial.

"Hey, what's up?" Lily's cheerful voice almost made me cry.

"Hey, I haven't been honest with you," I told her straight. "I need you at the store if you want to hear why."

Lily's silence spoke volumes. "Why now?" she finally asked.

"Because someone or someones broke into my house and the store and wrecked them both." I spoke over her barrage of questions. "And I can't do this by myself, I need you. But I can't ask for or expect your help without telling you what's been going on."

Lily was silent again and I had a moment where I was sure she might hang up, and then she spoke. "Are you okay? Were you there when it happened?"

"I'm okay. I wasn't at either place." The tears fell silently down my cheeks, and I didn't bother wiping them away.

"Have you called the police?" She sounded so calm.

"They've been to the house, seen the mess there."

"Where are you?" she asked, her tone clipped.

"At the store."

"Don't move. I'll be there in fifteen."

"Okay." My head rested against the wall. "Thank you."

"Don't thank me," Lily said, and I could hear her moving. "You and I are about to have a really big fight," she told me, her voice low and controlled. "Then you're going to tell me everything, and then you're going to buy me pizza."

"Okay."

"Okay." I heard her hesitate. "Should I bring my dad? To clean up?"

"No, I can manage."

"Okay. Sit tight." She said goodbye and then I was alone in the store, my life a mess around me.

As the night got darker, every shadow felt like a threat, every creak a warning that someone had been there and could come back. I listened to it all as the panic rose in my chest, and then I remembered what I had told Ned and Royce.

I was stronger than this, and I refused to let my own fear consume me.

Lily arrived like the whirlwind she was. A force of

nature that made everything get out of her way. She took one look at the store, at me, who had gotten off my ass and started to clean up, and she phoned in reinforcements.

My students, Lorna and Peter, arrived. Lorna's mama bear instincts took over, and within an hour of Lily arriving, I had spoken to two police officers, Lorna had called my insurance, basically forced me and them to agree she could talk on my behalf, and had given them my police incident report number as she explained the situation. She directed Peter to take photos of everything. Her husband was a carpenter, and he was taking measurements.

Lily's dad was here after all, and he was organizing new locks on doors. If I was honest, I was kind of pushed into a corner, given a cup of tea, and pretty much told to stay out of their way.

Which I needed. Because seeing my friends step in and take over allowed me to process the enormity of what happened, and I wasn't doing as well as I thought I was. Which was no surprise. Who would be?

No, I was grateful for my friends. Lily had given me a look that told me we would talk later, but for now, she was focused on fixing things. Lorna left with her husband when they found out my house was worse.

She returned to tell me she'd packed a bag and I was staying with her while her husband fixed walls, doors, windows...pretty much my house. She assured me it would only be for a few days, but their kindness and their support, it was too much, and I broke down.

They ushered me out of my store, an army of volunteers

busy putting everything to rights, and Lily drove the three of us to Lorna's.

Somehow, I was showered, in one of her son's beds, wearing jammies that weren't mine, with a plate of toast and a big mug of tea, while Lorna left "us girls" to rest, and she was going back to the store to make sure the "workers" were fed.

I felt guilty, but Lily shushed me when I started to protest. "Shh, she's not been this busy since her sons left for college," she whispered. "Let her do this."

We heard the door close, and I ate my toast quietly. I felt her get comfortable beside me, and when I'd swallowed my last bite, I met the look of my best friend.

"Start talking."

FOUR

Willow

It sounded so simple. Start talking—but where to start?

So I did what I'd want if the roles were reversed—I started at the beginning and didn't stop until I reached what had happened this afternoon. I kept out the fact they could change into animals. Royce had asked and I knew what it meant to them to remain unknown to humans like me.

"You're really drawing him?" Lily asked as she watched me. "Before you ever met him?"

"Yes."

She puffed out her cheeks and released a long breath. "I mean, I know you two had a thing, but I didn't realize *this* was the thing." She nibbled on the end of her hair, batting my hand away when I reached out to stop her. "It needs a trim, it's fine," she muttered absentmindedly. "And he left? With this psychic *connection* happening, he just thought he could leave?"

"I really don't think it's a psychic connection," I muttered, feeling uncomfortable under her penetrating gaze.

"Well, what would you call it?" she asked, shifting her position on the bed. "You're drawing him." Her expression became thoughtful. "Do you see what he sees?"

Thinking about it, I shook my head. So many of the drawings were of his past, but then, who was I to say I hadn't seen it from his point of view?

"No. I think I see moments that she wants me to see."

"She?" Lily's gaze sharpened, and I cursed myself for speaking too freely.

"My muse?" It was a wild, ridiculous stab in the dark that didn't mention their Goddess, but Lily accepted it readily.

"Of course! Like your inspiration, right?" I nodded along with her, but really, I just let her ramble. "It's so *interesting,*" she suddenly exclaimed. "I mean, I know why you kept it from me..." She gave me a look I knew well. "You *shouldn't* have, but I understand why." The look hadn't changed and was completely contradictory to her words.

I couldn't stop myself from asking. "You don't though, do you?"

The slap on my thigh was quick, and I was grateful for the covers between us. "No! Of *course,* I don't!" she snapped. "*Why* wouldn't you tell me? This is colossal, and you have all this crap happening to you, and you thought you could do it *yourself?* Are you crazy?" She didn't give me the chance to reply. "Yes, you are. I'm your best friend. We don't keep shit from each other. I don't care how sexy Caleb is, he does not trump friendship."

"It was a lot," I told her. "It had nothing to do with how he looks, Lil."

Her snort told me exactly what she thought of *that*. "You were thinking with your hoo-ha, and you know it."

Except, I hadn't been. He was a good-looking man, but the reason I went with Caleb and was still keeping his secrets was because it wasn't just *his* secret I kept. "Maybe," I murmured, holding back my displeasure as Lily accepted it without question.

Which is why when she hit me again over the covers, it was harder and hurt. "Ow! Why?" I demanded.

She rolled her eyes, clearly unimpressed with me, and I saw her frustration. Crossing her legs beneath her, she leaned forward, holding my gaze with an intensity that only Lily could manage.

"Do you think you're protecting me?" she demanded. "Is that it? Is that why you're giving me some story about a hot guy and your heart going pitter-patter when he gives you his brooding stare?" She leaned forward some more. "Something has happened to you. You could have been hurt, and you want to lie there and tell me it's about *just* a guy?"

Hearing the slight waver in her voice made me swallow hard as I studied her with the same intensity as she looked at me. Lily was scared. She was trying to mask it, but she forgot I knew her so well.

Like she knew me.

I let out a sigh, pushing my hair behind my ears, unsure how to deal with this and still keep their secret. "Lily, it's not that simple. It's not just about you and me. There are things..." I stopped. I weighed my options, tested my loyalty I had to her as my friend and to the shifters who may be the only way to break this link to Caleb. "Things are happening that I can't tell you," I admitted. "I promised. And honestly, I can't make you understand because *I* don't really understand, but I know that I can't tell you everything, and I have to ask you to respect that." Pushing myself to sit up straighter, I watched her. "Trust me that I'm doing this for you. It's for your own good."

The weight of the silence lay heavy between us, and I felt the pressure of it like a weight on my chest.

I think she saw my struggle because, for a brief moment, her expression softened before she looked away. When she looked back, her resolve had hardened, and I held back my groan.

"Then tell me what you can," she instructed softly. "Without the vagueness and BS you just fed me, tell me what's really going on. You can trust me," she reminded me, and I heard the slight reprimand that I had maybe thought that I couldn't. "No matter if you think it's crazy, tell me."

Looking down at my clasped hands, I watched them whiten as I gripped tightly. I'd told Royce I wouldn't tell her, but how could I tell her *some* of it without telling her *all* of it? But then, could I really drag Lily into this? Earlier, I'd been lamenting that my life was a mess; did I want to bring *that* mess into Lily's life? She didn't know what I had seen, what I saw when I closed my eyes. She didn't know what Caleb was running from.

Because neither did I.

"It's not that I don't trust you," I spoke softly. "It's not that I'm doing this to be a bitch or a dick. I gave my word I wouldn't tell you everything, on the proviso I could tell you *something*." I searched her face, seeing the confusion in her eyes. "Please understand."

"You think I can't handle it," she told me flatly.

"I don't think *I* can handle it," I blurted without thought, knowing I'd said too much when her eyes widened.

"Try me?" When I said nothing, she huffed out a laugh. "Fine, I get it. You're being *honorable* and shit."

Chewing the corner of my bottom lip, I felt the weight of doubt press down on me again. I was doing the right thing, I knew I was, but I was worried that by doing so, the secret—and it was a pretty big secret—would fray the edges of our friendship. "You accept I'm not telling you everything?" I asked, and despite the sigh, she nodded. "And you accept that I'm not doing it out of spite, but because it matters?" She nodded again. "And we're still friends?" I laughed when she laid her hand out flat, tilting it from side to side. "Okay," I accepted with a smile. "It's rocky, I get it."

Reaching out, I took hold of her hand and was relieved when she gave it a slight squeeze.

"I know you, Willow Harper," she spoke quietly. "I know that when you can't tell *me*, then you can't tell anyone. I hate that," she said with a rueful smile. "But I know you'll hate it more." Sitting back, she let go of my hand. "Let's go through it again, without the thing you can't mention, but with more of the details of what you can."

My heart raced with adrenaline, but also an overwhelming sense of gratitude. She deserved to know the truth or as much as I could tell her. Taking a deep breath, I began again—telling her about Caleb, the drawings, and the danger hunting me that I didn't understand myself. I laid it all out, except for the one secret that wasn't mine to tell.

She listened intently. I could see her reaction as she absorbed details I hadn't shared before, and I could see the wheels turning as she listened. When I finished, she sat there in silence with what I hoped was understanding.

"I think we need Dean and Sam," she spoke suddenly, and I smiled at her *Supernatural* reference. "Honestly, we need the Winchesters. There is too much otherworldly craziness here. You're psychic and linked to a guy you don't know, and we need to check for hex bags."

"This is why I didn't want to tell you more."

"And you thought I wouldn't be *in* this with you?" she asked me incredulously. "You know me better than this, Willow."

I couldn't help but laugh in relief, the weight lifting off of me. She didn't know it all, she knew it was more, and she wasn't flinching. She was still here. Still sitting beside me.

"Willow?"

"Yeah?"

"I know you made a promise," she said as she watched me, the intensity back in her gaze. "But when you can, you promise *me*, right now, if things get worse, you tell me everything. No more hidden truths. No more half facts. I want to hear you say we have a deal. Deal?"

I hesitated for a moment, that one secret I hadn't shared still sitting heavy on my conscience. But I nodded anyway. "Deal."

"Good girl." She beamed at me, and I noticed that my tummy didn't flutter like it had when Caleb said it. "So...let's figure this shit out. We need to know who was in your house, what they want, and how we get through to Caleb."

"We?"

"Of course *we*. We do this together, or I get you committed to a mental facility for being insane because you think you're psychically linked to a figment of your imagination."

The laughter burst from me, and it felt so good to laugh. "That's brutal," I told her, wiping my eyes when I finally calmed down.

"You know I will," she said with such pride that I started laughing again.

The sound of the front door opening sobered me, the reminder that I wasn't in my home, and that reminder hit hard. Other people were cleaning up the disarray in my business and personal life, while I sat on the sidelines, hiding.

Lily reached over and took my hand again, her eyes flicking to the door, but she said nothing. I knew we were both thinking the same thing. *What now?* Neither of us would have an answer until whoever was coming up the stairs told us. I felt trapped suddenly between my guilt and the feeling of exhaustion, as uncertainty on how to face it all hung over me.

I heard the footsteps approach, the tread light, and I exchanged a look with Lily, both of us prepared for Lorna to appear and burst the small fragile bubble of safety we had hidden in over the last couple of hours.

The door opened slowly, Lorna popping her head around, seeing we were both awake and stepping into the room with more noise. Her face was drawn, but it had softened when she saw us both.

"Girls, are you okay?" she asked, looking between us. "Everything in the store is as good as it's going to be tonight." She rubbed her forehead. "I'm so sorry, Willow, we couldn't save any of the art."

"It's okay, I knew that," I consoled her, even though it was my art. I'd known the moment I walked in earlier tonight that it was unsalvageable. I'd have to reach out to the other artists that I showcased and let them know.

"Noel, my husband," she added unnecessarily, "he stayed at your house. Called one of his workers in. The locks are changed." She fished in her pocket, laying out two new house keys. "Your dad," she spoke to Lily, "got the store locks changed. This is them." She lay another two keys down. "The house will take a little more time," she said softly. "You can stay here for as long as you like, okay?"

"You and Noel have done more than enough, Lorna," I told her gratefully. "I think I've already imposed as much as I should."

"You are welcome in my house," she told me firmly. "I want you to feel safe, and you won't feel that until you've had a good night's sleep and can face all this in the morning." She looked at Lily briefly but took a step forward. "We saw the knife on the floor, Willow. No one should have to hold a knife in their hand before walking into their bedroom."

I remembered the look Ned had given me. "I didn't. I put the knife down," I said with a scornful laugh.

"And that's okay," Lorna soothed me.

I nodded, but I felt the familiar tightness in my throat. The fact that it was a familiar feeling choked me even more. I wasn't able to stutter the words of thanks for the incredible kindness she was giving me. The acceptance from the other two women in the room, that I hadn't even been prepared to protect myself in my home, hit deeper than I wanted to admit.

Lily filled the silence for me. "Thank you, Lorna. Really,

we appreciate it." Her hand gripped mine tighter, and I knew she was frustrated that this had happened to me.

Lorna bent, picking up my discarded plate and mug. "You should try and rest, Willow. Your ME might flare up, and you don't want that."

No, because that would be just another thing to go wrong for me. Wow. How negative did I sound?

Yet the idea of rest...it didn't feel possible. My body was tired, but my mind was racing with everything that had gone wrong. However, the idea of lying awake, alone with my thoughts? I shuddered. A night of being haunted by the events of today would only be unbearable. I also knew I couldn't admit that to either of them.

"I'll try," I told Lorna with a small smile.

She beamed in response and then gave a not-so-subtle jerk of her head to Lily. "Your father is waiting outside."

"I'll just say goodbye," Lily told Lorna, and the other woman said goodnight to me. As the door closed behind her, Lily blew out a breath. "You put the knife down?"

"I was on the phone calling the police," I lied. Well, I'd been on the phone, so not a total lie. "I needed a hand to open the door. It was put the phone down or put the knife down."

"So you chose to put down the *weapon*?"

The outrage was real, and I bit back my laughter. "Seriously, Lily? What was *I* going to do with a knife?"

She thought about it. "Yeah, you're right, someone would definitely be in the hospital, and it would be you."

"That's what Caleb would've said too." I didn't miss her sharp look, but she said nothing.

"I better go. Dad's outside." She stood and I could see her

reluctance to leave. "If you didn't look so adorable in Lorna's PJs and comfortable in that bed, I would tell you to get up and come to my place."

I looked down at the red flannel jammies. "They're so soft."

"Okay, I'm going." At the door, she looked over at me. "You sleep, no visions, no muse invasions."

"Muse invasions?" My lips twitched slightly.

"No dirty dreams of Caleb either! I want you to sleep."

"I don't have dirty dreams of Caleb," I protested with a scowl, causing her to grin.

"I'll see you tomorrow. We'll check out the store and then your house. I'll pick you up."

"Lily, you work, you don't need to."

"Pfft. Dad will send me straight to you if I turn up at work, and you know it."

I didn't, but after tonight, I didn't doubt as much as I once would have. "Thanks. And thank you, for everything."

"Best friend." She pointed at herself. "Never forget it."

As if she would let me. I didn't say that; instead, I wished her goodnight, thanked her again, and when the door was closed, I switched the nightlight off.

And stared into the darkness.

I lay in the silence, going over everything that had happened that day. Friends had stepped up and given me their support. My fingers twisted in the blanket as I struggled with the fact that they shouldn't have had to, but I was so thankful they had.

I had people to count on, and that meant so much. I couldn't imagine life without Lily and my friends.

My mind flashed to Caleb in the sketch that Royce had

taken earlier. The shirtless one, where he was surrounded by nature.

Alone.

If this had happened to Caleb, would he have had an army of helpers to step up and lend a hand? *No.* He had no one. I remembered what I had thought earlier, and my resolve strengthened.

Not true.

He had me, and I knew I needed to make him realize that. Because people had been in my home and my business, and left a warning.

Was it a warning for me, or him?

FIVE

Willow

Waking up, I felt refreshed and well rested. Lying in bed, snuggled warm and cozy, I judged myself for how well I'd slept in a bed that wasn't my own. I mean, the sleep was *so* good I didn't want to get up, and it had nothing to do with hiding from my reality.

I'd genuinely had one of the best sleeps of my life.

The smell of bacon and coffee eventually lured me out of bed and down the stairs. Lorna was in jammies similar to mine. Granted, the ones I was wearing were hers, so it shouldn't have surprised me. Hers were blue, her slippers fluffy with bunny ears, and it just made me adore her even more.

Noel was at the breakfast counter, shoveling in his breakfast like a man possessed. He saw me lingering and straightened himself up, waving at me to come in.

"You slept well?" he asked, and Lorna turned, realizing I was behind her.

"I slept like a log," I admitted, walking to the counter where Lorna pointed with her spatula.

"We let you sleep a little bit longer," she told me as she served up bacon. "Noel's been to the house and store. All was okay, nothing further has happened. We have a town meeting to attend in about an hour."

I'd been in the process of helping myself to some toast at Noel's insistence, but I stared at her, my arm suspended in the air between me and the golden slices of toast. "A town meeting?"

"You've been targeted," she told me, flipping a pancake perfectly. "Your home and your business." She glanced up as the pancake settled back in the pan. "That's not random acts of violence," she told me slowly, like I hadn't thought of this already. "No, you've been targeted and we need to discuss this."

"At a town meeting?" I looked at Noel, whose head was down, and I didn't know him well enough to say for sure, but if I were to guess, I'd say he wasn't in agreement. "Did you...did you call this?" Noel glanced up and his look confirmed that would be correct.

"Willow, honey, we need to know what to do to stop this spree of violence."

Spree of violence? Oh damn, what had I done? Just last night, I was grateful for their help. This morning, I was wishing I'd kept my mouth shut. We didn't need a town meeting. I was pretty sure that the ones who had broken into my home and store weren't in the slightest bit interested in anyone else.

I couldn't say that though, because then I'd have to let them know I knew *why* it had happened, and I was not bringing that kind of attention to myself or shifters.

I needed to get hold of Lily. Lorna kept filling my plate

with her delicious home-cooked food, and I soon began to appreciate the speed that Noel ate at.

When I was finished, she told me to hop in the shower and we'd go to the town hall together. Upstairs, I closed the door and went to the furthest corner of her son's room. I called Lily, who answered on the second ring.

"I know, I know," she told me while sounding breathless. "Dad thinks it's best to stop the, and I quote, *wave of crime* before it gets out of control." I could hear her exasperation, and I echoed it.

"Lily, I can't tell them what happened, and we can't have this blown out of proportion!"

"I *know*," she hissed down the phone. "But we also can't do or say *nothing*. You called the police first," she reminded me.

"Because Royce told me to!" I wailed in defense.

"Well, maybe we need to ask this *Royce* how we get you out of this?"

Which may not have been a bad idea, but I'd told him I wouldn't say anything, and I could already see Lily being confrontational about their involvement. They would have no reason to believe that I'd kept my word.

"They don't need to hear about this," I told her quickly. "I'll go and just say as little as possible."

"Jesus, Willow, you do *that* anyway." I heard the sigh. It sounded determined. Dread filled me, and I knew I was in trouble when she said, "Leave it to me."

Which was exactly what I was afraid of.

I entered the town hall with Lorna on one side, Lily on the other, and Noel reluctantly bringing up the rear to stop me from bolting, I guessed. I could have been unfair, and he may be as genuinely invested in this meeting as his wife, but he didn't give me those vibes. Again, I could've been projecting my inner surliness unfairly towards him.

The town hall was buzzing with low conversation, and I genuinely was dumbfounded about how many people were there. Chairs scraped over wooden floors as people took their seats, and I tried to dig my heels in as Lorna marched us to the front. I felt Lily's grip on my arm and wasn't sure if she was trying to hold me back or just hold on.

I knew our town wasn't a big one, and when a meeting was called, most people turned up...but I hadn't expected it for me. I started to shake with nerves, and I felt Lily's grip tighten. I could feel their eyes on me as Lorna walked us down past the rows, and I wondered if this was what a bride felt. The weight of everyone's stares, being assessed and judged as she passed.

Get a grip. A bride wants to be here!

I needed to listen to myself. I started to take deep breaths, hoping to calm and center myself. I couldn't afford to freak out. Not when I needed to be evasive.

Sheriff Lincoln was at the front, off to the side, talking to Lily's father, and I turned to her in accusation and was met with a look of attitude.

"What did you expect me to do?" she hissed from beside me. "Say *no, Dad, of course I don't want to feel safe in my town?*"

"This is a disaster," I grumbled as I was finally led to a seat that Lorna deemed acceptable. I kept my eyes on the sheriff, and when he caught my eye, he gave a nod of recognition. Also something I didn't need, to be on his radar.

His eyes swept the room, and he must have liked what he saw, as he made his way to the front.

"Alright, we should start," he announced, his hand raised to quiet the conversations around us. "Some of you may know, but for those of you who don't, the recent spate of home break-ins has escalated, and yesterday evening, Canvas & Craft Collective was broken into and severely vandalized." He gestured to me. "Willow's home was also broken into, and substantial damage was inflicted on her property." The gasps rose into a rumble of murmurings. "Now, I know there's been some speculation, and I know that some of you are scared, but I assure you, we are looking into this and doing everything we can."

The murmurs grew louder, and I heard people shifting uncomfortably in their seats.

I'd been more focused on the term "spate." There had been more than one break-in? This had happened to others? Why was this the first time I heard about it? My heart raced, the sheriff's voice fading into the background as the weight of that word settled in. Had they all been done by shifters?

I glanced around the room, my eyes scanning the familiar faces. How many of them had been affected? How many had been keeping quiet? And more importantly—why?

I felt a knot form in my stomach. Whatever was going on, maybe it wasn't just about me, and that made me feel worse. Had the shifters who broke into my home known what was happening in town and used that as a way to get into my house?

That didn't make sense. Why would they need the subterfuge?

Mrs. Lippe, who always seemed to be front and center at these things, raised her hand, not waiting for the sheriff to open the floor for questions. She also didn't wait to be called on. "We deserve to know what's going on," she said. Her voice always made me think of what a hummingbird would sound like. High-pitched and painful to listen to. "People are talking about your department and lack of action. If we are in danger in our own homes, we have a right to know."

Mrs. Lippe was one of those people—one who would demand answers—and while she may hurt my ears when she spoke, she tended to ask the uncomfortable questions that no one else was willing to raise.

The sheriff's look was one of a man who had dealt with Mrs. Lippe for too many years. "I understand there are concerns. But we're still gathering information, and I assure you, when we know more, you'll be the first to hear it."

"And what about her?" a man behind me asked, and when I turned to look, he was pointing straight at me. "What about the break-in at her store? Is that connected to the home break-ins?"

I saw them all turn and look at me, and I felt my face flush. I hated being the center of attention, and I was a terrible liar, and I had no intention of telling them the truth.

What a fucking fuckup.

"Say something," Lorna encouraged me, digging her elbow into my side. Lily heard her and nodded at me. I looked at her with wide eyes, and she jerked her head, indicating I was to stand up.

This was a bad idea. When I looked at the sheriff, he had the same look of expectation as some of the others.

Shit.

Rising to my feet on legs that felt too shaky to keep me upright, I cleared my throat. "Hey." My voice broke and I sounded like a frog. "So, um, I don't really know anything, but um, my break-in felt kind of, um, personal." I gulped mouthfuls of air. "So yeah, um, I don't think it's connected."

The room was silent as they digested my words, and I started to sit down. I was caught in a crouch when someone asked me a question I didn't have an answer to.

"So...you're saying the people who broke into *my* house wasn't personal?" Her tone was accusing. "Because it felt *plenty* personal to *me*."

"What? No! Of course, I don't mean it isn't a personal attack—"

"Whoa, boy," I heard Noel murmur, and I glanced at him in panic to see him shaking his head.

The room was silent for a brief moment, and then the silence burst into a cacophony of voices, and I inwardly groaned. Sitting down, I faced the front, avoiding Lorna's frown and Lily's muttering about making things worse.

The sheriff finally regained control of the room, and I didn't raise my head to meet the hard stare I just *knew* was being directed my way. "Okay, let's calm it down, folks. As I said, we're investigating, and Willow's right, while her two incidents yesterday were unfortunate, there is a different feel to them." He took a moment and then confirmed what I already knew. "It's possible that what happened to Willow is not connected."

Not sure that made it better to hear it out loud.

"Everyone, just stay vigilant, make sure your homes are locked up, and keep calm."

I knew without looking that Mrs. Lippe wouldn't be satisfied, and from the grumblings that surrounded me, I knew she wasn't the only one.

"I know it's unsettling. We'll get to the bottom of this, and in the meantime, let's keep being neighborly and look out for each other."

The meeting broke up, but that didn't mean we could escape. Several people made a beeline for me, and I answered as little as possible, letting Lorna take control, with Lily jumping in now and again to save me from putting my foot in it again.

Finally, the end was in sight, and just as I was edging to the door, a hand on my arm halted my escape. Looking up, I saw the sheriff.

"Just a few minutes of your time," he told me.

"Right." I swallowed past the lump in my throat and nodded. "Of course."

Dread swirled in my belly. The real questions were about to start.

Lily took one look at me, saw the hard stare of the sheriff, and wisely ushered Lorna out without a word of protest as she left me with him.

"How are you holding up?"

"I'm okay, thanks." We stood in the aisle between the rows of seats, but he didn't offer for me to sit down, and I wasn't sure if I was allowed to. So instead, I switched my weight from foot to foot and probably resembled someone who needed to use the toilet.

"Sleep okay?"

"Yes, I had a great sleep," I answered quickly, relieved at

the simplicity of the questions, and I knew what I'd done even as the words left my mouth.

"Strange, I can never sleep in a bed that's not my own." His thumbs were hooked in his gun belt. The way he stood there, broad-shouldered and exuding authority, he screamed stereotypical sheriff vibes—the kind I'd seen in every TV show I'd ever watched. I almost wanted to ask him if he'd taken acting lessons. The whole stance was too perfect for it to be natural.

"I had a long day," I told him, breaking eye contact. "I was tired."

He nodded. "That's right, you have that illness, the fatigue one." My smile was tight, but I didn't elaborate on his *rustic* understanding of my illness. "I heard about that," he told me unnecessarily. "I don't think we've spoken before, have we?"

He knew we hadn't, and his act was pissing me off. "I don't believe so."

"Looked into you since last night," he told me casually. "Not much there, is there?"

"Do you mean in my profile or between my ears?" I should've been more careful, but the gleam in his eye when I sassed him told me more about the sheriff than anything he had said so far.

"Quite an inheritance the foster parents left you." He didn't react to my look of surprise. "Got anyone you can think of who may target you? To scare you?"

Yup. Some shifters who don't want me to paint anymore.

"My legal matters were settled." I held his stare. "Not that I thought you would have access to that information, sheriff?" If my accusation that he'd accessed my files without the proper measures in place bothered him, he didn't blink, and I decided I wouldn't either.

Sheriff Lincoln's smile spread slowly over his face. "Tough girl," he complimented me. "Good." He looked around the hall. "Can I be frank with you?"

He thought he'd been anything but that since we'd started talking? "Of course."

"Your break-ins aren't related," he told me. "The others? We know who it is, we just haven't caught them."

"Then why didn't you tell everyone that? Ease their minds?"

"Because I didn't want to." His tone held no room for argument. "Dunno why no one else has made the connection," he added with a sigh. "The vandalism at your place and the art store is on a whole different level. A lot of hate there," he added, "to shred someone's belongings like that."

"Everyone's an art critic," I murmured and once more was met with his hard look that saw through my bullshit.

"Makes me think you may know the person who did this?"

"I don't know anyone who would want to do this to me," I told him honestly. "Do you?"

"That level of destruction? Usually an old boyfriend, or relative wanting money." He shrugged. "Sound familiar?"

"No, sir."

"You lying to me, Willow?"

"No, sir." I wasn't. "I have no ex-boyfriend who would hate me, and as I am sure you know, I have no relatives."

We held each other's stare, and then I realized something when I thought about the *connection* he mentioned. "Alistair?" I asked him, lowering my voice, referring to the young boy who would use my key to hide for a few hours when his mom was *entertaining*. "The other break-ins are Alistair?"

Sheriff Lincoln's whole face changed, turning from hard-ass cop to resigned, weary man, who wished the answer was different. "It would be appreciated if you kept your thoughts to yourself."

"He has a key to my house," I told him, moving closer. "He wouldn't do this. To me," I added, since it was likely he *was* doing it to others. Probably the people who were hooking up with his mom.

The sheriff nodded. "Yeah, I know." He took his hat off and scratched his head. "Which is why I agree your break-ins are different. The fact it was your business *and* the house is why we had to take action here today, but if you're being targeted and have an idea as to why, you should tell me."

With my fingers crossed in my jacket pockets, I lied to his face. "Trust me, sheriff, if I knew what was happening, I would be the first person to tell you."

He walked me outside, and we parted ways. While Lily and Lorna grilled me more thoroughly than the sheriff during our short trip to go get lunch, all I could think about was Alistair, and I wondered how I could help him.

Which was a nice change from thinking about how I could help Caleb, until I realized that each was probably as miserable as the other, and that made me lose my appetite completely.

SIX

Caleb

I LAY ON MY BACK, AWAKE BUT WITH MY EYES CLOSED, AS I listened to the sounds of the mountain surrounding me. The sounds of nature used to soothe me; now all I heard were the echoes of emptiness. There was no pack here. There hadn't been in many years.

Ten years.

Ten years since I returned to a pack that had been slaughtered. Ten years since I had stood in this clearing that I now lay in the middle of. The air was cold, but I was a shifter and the chill in the air didn't really bother me. Nothing had bothered me for a long time.

Except *her*.

I blew out a low breath, the only outward sign that she affected me. I'd left her behind, so why couldn't I *leave her behind*? Instead, I thought about her *all* the fucking time. I had a lingering sense of regret that I'd left it the way I had, but when I thought about it, she was in safe hands. Cannon was the better alpha.

Alpha.

Only the shaman had called me that. I never had a pack to lead. The Shadowridge Peak Pack died the day my father did. I wanted nothing to do with this peak after that morning. There was nothing left anyway. The pack was dead. The ones who had betrayed them were dead. I'd killed any survivors of that morning, not that there were many.

The only one left alive in the Shadowridge Peak Pack was me. Any others, and there were so few, had changed packs.

I had never planned to return to this mountain, to the place I left behind what felt like a lifetime ago. And yet, here I was, every step I had taken those months ago had led me deeper into the landscape I had spent years trying to forget. The thought of returning was never part of the plan. But I hadn't left with a plan. A lone wolf doesn't need a plan—just instincts and the raw, unshakeable drive to survive.

I swore I would never return here, but that morning on Blackridge Peak, with the shaman and everything else, it stirred too many memories. Bringing things to the surface that I had wanted to keep buried. I didn't want to deal with those memories. Not then. Not ever.

"So why are you back here, Caleb?" I asked myself as I opened my eyes and stared at the blue-gray of the morning sky. I knew that answer. I had wanted to put distance between me and anybody that was pack. No one came here. This mountain was a monument to the dead.

My dead.

As the surviving alpha, no other pack could move onto this mountain until I gave up my claim of it to the Pack Council. I hated what happened here. I hated being here, but the thought of another pack here...bringing life and laughter to this land that my father died for...I hated that more.

The log cabin that Willow had focused on in her drawings lurked in the morning shadows, once a place of peace and love, now a memorial to everything I lost here.

I lost myself on this mountain.

I wasn't sure coming back here would allow me to find it.

Did I even want to find it? Who was I? An alpha without a pack? No, I was a *shifter* who had no pack. Who didn't *want* a pack.

I thought of her. Alone. Confused. No doubt she'd be feeling overwhelmed. I wondered if she was still on Blackridge. In my years off this peak, I'd kept my distance from pack, but no matter how hard I tried, I always came across someone. I'd heard of the alpha of the Blackridge Peak. Young when he found his power. Strong. His father was one my own father had hated. He despised his ways and how he ran his pack. I'd not been surprised to hear that the battle for alpha of the Black-ridge Peak Pack had been bloody.

There was little in our world that wasn't.

Luna had gifted us with the spirit of the wolf, and with that came the nature of the wolf. Cunning, resourceful, and complex. A creature that was devoted to family structure. What else was a pack than an extended family? Wolves were fierce, excellent hunters, and above all intelligent.

Wild and free, they lived uninhibited lives.

I hadn't felt free in a very long time. No matter how far I distanced myself from the mountain, its weight had never truly left me. It clung to me like a shadow, a constant, unmistakable presence. At first, every mile that I had traveled to put distance between it and me had felt heavy, as if the Peak itself was embedded within my bones.

In my soul.

My eyes closed as I fought off the shroud of remembrance. With a sigh, I got to my feet. My jeans, which were the only thing I was wearing, were well-worn. I only ever cared about my appearance when I was around humans. If you looked too much like a vagrant, they kept their distance; too polished, and either they assumed you had money already or they didn't trust you because you looked *too* good. It was a delicate balance, fitting in without drawing attention—a skill I learned with caution. A skill that had served me well over the years.

Now I only had one pair of jeans, frayed and worn. If I wanted to leave this mountain, I would need to get creative. I thought about leaving every day, and even though I wasn't happy here, the thought of leaving it once again felt strange. Foreign. Could I do it again? Looking down, I almost smiled. Could I do it with only one pair of jeans and nothing else to my name?

As I considered the idea of coming off the mountain, I felt them stir, a ripple in the air around me. The spirits that had waited for my return, ever-watchful since I had been here, they rustled like a breeze through the trees. I could feel them, patiently waiting, observing, eager for me to join them.

They'd welcomed me back the night I returned. When I thought about leaving, their presence grew restless, as if they disapproved, or maybe they feared what lay at the foot of the mountain and beyond as much as I did.

"Or maybe you've finally gone mad and think the spirits of the dead are around you," I spoke out loud to the empty air.

Yet saying it out loud didn't make a difference. It didn't sound stupid or crazy to say it. The feeling that this mountain wasn't finished with me yet remained. Was there any wonder I wanted to escape?

Pushing the feeling away, I knew I couldn't stay here forever. The spirits, or my memories, might try to pull me back, but I wasn't bound to this place—not anymore.

I knew that leaving wouldn't be like it was before. Before, I had a thirst for vengeance, and rage and grief rode me hard. I'd had a purpose when I left.

Now, what purpose did I have?

Her face floated across my memory. Willow? She wasn't my purpose. She had nothing to do with me. That thought felt like a lie.

They said that we were linked. Were we?

There weren't many people who would draw someone that they'd never met. Or sketch scenes from someone's past with such detail for someone who could never know those things.

I lay back down on the ground and stared at the sky. "Why her, Luna? Why a human?" I lay quietly as I watched a cloud lazily pass by. "Is that my punishment?" I asked the Goddess calmly. "I'm no longer worthy of a vision to a shaman; you send your message through a girl? A *human*?"

Stillness surrounded me as I waited for the answers. I'd have a long wait. I'd asked these questions every single day since I got here, and silence had been my only answer.

I lay in the same place, unmoving, staring at the sky. The gray-blue turned to blue, and blue bled to the grayish purple of dusk before the darkness swallowed the light.

When only the moon was visible in the sky, I stood. The

jeans were pushed down and discarded when I stepped out of them. I changed my form to my wolf and gave the moon a cursory glance before I turned away.

The spirits surrounded me when I was in this form, so close I could feel them brush against my coat.

My howl ripped through the silence of the night. I would ask my questions of Luna again tomorrow.

It was time to hunt.

The cool wind whistled over the peaks, sharp and biting as it burrowed its way beneath my fur. I started the descent, my paws maneuvering with confidence over the loose gravel and stones. The sound as the looser debris rolled down the slope was my only companion. Autumn hung heavy in the air. Snow would only be a few weeks away, maybe sooner. The air had a bite to it with more than a hint of promise. Cold winters, I was used to; it was the quiet I was struggling with. The depth of silence on the Peak was only making my thoughts seem louder.

I'd been a lone wolf for so long, but I hadn't been truly alone. The world of humans had been within easy reach whenever the silence became too loud. Lone wolves weren't supposed to thrive, and I hadn't, but I *had* survived. I wouldn't say I lived. I stopped living when my pack died.

As I descended the steep peak of the mountain face, I felt myself open more to the familiarity of my surroundings. Every rock, tree, and stream was as familiar to me as old friends. A reminder that no matter how much time had passed, I'd never truly escaped.

As I picked my way down the unstable terrain, I sought out new paths rather than relying on old ones. Like I had when I left. And what had I found? Nothing. The life of a loner was everything I wanted—and nothing like I'd expected. However, I liked having only myself to rely on.

Which was what the shaman was worried about. What Cannon feared but had not yet voiced.

A lone wolf was dangerous.

A lone wolf was independent. There was no pack to return to and nothing to tie you.

There was just...nothing.

Except for the loneliness. The wildness. The temptation to live too much as the wolf. To shed your humanity. Was I so close to forgetting who I was that they thought I was a danger to them?

To myself?

To Willow?

Cannon had put himself between us. Did they really think I had forgotten the ways of our Goddess?

The rage I carried with me since that fateful day ten years ago had nothing to do with Willow. The grief I held was mine to hold. It didn't make me weak. I'd been weak before, and the sting of betrayal was still as sharp now as it had been then.

Willow was not in danger from me. She never had been. Did it piss me off I'd been drawn to her while she had *drawn* me. Of course it did. I didn't understand it, and I'd never been someone to accept something I didn't understand. A fact that used to make my father clench his jaw tight and pray for patience from Luna. The memory made me smile. I could still see him so clearly.

Amos had been a proud man. A towering presence, both in life and the memory he had left behind. He'd been an easy alpha to follow. He commanded attention with ease and without question. I'd never heard him shout or raise his voice; he didn't need to. Pack knew his authority. It was how he carried himself, broad-shouldered and tall. I'd inherited his dark eyes, but I didn't think I would ever master the same piercing stare my father had controlled, the way he could see through the bullshit, and one look from him told you not to try any bullshit either.

I had my mother's light hair coloring. My father's was dirt brown, streaked with silver as he aged. It was a mark of his wisdom, my mother used to say. He used to say it was from raising me. His family was his life, and his pack was his pride. Amos was respected and known as a strong leader and an even stronger ally.

Balance is what made a good alpha. Amos was well-balanced. He was firm but fair. I remembered his ability to be fierce but kind. Calm but calculated.

And if you really, truly pissed him off...he was relentless. *That*, I'd inherited from him. The unrelenting need for justice. He would never have approved of *how* I achieved it, and for that, I was thankful he had never lived to see it.

There was a lot I'd done in the years since they passed that he wouldn't have approved of. He wouldn't have liked the situation with Willow. He would hate how I had been alone for so long. Amos believed that a pack centered you, and maybe once,

I did too. But now...now they were just a burden I'd never asked for.

Willow Harper, I'd never asked for her. I hadn't asked for any of this. This was the hand that Luna gave me. She didn't get to complain when I didn't play the way she wanted.

It didn't make me dangerous. It didn't mean I was a risk. It only meant I was content with my own company. Nothing more. I knew it didn't help that I'd left the way I did that morning in Cannon's house.

It would have confirmed their fear I was lost.

Maybe I had been. Maybe this mountain was the only place where I knew who I was, and maybe that would have to be good enough. I had changed over the last ten years. In some ways, I was unrecognizable. In others, I was so predictably the same that it made *my* teeth grind when I clenched my jaw.

I stood on a bluff overlooking the mountain, and I looked down and around, taking it all in. Possessiveness surged within me as I surveyed the mountain. *My* mountain.

Is this what they wanted, Cannon and the shaman, to have me back here?

Or...maybe they thought they could trick me?

Was that their plan? Push me far enough to renounce my claim here? To use a human to make me think there was a link between us. Why would a *human* have a link to Luna? *Or* me? It was preposterous.

Unthinkable.

Yet, I had believed it.

The thought made me step back. Had they thought to use my grief and my pain against me and, in doing so, it would make me *blind* to what was in front of me?

Did they think I was stupid? As I thought about all the ways they had plotted against me, I saw how they had pushed me into situations without me recognizing it for what it was at the time.

Manipulation.

As memories of their cunning deceit flooded back, my anger sharpened when I thought of Willow's too *obvious* acceptance of shifters in her human world.

The air around me grew heavier as I felt the spirits form closer around me.

Their presence was similar to the night of my return, swirling in the air like smoke. They fed into my rage, making me stronger. As my anger strengthened, so did my connection to them, forming a bond that I didn't understand, but I welcomed it.

This mountain was mine.

The Pack Council couldn't take it from me. Not unless I gave it up. Either in life or death.

I'd never give it to them. I'd die before I let them have it.

Seething, I considered my options.

Did I play along? Or did I stay away? The smart play was to stay away. They couldn't manipulate me anymore if they couldn't get to me.

But as my father had told me for much of my adolescence, no one ever said I was smart.

I just needed a plan.

SEVEN

Willow

I woke up in bed to the smell of fresh coffee, and I was already smiling. Lorna may talk a mile a minute, and she may have missed her calling in life as a police detective, or possibly an inquisitor from days of old, but the woman knew how to look after her guests.

Getting up, I swayed a little, fatigue still clinging to me, unwilling to let go. Once I was feeling steadier, I went to the bathroom, made sure I didn't look too bad, and then eagerly went to find Lorna and breakfast downstairs.

"Morning!" She beamed at me as I rounded the partition that separated the hallway from the kitchen and dining area. "You look tired still. Do you want a tray to go back to bed?" She didn't wait for an answer. "Noel, Willow needs to go back to bed."

"Noel!" My voice was sharper than I intended, and he paused mid-rise from his chair. "I do not need to go back to bed. You have done far more than you ever should have needed to," I told him with a smile, and I watched as his eyes flicked between me and his wife, gauging who he should listen to. "I'm okay," I assured them both. "I'm going to have breakfast, and then I am going to go to my shop, and then"—I cut off Lorna's protests—"I am going to go home and sleep in my own house tonight."

Lorna looked crestfallen. Noel looked nonplussed, but he did resume his seat and took a drink of his coffee.

"But you don't have to leave," she told me. I watched her pour the batter into the pan, and I pulled the bowl of fruit she had already prepared towards me. Taking a seat opposite Noel, I started to eat.

"I do need to leave, although I will miss how incredibly well I've been looked after." Lorna looked at me, her expression still one of disappointment. "Lorna, you have been amazing. You both have." I turned to look at Noel, who raised his cup in acknowledgment. "But I need to go home. I stay here much longer, and your boys will need to share a room, as I'll have moved in." I hoped the light teasing softened her mood. "Honestly, I'm not joking, I want to stay here and be pampered! Leaving is for *your* sake, trust me."

She did laugh at that, and I felt the small knot of anxiety lessen.

"It's nice to have someone to get up for," Lorna admitted softly, and I saw Noel's head dip to hide his frown. "Noel's usually away before I rise, so there's no one to cook for."

"You're losing work because of me?" I asked him, feeling guilty all over again.

"Not at all," he assured me. He stood and carried his plate and cup to the sink, where his wife hovered. Kissing the top of her head, she leaned into him a little. "Sometimes I work further out, but I was on a job in town, not been a problem to help you out."

"I will pay for your time, you know that, right?"

"You will not," he said firmly, squeezing his wife, who had been about to protest for him. "This nasty business of yours, I just worry if it happens to Lorna when I'm not here. No, I'll be closer to home until this mess is sorted and you're fixed." He opened the fridge and pulled out his lunchbox. "I'll do your house first, then be at the store this afternoon, okay?"

"Okay, thank you." I decided to discuss money with him when his overzealous wife wasn't listening. Noel was a businessman, he'd see sense.

Lorna busied herself in the kitchen, serving me breakfast, and then she tidied up, always refusing any help. I knew she was happy having someone to look after, and it made me feel sad. I already knew I would never charge her for another art class again. I just hoped she'd accept my decision when I told her.

Maybe that was something I should also discuss with Noel. Food for thought.

Ready for work and dressed in jeans, a sweater, and my padded jacket, I shoved my feet into my boots at the front door of Lorna's house. She was a "boots off in the house" homeowner, and I respected her wishes.

"And you're sure you don't want me to come?" she asked, hovering at the door.

"I am sure I want you to go to Zumba and have fun." Reaching out, I took her hand. "You have been amazing, and you don't know how grateful I am for a friend like you, and I mean that."

She blushed with embarrassment at the praise, but she squeezed my hand tightly. "You're welcome, honey. I'll see you later," she told me, and anticipating my protest, she shook her head. "No, I know you won't eat if I don't come and bring lunch." She looked me over. "You really do look healthier with me feeding you for the last few days, you know. I think we'll have to discuss this with your doctor, Willow."

The "mom" look was back, and I had to admit, I didn't hate it. Suppressing a smile, I looked at her as I scrunched my nose up, already opening the door. "Maybe," I acknowledged. "Maybe you take better care of me than I do myself. But...I won't admit I said it!"

Laughing, I ran out the front door, hurrying down the path as she shouted after me that she had a recording device at the front door for her boys sneaking in, so she had it all on tape. I laughed louder and she waved at me as she yelled she'd see me later.

I was still giggling at her use of "tape" as I walked to work. Who said "tape" anymore? She was so funny. With my head in the clouds, a feat I placed firmly at Lorna's door because of how much she had cared for me the last few days, I didn't see the man rounding the corner who I walked into until it was too late.

"Ow! Sorry," I added as I looked up at him and took a step back. I thought Cannon was big; this guy was huge.

"You should watch where you're going."

Looking between him and the corner, I pointed. "It's a blind corner. This is as much your fault as mine."

He was white, with dirty blond hair, a full beard, and hard

hazel eyes. "Watch where you're going in the future," he grunted and resumed walking.

"Jerk," I muttered under my breath as he walked away, my breath hitching when he turned swiftly to scowl at me. With my head down, I hurried on my way to work. I didn't think they got bigger than Cannon, but that guy would definitely give him a run for his money.

On Main Street, my steps had slowed so much I was making hardly any progress. He was big and powerful, with really good hearing. Or maybe he hadn't heard my name-calling, but I thought he did. Which meant he was a shifter.

Or I was overexcitable and thought everyone was a shifter now. Or *was* everyone a shifter now?

Opening the store, I didn't bother turning over the "closed" sign. Noel and his guys weren't finished yet, and until they were, there was no point opening. The insurance also sent someone out to inspect, and we had documented everything, so now all I had to do was wait. While I waited, I could draw.

The scene was one I had been reliving for the last few nights. Caleb lay on his back, his eyes on the sky above him, wearing nothing but jeans. His feet were bare, his abs on display, his hair disheveled around his head as he fixed the sky with an impenetrable stare.

The first time I saw the log cabin, I thought I was drawing a scene from his past, but the second time I saw him there, I just knew it was *now*. Like right now.

My finger traced the line of his body laid flat out against the cold ground. Loneliness emanated from the page, and I wished I could reach in and grab him and pull him out to me and have him here at my side.

I missed his grumpy ass. Did he miss me?

"Stupid, Willow," I scolded myself. "He couldn't wait to get away from you, so how would he miss you?" Even though I knew I was right, I still wanted to take hold of his hand and tell him we would find the answers together.

The knock on the door caused me to jump. Looking up through the window, I saw two familiar faces. Hurrying over to the door, I opened it for Royce and Doc. "You're here so soon?"

Royce walked in, surveying the damage, Doc following closely behind, and I locked the door behind them.

"Place looks almost like new," Royce complimented me, already walking to my easel. Noel had fixed them first at the request of his wife. "When was this?" he asked, his eyes on Caleb.

"The last few nights," I answered honestly. "This is the first time I have drawn since the break-in. There's no others for you to worry about."

Royce peered at the sketch. "Why does he have mini tornadoes around him?" He exchanged a look with Doc. "Weather's still good on the peaks."

Joining them, we all stared at my sketch. "I don't think it's weather," I told them slowly. "I don't know what it is, but I don't think it's weather-related."

"Looks spooky," Doc said finally. "What do you think it means?" he asked me.

"I wish I knew."

"You ready for your physical?" Doc changed the subject, and I saw Royce roll his eyes.

"Today?" I wanted to tell him no, that Lorna had some

insights, but how could I explain my human friend's insights to my doctor?

Doc looked around my empty, almost fully repaired store. "Got anything else you need to be doing?"

"Rude," I murmured, walking to the back of the store.

I heard them both chuckle, and I remembered the man from this morning. "I have a question, and it's going to sound… stupid…but if I ask, will you promise not to ridicule me?"

Royce lost his smile a little. "We would never make fun of you for wanting to know about us," he chided gently.

I felt guilty again. I was definitely winning on the "thinking bad thoughts of your peers" day.

"I walked into a guy today. But he was big, bigger than Cannon." When neither of them looked impressed, I carried on. "He was rude, and as I walked away, I called him a jerk."

"I thought you said *he* was rude?" Doc teased.

"I said it so low he could never have heard me if he was… well, you know."

"Human?" Royce supplied, and I nodded. "Describe him."

I did as I was told, and Doc must have thought that me agitated and fully invested in my topic with Royce was the best time to examine me. I didn't protest as I got poked and prodded, still discussing details with Royce.

He asked for details no one would notice or even know they had noticed. The one on the smell of his aftershave caused me the most consternation until I concluded he must not have been wearing any. That answer wasn't supposed to make them react like they did.

"I'm going for a walk around town," Royce told Doc. "No one gets in, okay?"

"Roger," Doc confirmed as he fiddled with an ear thermometer.

"I have friends coming to work on the store," I told Doc.

"That's fine. He means the ones you don't know."

Right. God, how was this my life? "Should I be worried?"

Doc looked up at me as he placed a cover over the ear prod. "Are you?"

"Yes?"

"It's normal." He stuck the thermometer in my ear. "How have you been feeling?"

I heard the machine beep to indicate it was done. "I've been okay, considering." I thought about Lorna. "I've been staying with a friend. She was a student here. An older lady, got two sons, they're in college, so she's missed looking after people." I gestured to the shop. "Her husband's been doing the work here actually."

Doc nodded as he looked around. "Handy friends."

"Yeah, um, Lorna, that's her, she said this morning that I look better for staying with her, and being well...looked after?" I saw him studying me, and I looked away as I continued. "She thinks I look healthier."

"Your symptoms?" Doc asked me, taking out a small notebook. "I have here a pattern of sorts that I've been observing." He gave me a quick smile. "It's a bad habit of mine, I do it a lot. So, here, I have your sleep patterns, your feelings of fatigue, listlessness. Eating habits. Your temperature from the few days you were with the pack."

"Oh my God, how long were you *observing* me?"

"When you were in the bunker, a couple of times before, you know. Normal stuff."

We held each other's gaze, mine inquisitive, his looking dodgier by the second. "Caleb?" I guessed. "He took notes for you?"

"He's very observant," Doc mumbled, flipping his pages back and forth. "His observations were quite informative."

"I bet they were," I snarled as I started to pace. "What else did he *observe*?"

"Just things that he asked me that he should look out for. Your illness isn't one a shifter would come across before. Being told someone suffers from constant *fatigue*, it's the exact opposite of a being that is continuously energized and *active*. You're the polar opposite of a shifter. He had no idea what he was looking for. You were unconscious for days, he needed guidance and told me he had already had a doctor consult, and he needed more. He had your notebook, but he didn't understand your code."

"He could have asked."

"You were unconscious."

"Then he should have waited for permission."

Doc tilted his head as he studied me. "Are you really that upset he went out of his way to care for you?"

"Well, when he just up and walks away, yes, I am. Because I don't believe he cared."

Doc nodded. "So your feelings are hurt."

"Yes, he hurt my feelings! He walked away and left me with a wolf pack who could have locked me in a bunker and never let me out!"

Doc laughed. Right in my face. It was as sudden as it was genuinely amused. "I thought we'd been nothing but hospitable," he said with a smile as he tidied his small pouch of medical equipment up. He then drew out a syringe and a vial. "May I?"

"Can I say no?" I was already rolling up the arm of my sweater.

"You could." He wrapped a blood pressure cuff around my arm. "But why would you bother?"

Meaning he would take it anyway. Comforting. To be honest, I didn't mind. I actually found Doc a very proficient healthcare provider. I wondered if he had any job satisfaction with a pack of wolves who rarely got sick as his caseload.

"What's the average age of a shifter?" I asked while he found a vein and got ready to pierce my skin.

"They stop aging, unlike humans, once they reach maturity." Doc was distracted, my vein proving to be more elusive than he would like, so he didn't see my look of surprise.

"He's immortal?" I'd gained a range of several octaves higher than was normal.

"What? Who? Immortal? What?" Doc blinked up at me, the first drop of blood hitting the vial. "No one is immortal, that's ridiculous. Though the shaman is over two hundred years old, so I would say he may feel that way sometimes."

"Two hundred..." I was shaking my head, and Doc was grinning at me again. I wished I wasn't such a source of amusement. "You're pulling my leg. I know he's old, but eighties at the most. Maybe ninety."

"Two hundred plus." He pressed a cotton ball against my skin. "They hit maturity, and they slow down getting older."

"Wolves live to like thirteen."

Doc raised his eyebrows as he waited for me to get where I was going. When I said nothing else, he hid his smile. "You're looking at animals. Shifters have the Goddess Luna's magic in them."

"What age are you?" I demanded, refusing the Band-Aid and rolling my sleeve down. "Fifty?"

"Ouch." He rubbed his jaw as he mock glared at me. "Thirty-eight human years."

"That's insane. And also really, really unfair."

He patted my knee in sympathy. "So now you know why I observe, why I told Caleb to take these notes." Straightening, Doc looked at his notebook. "I have to admit, I think your friend Lorna may have a case; you're healthier with her than you are alone."

I looked away and fought the familiar feeling of irritation. "I do look after myself. I don't need a keeper."

"I know, and you are very conscious of being healthy," he agreed. "But let's not write off the power of being cared for."

The door got knocked and Doc crossed the room to open it for Royce. The bigger man walked in and looked at me grimly.

"We have more shifters in this town than we need."

EIGHT

Willow

"What does that mean?" I asked warily, getting off my seat. "What does *more* mean?" I looked between them, worry gnawing at my gut. "Are they here for me?"

Royce shook his head, but he didn't look convinced. "I don't know," he said, which I hadn't been expecting.

He looked like he wanted to deny it, but then he said that, and that was confusing and I decided I needed to sit back down. "Mixed messages, big guy," I grumbled, perching on my stool. "Did you speak to them? Did you see the big guy? He's really huge."

"I didn't see any of them," Royce answered me, sharing a look with Doc. "I can smell them."

"They smell bad?" I asked, confused.

"No, Willow, I can sense they're shifters," he explained patiently.

Right, because that was normal. I thought about it. It *would* be normal for him. "Have they left? Are they coming back? Why would they be here? Did Caleb send them?"

"You're getting excited," Doc warned me, coming to stand beside me and getting his pack of tricks back out.

"You didn't see this guy. He would break me like a twig," I snapped.

"They could be here for any reason," Royce reminded me. "Caleb's been here, we're here, Cannon's been here too. Whispering Pines has seen a lot of shifter traffic recently."

"And you're not here for the hiking," I bit out in agitation. "Are you suggesting they are?"

"Calm down," Doc said as he stuck the thermometer in my ear again. "Don't undo all of Lorna's hard work."

Chastised, I sat still and willed myself not to overreact. "I thought I could go home tonight," I told them both dejectedly.

"Willow's been staying with friends," Doc explained. He noted my temperature in his book, and tapping it against his hand, he looked me over carefully. "One more night taking advantage of someone who wants you there wouldn't hurt, would it?"

I wanted to argue, but what was the point? *Taking advantage* was harsh, but there was no denying it. We knew I was going back, and even if I did protest, I was pretty sure Royce would carry me there himself.

"It beats the bunker," Royce joked gently, again confirming my belief that shifters were mind readers.

"You could confront them?" I suggested. "Caleb would."

Royce raised an eyebrow. "Caleb may be why they are here. Let's not pin the hero badge on him just yet."

"Royce." It was Doc's turn to reprimand. "We don't know what the circumstances are for him leaving."

"Cannon knows," I blurted, causing both of them to turn their attention to me. "Can't we ask him?"

"It's not for us to know," Royce told me smoothly.

"Which means you know and won't tell." My shrewd look didn't even warrant a flush in his cheeks for his obvious fib.

"We should go," Doc said, repacking his things. "We bring attention to Willow if they really are here for no other reason than passing through."

Royce didn't need to voice his thoughts. They were the same ones that I was having. Passing through for what? They were shifters, they didn't need to come to town. They could *pass* right on by running *through* the woods in their wolf form.

Royce was in my sketchbook. "I'm going to take this with me," he told me, taking it without me saying yay or nay. "I think Cannon will need to see this one."

"Fine." I heard truck doors opening from the street. Voices I recognized. "That's my friend who's working on the repairs."

"We'll use the back door," Doc told me. "Go to your friend's tonight. We'll take a look into the others who are here, and we'll let you know. Okay?"

I nodded, because if I spoke, I may have begged them not to leave. As they left, I caught Royce's arm, halting his progress. "Can you reach out to Caleb?" I pointed at the sketch rolled in his hand. "Ask him if they're friends of his?"

The look was so full of pity that I almost cried. "He's lost, Willow. He's not the man you want him to be."

I wanted to protest. Fight for Caleb, like Caleb may have fought for me. Instead, I let Royce go, and while the back door closed, I hurried to open the front to Noel and his colleague.

After Noel told me what they had planned for today's

work, I made the excuse of going to get them a treat from the bakery for thanks. I needed a reason to leave and mull over what Doc and Royce were saying about Caleb by *not* saying.

I sorted out the facts as I knew them.

He came here as he was drawn to the town, to me, and to my weird ability to see him when I had no business knowing about him or his kind. Caleb may not have known who I was, but he *knew* me when he got here.

How?

I could see him in my dreams; could he see me?

I wasn't a shifter. A doctor and a spirit guide, or shaman as they called him, had confirmed that I was one hundred percent human. There was no reason why Caleb would be tied to me.

But he was.

How?

I was normal, the whole psychic thing aside. That wasn't even right. I wasn't psychic. If I was, I'd have picked some numbers for the lottery and already been on the beach in the Caribbean by now. No, I wasn't "gifted."

So why the heck was I linked to him? Luna? What did she need me for? Because I could draw? I was sure there were plenty of shifters who were just as talented as me.

What did I offer that they couldn't?

My humanity?

No. Shifters may not be human, but they were not monsters. They didn't need me for their moral compass.

Caleb had no family left, and neither did I... Was it because we were both orphans? From the little they had told me, his dad died ten years ago, so was that his last familial tie?

Surely he would "go rogue" then? A person can do extreme things because of grief. Had Caleb?

He called himself a murderer. Who had he killed? Was it figuratively or literally?

My God, I had so many questions. The most important being *why me?* The next, *why him,* and the follow-up, bonus round questions, *where is he* and *how do I break this link?*

Another follow-up question would be *what is wrong with him?*

The shaman had called it *rogue.* To me, a rogue was someone mischievous, perhaps morally gray, a rebel maybe. To shifters, it seemed it was far more dangerous. I remember someone, possibly Royce, telling me that it meant the rogue had turned their back on pack life. That they had embraced the darkness that came from being alone too much. That their anger and hate had morphed them into a shadow of themselves. Which sounded terribly dramatic and kind of far-fetched.

I couldn't imagine Caleb giving in to that. He was so stoic and *strong.* He was more likely to be avoiding all their negativity.

Couldn't we all feel "dark" if left with no social connections or interactions? It didn't mean we were dangerous. When I asked that, I was told I wouldn't understand because I wasn't a shifter.

Patronizing, but maybe it was true. I wasn't prepared to give up on him though, and while they said they hadn't, I didn't believe them. I thought of the sketch from this morning. What had been surrounding him? Wind? It felt more than that...like the manifestations of our thoughts.

"That's deep, Willow," I said with a shake of my head as I approached the bakery.

Manifestations...I stopped walking. Like spirits?

Turning in the street, I looked down Main Street, sure that I would somehow see a sign that I was right. Instead, I saw my fellow residents, carrying out their normal day-to-day lives.

Chewing the corner of my bottom lip, I detoured from the bakery and headed to the library instead. I needed a book on spirituality before I started talking about shit I knew nothing about. As I walked, I couldn't stop thinking about spirits and Caleb. By the time that I got to our small public library, I was convinced I was right.

He wasn't lying on the ground, watching the elements; he was lying on the ground surrounded by the spirits of those he had lost. No wonder he was miserable.

I needed to help him.

"You've been quiet," Lorna said as she tidied the dinner table. "Are you okay?"

Looking up from my empty plate, I nodded. Pushing my seat back, I got up to help. "Yes, disappointed that the *independent woman* didn't happen today," I told her truthfully.

Reaching over, she rubbed her hand over my arm in a soothing gesture. "You're an independent woman, honey. Admitting to yourself you needed one more night isn't a weakness. It's a strength."

"You're too kind." I started handing her dishes, and thankfully, she'd apparently gotten over the need to do everything for me. I followed her to the dishwasher, and I rinsed as she stacked.

"I'm not kind," she told me, taking the dirty dishes and putting them into the dishwasher with the care and precision of a heart surgeon carrying out a triple bypass. "The boys rarely helped me, so it's nice to have a hand."

Frowning, I looked at her to see if she was serious. "Bad parenting," I scolded, only semi-joking. "They should have had chores."

"Oh, they did," she told me earnestly. "Noel made them work for it. Yard work, they did lots of work in and around the house. They did extra practice with their dad, so they did a lot. But the kitchen chores never stuck."

I kept my mouth shut because it sounded very much like the housework was deemed not acceptable for the men in the house. Not my business. But still, when Noel came in from the den to ask if Lorna was making more coffee, I had to bite my tongue to tell him to make it himself.

The man had stopped jobs to fix my house and store. I should be making him his coffee.

"Are you feeling better?" he asked me for the second time.

"Yes, sorry about earlier."

"It's fine, just had me worried for a couple of minutes there when you didn't come back."

I'd left him to go to the bakery. Instead, I went to the library and lost track of time. I had checked out two books, which were stuffed into my tote so they couldn't see them. Not that I was ashamed, I just didn't want to explain my sudden interest in the supernatural.

Explain that the two books had taken precedence over the

thank-you pastries. I had picked up one on spirituality and the other aptly called *How Do You Know If You're Psychic*. I planned to read them both in bed later. Not cover to cover, just skim.

It had been a good plan, and like most good plans, it went wonky when, instead of skimming them, I read them cover to cover, and when I heard Noel rise for work, I realized I had spent the whole night reading. My ME would not appreciate this, and I hastily shuffled down the bed to catch a couple of hours of sleep before the smell of bacon lured me from slumber.

I fell asleep immediately, but it was not a restful sleep. Almost immediately, image after image of Caleb flooded my mind.

The images had come to me in fragments, pieces that were hazy and unclear at first, but little by little they came into focus. Caleb was alone in the middle of that clearing I now knew as well as I knew my own home. It seemed so *empty*. The clearing had that huge log cabin in the corner and was surrounded by trees, but there was just the feeling of *nothingness*. He looked different, even in so short a time. He looked... haunted.

Caleb was tall, six three, and he always seemed taller because he had excellent posture, standing tall with confidence, and never slouched. His whole persona was one of sureness, and in the vision, he looked *less* than that. Less than him. He looked dull like his light was extinguished.

I felt as though I could see the isolation and loneliness that reached for him, eager to surround him like a blanket that offered no comfort. His head was bowed, his shoulders slumped, and when he turned his head to look my way, I saw the vacant stare, looking right through me as he stood there looking like he had given up.

I wanted to reach for him, comfort him, and tell him that even though he had isolated himself, he was not alone.

But as the fragments joined into a clearer picture, even I couldn't put a positive spin on how utterly defeated he looked. There was no sign of life around him. He was alone, no pack, no friends, no one beside him.

Only the darkness.

At first, I thought it was shadows from the tall pine trees, but then I realized it was darkness that reached for him while it stretched out impossibly far in front of him.

Image after image flooded my dreams, and as they filled my head, I began to see what I had missed before.

The darkness wasn't around him; it was *inside* him. Was it in him and wanting out, or was he taking it into himself the more he stayed away? I didn't have the answer, but I knew I couldn't bear to watch him as his strength ebbed away and he embraced the solitude that was crushing his soul.

He was fading.

Despite knowing I wasn't awake, knowing in my own subconscious that this was a dream, I still called for him. I yelled at him to rally, not to give up, but the more I yelled, the more I saw it tighten around him, almost seeping into his pores, embedding itself under his skin.

I could see it wearing him down, and Caleb—he didn't fight it. As the images slowed, I saw him weaken. I watched as he sagged further under the weight of misery that clung to him. I saw his body crouch and almost curl in on itself.

Horror gripped my throat as I saw the very ground on

which he stood turn black and boggy, ready to pull him under, pulsing in anticipation of claiming its prize.

The ribbons of darkness spun out from him, reaching to the sky and meeting...nothing. What had they said to me...he needed a pack? Is this what happened when you had none? When there were no connections to a pack or another person, effectively cutting yourself off from everyone. And only you remained, cloaked in an isolation of your own making.

The images changed, morphing in front of me, twisting into something more than a man bowing in weakness, changing to slashes of blackness that shimmered with night as they covered his body. Had it been an actual sketch, I would have drawn thick, black, heavy lines across the page, erasing the details of *him*.

Tingles of fear peppered down my back as I understood the message for the first time. Caleb wouldn't hold on much longer. He was in a battle for his soul, and he wasn't even fighting. Once he let the darkness take him, there would be no coming back, because he would be powerless to stop it.

Caleb was slipping away. If he remained there any longer, he would be lost to me forever.

I woke up in tears. I didn't care where I was, I didn't care whose bed I was in, I didn't care that Lorna would be watching the clock for me to come down. The urge to draw, to record what I had witnessed, consumed me. I reached for my sketchbook and pencil tin and began to draw everything I had seen.

My fear at what he would become, and my anger that he was letting it happen, poured out onto the page. When I was done, I sat back and looked at what I had created.

More tears spilled over. I could sense the desolation reaching out of the page for me.

Whether it was real or my brain had been fueled with my nighttime reading, I wasn't sure. Either way, I knew I was ready to leave.

I didn't have a car, and I didn't have a license. Although Lily had her truck back, the fact Caleb had put so much mileage on it hadn't gone unnoticed. I didn't have confidence in the fact I would manage to talk Lily into lending me another vehicle, especially when she knew I couldn't really drive.

But I had to find some method of transport. I knew I had to go and find out where he was and then find him before there was nothing left of Caleb to bring back.

NINE

Willow

"I CANNOT BELIEVE YOU WENT TO THE LIBRARY AND checked these books out." Lily was in my bedroom, helping me move back in. I'd been an additional two days with Lorna before I left her to come home. I took two days longer for the main reason I *had* thrown all her good work out the window when I spent all night reading the offending book in Lily's hand and then having horrible visions of Caleb.

"I thought you were making the bed?" I asked her, straightening from unpacking my backpack. "You've been sitting on it for the last five minutes."

Lily ignored me. "Listen to this: 'Determining whether you possess some form of extrasensory perception can be subjective.'" She paused in her reading to give me a dry look. "I bet it can," she muttered before she continued. "'It is often based on personal experiences, and for people who *believe* they *may* have psychic abilities, they report specific signs or feelings.'" She gave me a loaded look as she turned the page. "'Here are some examples of psychic experiences.' Are they kidding?" She didn't wait for an answer. "'Strong intuition.'" Again, she looked up at me, rolling her eyes. "Duh."

"Lily," I scolded her lightly, "there are people who believe this."

Her look spoke volumes. "Two, clairco, no, wait, clair-cogniz... Niz? Claircogniz...ance... claircognizance? Easy if you can say it," she grumbled. "Oh, it means unexplained knowing. Unexplained... What?" She held her finger up to stop me from speaking as she continued reading. "'You may *just know* information, without prior knowledge or learning. Or the *sense* of knowing could appear in dreams or spontaneous thoughts which later prove to be true.'" Her eyes met mine, and I already knew what she was thinking. "'Psychic people may have premonitions or visions.'" Her eyes widened as she read on. "'They may have vivid *dreams* or *visions* that later come to pass. The visions can feel out of place at the time but later become clear after the events unfold.'" Lily laid the book in her lap, her face thoughtful. "Wow. You could say you have clair-whatever and the premonitions."

"I thought you were a skeptic?" I teased, unloading my toiletry bag. "You read three possibilities, and now you're a believer."

"Shut up." She picked the book back up. "There's also, clair...good grief, they're obsessed with Clair!"

"Clairvoyance," I murmured and was rewarded with a throw pillow being *thrown* at me.

"Clairsentience is heightened empathy. Oooh, telepathic experience, knowing when someone is going to call or text you." She looked up at me, puzzled. "I always know when you're going to text."

"Mm-hmm." I folded my laundry.

"Ooh, I wonder if telekinesis is one?" I watched her skim the page, and the flash of disappointment on her face when she couldn't find it, made me grin. "No, just a strong connection to spirituality." She hesitated, peering over the top of the book. "Do you see dead people?"

"No."

Lily sniffed dismissively. "Boring. Okay, where was I? Experiences of déjà vu, pfft, we all get that." She scowled at the book. "Sensory disturbance where you hear or see things that others don't...yikes, creepy. Psychometry, ooh this one's cool. You sense things by touching people, objects, oooh, like a tracker dog."

"Lily!"

"What? I'm being serious!" The problem was, she probably was. "Have you astrally projected?"

"No."

"Hmm, it says you could leave your body and be in two places at once. That'd be handy. There's more. One's something I'm more likely to have, something to do with patterns and numbers." Lily closed the book. "So...psychic? Cool." She held out her hand. "When do I get married and how many kids?"

Standing up, I brushed off my jeans. "Weren't you a skeptic five minutes ago?"

"Yes, but the book says, if you feel you have abilities, you have to experiment." She held out her hand and shook it a little. "Experiment."

"The book also says that a dream journal and meditation are also things that may help."

"It also *says*"—she narrowed her eyes at me—"that there is no definitive test and to explore your potential." Her hand was back off the bed. "*Explore*."

"You're impossible." Snatching hold of her hand, I studied her upturned palm. "Oh yes, I see it. At least three husbands... no, wait...four husbands, and sixteen children."

Lily snatched her hand back. "My poor va-jay-jay! *Why* would you want to hurt it?"

"I'm not the one popping out sixteen kids." Flicking my hair back, I popped my hip out as I made a silly pose. "Ladykiller."

"Is that why there's four?" she asked excitedly. "Do I kill them?"

My arms dropped to my side. "You know I'm joking, right?"

"Yes!" Lily picked the book up, turning it over in her hands. "So, what d'ya think? The visions, the sense of knowing, that kinda fits, right?"

"I guess." I shifted my attention to my sock drawer.

"Weird that it's just Caleb."

"Mm-hmm."

"Do you think he sees you?"

The question was one I'd asked myself. "No."

"Then how did he know it was you?" Lily leaned back on her elbows, getting comfy on my unmade bed as she asked the question I asked myself...a lot. "How did he know you were his girl?"

"Misleading," I protested weakly.

"Meh." She was wearing that look, the one she got whenever she was plotting or piecing together a puzzle. Or worse...a theory. Her brow furrowed in concentration, her lips pressing together to form a line, and I could practically hear her thinking. "Okay, I accept it. You're psychic."

"Hadn't we established that with the whole *read my palm*?"

"A test," she quipped. "You failed." Grinning at me, she sat up. "You keep having the visions, and they're too specific to be just random dreams, and of course, they have your recurring Hotcakes in them." She turned pensive. "And you maybe know more things about Caleb than you should...so, yup. Psychic."

I let out a shaky laugh. "Or we're just reaching."

"What would you call it? Premonitions? Gut feelings? The book"—she tapped the cover—"says that happens." Lily sighed dramatically once more. "You're the one who went and got the books!"

"I know." I saw her face. "I *know*, but maybe I'm not ready to shout it out."

She gave a half shrug. "Okay, fine, you're probably not Matt Fraser but there's definitely something. You need to get in contact with Caleb."

If only you knew how much I was trying to.

"I don't know where he is."

"Um..." She tapped the side of her head. "I think you do." She gave me a pointed look. "I get it, I do, you're really reserved and this is way out there, even for me, but there's something between you, right?"

I didn't expect such a simple question to make me feel as emotional as I did. There *was* something between us, and I knew it was more than either of us was admitting. The more I saw of him in my dreams, the tighter I felt the link between us grow.

"Perhaps." My whisper was barely audible.

She looked at me with sympathy. "You're in this together. Neither you nor he can keep brushing this off. You need to find him and talk."

"He left, he doesn't want to be found, and I don't even know where to start looking." I sat down beside her on the bed, and she reached over to place her hand on mine.

"Then we start with what we know and work from there."

I side-eyed her. "You're making it a project, aren't you?"

"I *love* a good project," she exclaimed with a gleeful squeal.

"Whoa, boy." Pushing myself off the bed, I left her to it as I went to the kitchen for some water.

Shaking my head as she shouted out not to be shy to share the lottery numbers, I opened the fridge to get the water. I couldn't help but pause as I reached for the bottles. Something was happening to me, and I needed to face it.

Face *him*.

I knew it and so did Lily, and she didn't even know the whole picture. Surely, Caleb would be easier to convince if I could talk to him?

Easier to convince him if I could *find* him. Grabbing us water and a bag of chips that I knew I hadn't bought and was sure Lily must have, I went back to my bedroom. She was exactly where I left her, sitting on the unmade bed, the book open again on her lap as she flipped through the pages.

"Lily, you should move so I can make the bed," I scolded, dumping the bottles and chips on my nightstand. She got up off the bed, reading a page, and missed the look of exasperation I gave her.

Quickly I made the bed, biting my tongue when she sat back down on the freshly straightened cover.

"I think I may know where he is, but I need to go to him, not the other way around."

Lily looked up, reaching over and dipping her hand into the bag for some chips. "Okay, where is he?"

"With friends." *Lie.*

"Hmm." She popped a chip into her mouth. "I thought he was a loner? He has friends?"

"Mm-hmm. A few."

She shrugged as she accepted it because she had no reason not to. "And they know where he is?" She looked up at me. "Did they tell you?"

"Kind of."

That calculating look was back. "Why are you being so... evasive?"

I'd been called out and there was no avoiding it, so I took a deep breath and told her the truth. Kind of. "I need to go to *them.*" My voice sounded surer than I felt.

I watched her closely, steeling myself for her reaction. I had a fifty-fifty chance of how she would react—either casual acceptance or full-blown outrage. I'd prepared myself for either, getting ready for the tirade if she went for the latter. I was completely stunned when her face lit up with excitement.

"That's a *brilliant* idea!" She looked like a kid who'd just been told they were going to Disney.

It was? Thrown off balance, I scrambled to catch up. I hadn't expected *enthusiasm.* Wait, was she being sarcastic? "It is?"

"Of *course* it is! This is a perfect time for you to go! The store's being redecorated, and you need a break, and let's be honest—those weirdos who wrecked your home and business could come back." She nodded vigorously, her excitement palpable. "It's a *great* idea."

Staring at her, I still felt a little speechless, trying to wrap my head around how I got this so wrong. She wasn't supposed to *accept* it. "You think it's safe to go?" I asked, my voice wavering a little as I tried to remain casual. "Those weirdos, as you call them, could come back, and this time, I won't know what damage they do."

"Which is *exactly* why you go." Lily's voice was firm. "Give the sheriff the time to look into it and hopefully catch the asshats."

That made sense. But going back to that mountain where Cannon's pack was had been gnawing at me. Would they help me? They owed me nothing, but I think, I really did think, that Cannon cared about Caleb. Maybe not as a person; I mean, he was pretty unlikable sometimes, but he was an alpha. So was Cannon, and I think that mattered to them. "You think so?"

Lily shrugged, completely unaware of my inner musings. "I think you need to go find him, and I think you need to find out what's happening between you. I think whatever mysterious link there is, it needs to be broken." She gave me a look so much wiser than her years. "You need your life back. Caleb left with a lot of questions unanswered and, I think, a few things between you two that need to be addressed." She gave me a sly smile. "I think it will do you good to get away from all this."

"All this?" I looked around at the bare empty walls.

"Yes." Her look was tinged with sympathy. "The break-in at the store, the house, it's wearing you down. It's been a lot, and I think you getting away from here will give you some perspective." Lily tossed her hair. "Don't think I don't see that you've been different since coming back. I know you." She fixed me with a stare. "I *see* right through you, so don't even try to deny it."

I didn't open my mouth. She was right, I had been different. How could I not be? There were *werewolves* in the world. Plus, the visions, the dreams, the break-ins, and the feeling that something larger was closing in on me. *Weighing* on me. I felt as if I was being pulled in different directions, and I couldn't concentrate. No matter how much I denied it, the fact was that every waking moment, I was thinking of Caleb.

"Maybe," I conceded. "But can I really just leave here, not knowing if everything here is okay? That my business is going to be okay?"

"Hello." Lily gestured to herself. "I'm here, and I don't know if you met her—you were at her house for the last week—but, hello, *Lorna!* This is the *perfect* project for her. We tell her you need a break and that you trust her to run things in your absence. Girl, you will make her year."

"Lorna?"

Lily rolled her eyes at me. "Please. Save her marriage, and think of Noel. Do you think he wants to hear about Zumba, baking, or God only knows what else she's doing? The woman needs a job. Plain and simple. This is *your* chance to make a difference in her life." She gave me a look that made me brace myself for whatever she was about to say next. "And I think a certain brooding man is probably missing you more than you think."

I was already shaking my head. "This isn't about Caleb."

"Uh-huh," she said, completely unconvinced. "Sure, it's not."

I didn't push it anymore. This is what I wanted, to go and find him, so why I was now resisting my own idea made no sense. My reasons for going were different than Lily's, but she'd raised valid points. The store, the break-in, the constant worrying about Caleb or what was going to happen next—it was exhausting. And it wasn't until my friend raised it that I noticed how much it was taking out of me.

"You're right," I admitted. "I could use a break, and Lorna is the perfect choice. I hope she says yes." Lily huffed out a laugh, and I poked her leg in reprimand. "Be nice, and also, I want you to know, this isn't about running away."

"Oh, you're not running *away*," she said with a smug smile. "You're running *to* some*one*."

With a groan, I pushed myself up off the bed. "You're ridiculous," I muttered, shaking my head.

"When you're getting all hot and heavy with Caleb, you're going to thank me." Lily bounced up, full of enthusiasm. "I'll help you pack. Now, go phone Lorna, and remember to lay it on thick. She needs to know how much you appreciate her."

"I *do* appreciate her," I protested defensively. "She's been amazing, Noel too."

Lily snapped her fingers as I spoke. "That! That right there, make sure you say that." She was already in my closet, rummaging through my clothes with reckless abandon. "Where's your sexy underwear?"

My brain stuttered and I felt my mouth drop. Shaking my head, sure I had misheard, I felt my face reddening as a sweater got tossed onto the bed without Lily ever turning around. "What?"

She must have registered the tone of my voice, because she

shot me a look over her shoulder, completely unfazed. "Your sexy underwear, you know, the *nice* stuff." She looked me over. "Willow! You need to be prepared for *all* scenarios."

My mouth opened and closed a few times. "Lily, this is not —I'm not going to—" I stumbled in my need to protest. "I'm not leaving so I can have sex with Caleb!"

The flat stare was unimpressed, and she missed my glare when she turned her attention back to the closet. "Why? I would. You want to. He probably wants to. You need more confidence in yourself."

Her patronizing tone only made it worse. "You are being ridiculous—"

"Ridiculously right, you mean," she said with a grin. She turned around, holding up a black lace bra triumphantly.

That was my cue. "Yup, I'm done." I backed out of the room before she found anything else like, God forbid, my matching panties.

Her laughter followed me as I made a hasty exit. In the kitchen, I picked up my phone, ready to call Lorna and ask for her help once again. A particularly loud yell of glee made me wince.

As I called Lorna, I made a mental note to check everything Lily had packed. I had enough problems; I didn't need Caleb thinking I was trying to *seduce* him.

It didn't matter that deep down a tiny little part of me was disappointed at the thought he probably wouldn't notice even if I did try.

TEN

Caleb

October had arrived on Shadowridge Peak. The wind howled through the trees as it swept over the peak, bringing with it the scent of pine and dank earth. Shifters ran hotter than humans, so the cold didn't bother me.

Nothing bothered me anymore.

Restless, I moved easily over the terrain. This mountain, once my refuge, felt more and more like a cage. The solitude I had carved for myself over the last ten years now settled around me, weighing me down.

At the ridge, I stopped, staring over the valley and the familiar dips of the mountain. Still, the view never failed to take my breath away as I took in the stunning vistas of my home. Since I had realized the betrayal of the others, the hollow feeling in my gut had been hard to fill. The tightness in my chest had been gnawing at me for days.

A voice whispered in my mind that the isolation was causing me unease, but I knew it was better than the alternative. It was better than looking at them in their faces as they lied to me about their concerns. I hadn't figured out how they got to Willow, to make her compliant with their plans, and as I scented snow on the air, I reminded myself that I had decided it didn't matter.

That *she* didn't matter.

My eyes closed briefly at the thought. No matter what I told myself, *raged* at myself, I couldn't shake the feeling that I was wrong about Willow. Her innocence was so...raw. I doubted my own conviction that she could fake it.

Shaking my head, I turned away from the breathtaking backdrop and continued back to the cabins. As I made my way there, I contemplated what to have for dinner. Rabbit was tasty, but I had a hankering for some venison.

I yelped when without warning, it hit me—*her*.

Willow appeared so vividly in my mind that I staggered, my paws slipping on the ground as I tried to catch my balance, checking my surroundings, momentarily wondering if there *had* been something that physically hit me. But I was alone.

At first, I thought it was nothing more than a memory. I had just been thinking of her, so it would make sense. Her face, her voice, that stubborn determination that frustrated and fascinated me. But...this felt different; this was not a memory.

I was outside her...house? My form changed from wolf to man. I needed to see clearly. I needed to be human so I could make sense of what was happening.

The scene changed; her house was still there, but I could see the rest of the houses in the row. It was still daylight but silent in the sunlight. She lived on a quiet street, but this...this was too quiet.

Crouching low on the trail, immune to the cold that nipped

at my bare human skin, I blinked hard, squeezing my eyes shut and shaking my head to clear the vision. When I opened my eyes, I could still see the image clearer than the forest and rocks in front of me. The scene was clearer now, crisper.

The front door to Willow's home remained shut. But my feet took me to the back of her house. I wasn't moving—alone and naked on my Peak, I wasn't moving—but I was *moving* closer to her house, walking past her window, crouching low.

Why I crouched, I didn't know.

Her bedroom window was open, and even in the shade, wolf sight showed me the chaos that lay inside.

Suddenly, I couldn't breathe. But I needed to see more, so I rushed to look through the back door.

I saw her face. I saw the fear in her eyes. The tremble in her hands as she took in the mess, the tears shimmering as she looked around in shock. The horror registering as she realized someone had been inside her home. Her sanctuary. Violating the place where she felt safe.

Willow began to pace, her lips moving, and then she spun on her heel and went to her studio.

I could feel her panic, her frustration, and then the absolute devastation as she took in the destruction of her home studio.

I dropped down, my knees resting on the cold earth, my fingers curling into the dirt, grounding myself to the mountain as if by doing so, I could sever the connection. Instead, the connection, the *link* to her, felt stronger. Her emotions washed over me, settling around me, blending with mine, and I could feel her, everywhere. I'd never felt it this strongly before. Previously, in the past, I had felt a pull towards her, but this, this was more than a pull. This was like I was being dragged through the miles that separated us to witness what had happened to her.

"What the hell is happening?" I muttered, knowing I was on the Peak but seeing Willow's house.

Lurching forward, I felt nauseous as the scene shifted once more. Willow wasn't in the house, thank Luna, but I could see the shadows moving—dark and faceless figures moving out of the trees at the back of her house. I watched as they took entry into her home. Her space. My claws broke free of my skin with painful slowness as I fought my instincts to *run* to her, my body screaming in agony as I forced myself to be still and *watch*, to see *who* had invaded her home.

I saw one of them move closer, and my heart thumped in my ears, the blood pounding in my veins. He was a shifter, one I didn't know but one I would never forget. I drank in his features, his height, the length of his hair, and the fact he favored his left leg. Was that an injury? Permanent or recent? I knew as I kneeled on my mountain, that I would permanently wound them when I found them.

My pulse rocketed as the connection held me like a vise as I watched them move to her bedroom and touch her things. I saw one pick up a pair of her underwear, raise it to his nose, and inhale. Rage coursed through me, and I heard my snarl echo in the air around me.

My howl of rage ripped free of my body, and suddenly, the connection snapped.

Panting, my breath was coming in too short a gasp as I fought the adrenaline racing through me. I wiped the sweat from my face as I came to terms with what I had seen. My hands were submerged up to my wrists into the earth, and I could feel my claws were out.

"What the fuck was that?" My voice sounded hoarse, and I looked around, knowing there was no one here to give me answers.

Standing, I didn't enjoy the feeling of weakness in my knees. My legs felt shaky, and I wasn't sure they would hold me. Only once in my life had I felt so unsure on my feet, and I had sworn I would never feel that helpless again.

My body was streaked with dirt, which made no sense, but it was the least of my concerns. Shaking some dirt from my hands, I tried to make sense of what I'd just seen.

I wasn't supposed to see this. I wasn't supposed to be linked to her. *I* wasn't the psychic.

Only a shaman could see visions. I was no shaman, and Willow Harper sure as fuck wasn't Luna.

Neither of my parents held any other gift. My father was an alpha, and my mother was simply his mate. That was all they were. I felt a twinge of guilt; they were *so* much more, but in terms of *gifted*, they were normal.

Yet, I couldn't deny what I had seen. What I had felt.

Her fear.

So sharp I could taste it. Danger surrounded her, and I *wasn't there*.

My fists clenched at my side at the thought. My anger felt as if it would boil over. I'd seen their violation as if I was seeing it in real time, but when I had stood in front of her house, I knew that this hadn't happened today. I didn't know how I knew that, but I did. A week at most had passed.

Why hadn't she told me? Why hadn't she told Cannon? *Why had no one told me?*

Was it a trick? I rejected that as soon as I thought it.

I should ignore this. I *could* ignore this. But...what if it was real? Shifters were in her house, wrecking it, looking for something.

What were they looking for? What would they do to Willow to find it?

I took my wolf form, my body moving and running as if on autopilot as I ran to the clearing. I needed to get to Willow and make sure she was safe. I feared that whatever was coming for her was connected to me, and the idea that she would pay for something that had nothing to do with her, I couldn't have that.

Quickly, I checked the ground I had slept on for weeks. The cabins I had never gone inside. Those homes were not mine. I'd returned to this mountain, driven by the need to be here, to defend it, but now every fiber of my being was telling me I needed to protect *her*.

I didn't understand this or what was happening between us, but I couldn't shake the sight of that bastard holding her underwear to his nose, and I knew one thing was very clear—I couldn't stay here.

Willow needed me.

THE DESCENT DOWN SHADOWRIDGE PEAK WAS NO LESS brutal than the climb up. It didn't matter what form you took, it's not for the fainthearted. Which is why Shadowridge Peak was such a dream to defend.

The rock shifted underfoot as the cold wind needled under my fur. I felt the pull to get to Willow, but I could also feel the tug in my bones to turn around and head back up the way I had just come.

But I wouldn't turn back. I couldn't do that, not after seeing the fear on her face.

The tall pines that I had moved so effortlessly through now felt claustrophobic as they closed around me. The wind shook them, and the shadows gave the impression the branches were claws reaching out for me. My serene solitude now felt wrong.

I could see her as I had *seen* her. The frightened look, the unshed tears as she struggled to accept what had happened to her. The danger that surrounded her. I closed my eyes, and I could see her. With my eyes wide open, I could see it. See her, standing in the middle of her house as police questioned her. She stood straight and tall, trying so hard to be brave, trying so hard to hide how vulnerable she was.

Wherever I looked, I could see *her*.

Whoever it was that had walked into her home and destroyed it, they were still out there.

I knew it. I could *feel* it.

I could feel the link between Willow and me. It was stretched so tight, but the moment I accepted it was between us, I felt it become thicker. Stronger. The more I saw her clearer in my head, the tighter and stronger the link became.

It no longer felt fragile. No longer like it could snap at any time.

I felt like I could reach out and touch her. Was that how it was for Willow? When she drew me, was that how real I felt to her when she painted? I wished it were as simple as being able to reach out and touch her and pull her to me, to safety.

Instead, I knew there were many miles between us.

The ground beneath me moved, and I was brought back to the present, to the uneven ground beneath my paws, as the rubble and debris of the mountain warned me to slow down as my descent became steeper. My back paw slipped on a stone, and I skidded, catching myself sharply before I went sprawling. Tentatively my wolf became still, claws digging into the ground below.

I needed to focus. I would be of no use to Willow if I lost focus and ended up bloody and broken at the foot of the mountain. I ignored the reminder it wouldn't be the first time. You don't grow up on Shadowridge Peak without taking a tumble down the mountain one or two times.

It would take me days to get to Whispering Pines; did I have days? I'd come here believing that it was for the best, but now the distance between us felt like a curse.

The ground evened out so suddenly it caught many unprepared, but not me. I knew every crag of this mountain. Picking up my pace, I ran to the lower slopes of Shadowridge Peak, knowing soon the densely packed trees would even out.

Voices on the wind whispered to me as I ran, trying to slow me down, urging me to turn back, telling me that I wasn't ready. That I wasn't the hero Willow needed. That I didn't deserve to return to her. Maybe I should've listened, but I didn't.

I'd never wanted to be a hero.

What tied us together needed to be understood, but I had

left, the past too heavy for me to confront, and now my cowardice was costing her. Willow needed me.

The morning that I kissed her flashed in my mind. The way she'd responded. The taste of her on my lips. I shouldn't have left. I'd thought I was doing the right thing. Seeing her draw the darkest moments of my life had been too much. Closing myself to those old memories, I concentrated on getting to her now. What if by leaving her, I was the reason she was in danger?

The very idea of it made me feel sick. It also made me run faster, and soon I was descending the last steep incline.

The shadows of my past called for me, desperate to cling to me, but I felt a different darkness now. Something cold, and obscure, skirting the edge of my awareness. I'd seen it in Willow's house as she looked at the damage to her home. I felt it within me now. A new darkness, so different from the one I was used to, and I hated it. Hated that it was closing in on her, reaching for her, ready to tear apart her life.

And I had already wasted so much time.

Finally, I reached the bottom of the mountain, and I headed south towards the nearest town. It was miles from where I was, but it was the first place I would find clothes. I'd need to steal a car. That also wouldn't be the first time, and I doubted it would be the last. All that mattered was that I got to Willow before anything else happened to her.

I had a fleeting thought that I would be better off contacting Cannon and his pack and telling them I needed them to protect her, but the lingering doubt that they couldn't be trusted still clung to me.

I didn't have any confidence in them. I wasn't ready to face them. Right now, I only cared about getting to Willow.

Gritting my teeth, I pushed harder, my muscles burning with effort, but I ignored the burn. The road in front of me was a blur. All I could see was the vision of her—standing alone, fear in her eyes as the shadows surrounded her. She didn't know I was coming for her. She didn't know I had seen it or that the link between us, the thin thread that connected us, had become taut and stronger, pulling me back to her.

She thought she was alone. She was wrong.

ELEVEN

Willow

It shouldn't have bothered me how easy it was for Lorna and Lily to replace me, but it did.

Replace me was perhaps melodramatic, but as I stood in the corner of my own store and watched them bouncing ideas off each other, I couldn't help but feel slightly disgruntled.

Hanging up a new piece of art that had come into the store a few days ago, I was grateful for the fact it filled up the too empty walls. I clearly marked that it wasn't mine, making sure the label was obvious to anyone who cared to look. It was a small hope, probably a naive one, but if the same people who broke in before came back, they would see the label and leave this piece alone. It didn't deserve to be destroyed because of me.

While I knew I couldn't count on much anymore, I really did hope that this one tiny label would save this piece from the destruction my own work had suffered.

"Willow, if there are any sales while you are gone, how do I deal with that?" Lorna asked, turning from my computer. "I found the packaging tape and everything, but I need more information."

Standing back and looking at the newly hung piece, I admired it for a moment more before going to the counter to show Lorna how to log inventory. It shouldn't be too taxing. The walls were sparse, and any art I had produced myself I hadn't shared with anyone. I'd taken a couple of photos on my phone of ones I was sure Cannon and the others needed to see, but the rest I had destroyed.

Caleb Foster owed me compensation for the number of sketchbooks, pencils, and charcoal I had gone through. I'd bypassed paint. I had a harder time destroying canvas. The artist within me protested loudly. Plus, burning canvases brought unnecessary attention.

I knew it was silly, that I was being paranoid because of what had happened, but I had the constant itch between my shoulder blades that I was being watched.

I hadn't told anyone of my fear. They would never let me leave if they thought I was being watched. It all sounded incredibly dramatic. I was a twenty-six-year-old woman, I had no parents, and I was an adult. No one *let* me do anything. I did what I wanted.

Which is why you keep asking for permission, I snipped at myself in the same surly tones as a teenager. The thought made me smile. I did ask Lorna *a lot* if something was okay, and she took everything in her stride so easily it was a difficult habit to break.

Noel was delighted that I'd asked her for help. While she had joked when she first came to my class that she was doing as many things as possible to keep her marriage from imploding since her boys were at college, I did think there was some truth in that. Only, I think the way she had done it was perhaps the opposite of what her husband had wanted.

Noel wanted her to be happy and busy, but not too busy to avoid actually spending time *with* him. The funny thing was, I think *that* revelation had completely passed her by.

Of the three of them, Noel was the hardest to convince that my taking a break was a good idea. Well, that was unfair; he agreed with the break, but he didn't agree with the leaving town part.

I smiled as I watched her repeat the information she had just learned back to me for confirmation that she had understood it correctly. She also wrote everything down, a quality I admired. Both Lorna and Noel made me feel cared for. It was something I had rarely felt in my life, and I was clinging to it for as long as they let me. It had been a long time since I had a parental figure in my life, so the fact I currently had two made me feel rich.

"Are you all packed?" Lorna asked me, her attention on her notepad.

"Yes." I had one backpack, and that was all I was taking.

"And your friend is meeting you in Baywater Creek?"

I shook my head. "No, Kettlebridge," I told her. "Then we go to Baywater Creek." I'd never heard of the town, but Cannon had suggested it, and his tone held a fondness I didn't understand, but I didn't argue.

When you need a diversion, you take the diversion offered.

The truth was, I was going to pretend to make my way to Baywater Creek, and after two of the four buses I needed to get there, I would get picked up by Doc, who would take us to

Blackridge Peak. All very elaborate, but Royce was sure I was being watched, and I was sure he was right.

I would leave town, and if I was followed, they would follow the bus. Why I would be followed was as much a mystery as why they would break into my home and store.

Cannon was tightlipped when I asked if it was Caleb they wanted. With neither a confirmation nor denial, I was left to my own thoughts.

For someone like me, that wasn't the best option. It didn't help that I was seeing him everywhere. Caleb, not Cannon. Obviously. I scoffed at my stupidity. They all thought a break was the best thing for me. If they had asked me what I really wanted, it was to rest. I wanted to sleep undisturbed and wake rested with no new sketches to draw of the man who left me.

I really was on a roll for being a drama queen today.

"I've never heard of Baywater Creek," Lorna told me, and I snapped out of my inner musings.

"Mm-hmm." What could I say? *Sorry, I haven't either, and I only heard of it when a six-five giant told me to use it as an alibi?*

No thanks.

"It's in Colorado?"

Was it? I had no idea. I knew it was a town located along the route of the Rockies, but they stretched for over three thousand miles, covering six states and into Canada. Which state in particular Baywater Creek was in was unknown.

"Yup, it's small." I was fairly confident it wasn't a sprawling metropolis.

"Isn't it amazing how much we don't even know about our

own country?" Lorna shook her head slightly as if she couldn't quite believe it.

Knowing there were shifters out there, living among us, men and women who could *shift* into wolves, I decided to not tell her how much she didn't know about her country.

"It is a little." When in doubt about what to say, I found it was easier to agree.

"And your bus is what time again?"

Now, I narrowed my eyes at her. She knew darn well what time my bus was. She had my itinerary memorized. "Okay, what's going on?" Folding my arms across my chest, I fixed her with a steady stare.

She had the decency to blush. "I'm sorry, Willow, I'm just a worrier."

Leaning towards her, I closed the distance between us and gave her a quick hug. "I'm going to be okay," I told her, hoping it wasn't a lie. "If you don't want to do this, it's okay, I unders—"

Lorna's eyes were wide with alarm. "No! I *want* to do this. I am really looking forward to it," she admitted sheepishly. "But I worry about you, sweet girl, all alone after what's happened to you."

"I've been alone for a long time. It's fine, I'm used to it." It was an innocent offhand remark.

It did not need to take twenty minutes to appease my friends, assuring them that I hadn't meant to insult them or our friendships. When they finally had their ruffled feathers back in place and were suitably soothed, I thought maybe a break would be a good thing after all.

Buses were strange things, I decided that morning. Convenient, more eco-friendly, kind of, but they just housed such a mix of travelers. Take me, a mid-twenty-something-year-old educated business owner. Most people in my shoes had a car and, more importantly, could drive it. Compare me to the older lady two seats down from me, who was reading a book, an actual paperback and not a tablet, who had her knitting beside her. When she wasn't reading, she was knitting, the click-clacking of the needles soothing.

Both of us were maybe typical bus users? I wasn't sure. Or was it the younger guy sitting diagonally behind me? His eyes had been trained on me for a while, and it was making me uncomfortable, but not in a predatory way. He just seemed to have staring issues. Then there was the guy at the very back who burped his alcohol-fueled breath for us all to enjoy.

This was the same bus, well, maybe not the exact bus, but the same route that took me to Whispering Pines. I had felt sad as we left the town, and then had spent the next ten minutes settling down into my seat with my bag and snacks for the journey. Then I turned my attention to studying my fellow passengers because my paranoid brain wanted to make sure that there were no obvious stalkers. Which is why I kind of knew who my companions were.

Plus, I liked to make up stories about them. The older lady was most definitely a grandmother and was knitting scarves for her grandkids to get them ready for winter. The younger guy, the one with the staring issues, had anguish all over him. I was sure he was recently brokenhearted, and I reminded him of that person. The drunk in the back, well, it depended on how loud his burps were. Sometimes he was down on his luck and heading home to put the pieces of his life back together. Other times, I imagined that he'd been run out of town, his past catching up to him in one way or another.

The bus was a story all by itself, warm but worn. Every creak and rumble echoed with the countless miles it had traveled. How many people had sat in these seats, carrying not just their physical baggage but all the extra invisible weight of their stories, hopes, and failures?

My idle musings kept me entertained and distracted for the first leg of my journey. The people, the stories I invented for them, even the bus itself—everything blended into a soft, harmless daydream that passed the time. But when I got off the bus at the station, as I stepped off the small step, something shifted in the air.

Scanning the platform, I searched the shadows until my gaze landed on the really large guy standing in the far corner. As I noticed him, he noticed me, his eyes locking on mine, unblinking and direct. Unease settled low in my belly, a coil tightening into a knot of apprehension as I fought down the feeling of panic.

I kept repeating to myself that I was overreacting. My imagination had been on overdrive over the last few hours, and this was probably just a guy waiting for the next bus. Trying to shake off the uncomfortable feeling, I moved to stand nearer an exit, and I felt his eyes follow my every move. Gripping the strap of my backpack, I debated whether I could outrun him if I suddenly legged it. I knew I didn't have the speed or strength needed to shake him off.

My next bus rolled slowly into the station, and I surreptitiously glanced at the station clock. I'd planned the journey out roughly for presentation purposes, knowing I wasn't completing it. I hadn't looked too much into the schedules if I missed a connection. I was now regretting not being more meticulous in my fake journey planning.

I debated my options. I could run. No. I just knew I couldn't. Scratch that. I could get the bus that I was supposed to. What could he do to me on a bus? I'd be surrounded by other passengers, and any physical harm would be restricted. Blowing out a breath, I wondered if that was the best option. Doc was meeting me at the next stop, and I had help if I needed it.

Or I would lead them straight to Doc.

Why are we suddenly at "them?" The voice in my head sounded like Caleb, and the mix of curiosity and amusement in the tone made me miss his presence even more.

I didn't know what to do. The sudden sound of the hydraulics of a door closing from a nearby bus made me spring into action. I didn't run away to be chased. I didn't leap onto the bus to lead them to Doc.

I dived for the bus that wasn't mine, making it just in time as the driver was closing the doors. My heart was pounding as I barely squeezed through, catching myself from face-planting and flashing my ticket with shaky hands. I hoped the driver wouldn't look too closely at the wrong destination printed on it, and thankfully he didn't. He did give me a look of exasperation as if to say he just saw me standing, purposely *not* getting on the bus until the last minute, but I didn't engage.

Hurrying to the back of the bus, I sank into the seat, knowing I had gotten away with it when I saw the big guy standing on the platform, scratching his head as he watched the bus depart. It looked like he'd chased me in vain. It was a small distance between us, which was a relief, but I had no feeling of safety despite the fact the bus was moving out of the station.

Glancing out the window, I saw him take a phone out of his pocket, and I wondered who he was calling. Was I actually of any interest to him? Had he been focused on me, or was I losing my mind? Firing out a quick text to Doc, I explained I was on a different bus and then had to ask a fellow passenger where I was actually going. My text to Doc was concise, I didn't want to explain over a text why I was on a different bus, in case he thought I needed a psych evaluation.

The bus was going to the same destination, sort of. It was just taking a more scenic route, and my stop wasn't the last stop on its journey, which was fine. As my pulse slowed, the panic that had gripped me mere moments before began to feel distant. I began to think that my behavior hadn't been rational, and now safe and warm on the bus, I felt a little foolish. The guy probably hadn't even noticed me—I mean, why would he? I'd probably misread the whole incident.

Almost as if in a daze, I reached into my backpack and pulled out my notepad, dropping it open on my lap. A quick search and I found a blunt pencil, and without thinking too much about it, I started to draw. The lines were rough at first, but with each sure stroke, the tension I'd been holding onto started to fade. Shapes began to form, and slowly those lines began to take a life of their own.

Broad shoulders sat atop a bulky torso, heavy with muscle, slowly taking shape on the page. The posture was rigid, and the set of his shoulders was stiff, but there was something familiar in the way he held himself. A wide chest and long arms hanging at his side, it wasn't until I started adding the facial details that I knew who I was drawing.

The man from the platform.

His eyes stared at me from the paper, as they had at the station. My pencil hovered uncertainly over the drawing as I noticed details about him that I had missed before. His eyes were hard, unblinking, and completely emotionless. His square face was hard angles and planes, not softened by his crew cut. His button-down shirt was pulled tight under his lightweight jacket, which I wasn't sure he needed if I was correct in guessing what type of man he was.

His arms, which I had thought were simply at ease at his side, I now saw were taut with tension, his hands curled, almost as if he was fighting the urge to clench them. His stance was wide, feet apart as if he were braced for something, grounding himself in anticipation, as though he was ready to spring into action at any moment. As I looked at him, I knew I wouldn't have outrun him.

But had I outsmarted him in my desperate bid to flee?

A shiver slithered down my spine as I held his stare, fear once more knotting in my belly. Not wanting to look at him any longer, I closed the notepad and my eyes, willing myself to forget.

It would be better when I got to the others. I repeated the thought over and over, trying to convince myself it was true. Once I was with them, I would be safe. I needed to sever this tie to Caleb and his world—his secrets and the dangers that surrounded it. Maybe then, just maybe, I would be of no interest to any shifter.

My life could return to normal once more.

Normal. The word felt as foreign to me as *shifter* had only a few weeks ago. But normal was all I had left to cling to. This sense of danger and unease all the time wasn't for me.

I liked safe. I liked routine. My life had always been built around simple, almost predictable patterns. I needed stability. I liked things that made sense. Which I felt was probably the very opposite of a shifter's existence. For the hundredth time, I wondered why the hell it was *me* who was tied to someone as unpredictable as Caleb.

He was everything that I wasn't. A drifter, whereas I liked a place to call home. I wasn't built for this kind of life. This excitement and worry weren't for me, and I knew my ME would let me know about it sooner than I was ready.

Yet, here I was, on a bus with the wrong ticket, unable to let go.

With a sigh, I rested my head back on the seat, willing myself to rest so I was ready for the next step. I still had a mountain to climb. Literally. With a groan, I pressed the heel of my hands into my eyes, trying to chase the remainder away. Caleb wouldn't be there this time to carry me.

Caleb.

Always Caleb.

No matter how much I ignored it, no matter how many sketchbook pages I covered, the pull between us felt so real that I wasn't sure if I wanted to cut it, even if I could.

I did know one thing. If there *was* a Luna...I hoped she heard me as I thought about what a sick and twisted sense of humor she had.

One other thing I would tell her...she could take her amusement and shove it up her ass.

TWELVE

Willow

The bus journey wasn't as long as I thought it was. When Caleb and I traveled in Lily's truck, it felt like we were *always* in the car. But then, at the time, I wasn't taking into consideration the fact that Caleb had taken detours from his destination and then double-backed on himself.

We'd had the whole wolf-in-the-road incident, and as I journeyed on the bus, I thought about that. How naive had I been? He'd told me that he saw a program where alpha wolves were dominant and you needed to stare them down. It had sounded plausible.

Had it?

No. It had sounded like he was batshit, but had I challenged him? No. Why? Because the alternative for an explanation of what to do when in a face-off with a wolf is not *I'm a shifter and can communicate with them.*

No one was *ever* going to come to that conclusion naturally. So maybe I needn't be so harsh on myself for believing it.

Maybe.

I flipped idly through my notebook, reviewing the sketches and drawings that I had done since getting on the bus. The man from the platform was featured in detail on two pages, but there were other images and snippets of scenes that made no sense to me.

There was nothing of Caleb, and I found myself flipping back further until I found a simple sketch I'd done of him where he was shirtless, jeans hanging low, and feet bare. He was looking to the south, and I wondered what held his attention so often, as it was a familiar pose for him to be looking in that direction.

I knew it was south, I didn't know why.

I knew it was a direction he focused—fixated—on a lot. Caleb's gaze always seemed to drift that way, and I had spent too many hours wondering what unseen something pulled his focus so. Because I knew it wasn't a casual glance. The intensity of his focus was in his posture, in his narrowed stare, and I wanted to know the answer as to what place it was that he couldn't let go of.

Or who.

Was it another part of his past? The past he kept from me. *Kept* was an exaggeration. Caleb owed me nothing. Well...he owed me a huge explanation about a lot of things, but his past? Was it really something he needed to share?

He was a loner, always distant, even when we were in a truck driving for hours. I couldn't help but wonder what made him that way. What had happened to turn him into someone who thrived on solitude, who kept everyone at arm's length?

Would I ever find out, or would part of him always remain distant and a mystery?

But as the bus ate up the distance, I was honest with myself and asked possibly the most important question of all. Did I need to know? Would understanding what broke him change anything between us, or was I just fixating on him like he fixated on that direction south?

Caleb Foster fascinated me.

Even without the knowledge he could change shape and become a wolf, he would have been intriguing. There was something about him, raw and magnetic, that drew me to him long before I knew the full extent of his secrets. Caleb had a quiet intensity. The way he looked at me, and others, like he was already thinking a step ahead—it captivated me.

I wasn't one for psychic connections and star signs and all that, despite my current circumstances, but I did feel like there was an aura around Caleb, one that made you feel like there was so much *more*. Even with his quiet ways, there was a weight to his silence, and I wanted to know what it was that he found so heavy to bear the burden of. It was that mystery and depth that would have made anyone want to peel back his layers and look closer.

Doodling a few simple flowers beside the drawing I did of him before, I wondered if the fact that I was drawing scenes of him was more than "peeling back layers."

In this, I was the intrusive one. He had no say in the matter, and to an extent, neither did I. With one last look at the sketch, I closed the sketchbook and turned my attention to the countryside. The bus rolled steadily along, and through the dirty window, streaked with fingerprints from passengers before me, and dirt from the road, I watched the Colorado landscape stretch out before me, and my fingers itched to paint it. Tall pines towered over the highway, the afternoon sun showing the deep dark green of the needles. The mountain peaks of the Rockies loomed in the distance, snow evident on the highest peaks, a reminder that autumn was here, and winter wouldn't be far behind. Looking at the peaks, my eyes taking in the details like never before, I wondered which one Caleb was on.

As the bus climbed higher, the dense forestry thinned a little, opening up to wide expansive fields, and somehow their vast emptiness added to the beauty of the land. I needed to learn to drive, I promised myself. One simple road trip, and the car would be overflowing with paintings and art.

A few ranch houses were scattered across the landscape, breaking up the scenery. I saw some cattle, but other than them and the cars on the road, it was all very serene. As the bus took me further away, I felt the bubble of anxiety that I had been holding onto since the bus station dissolve a little. Even the air inside the bus felt cleaner, and the silliness of the thought made me smile.

It was so peaceful, a complete contrast to what was happening in my mind, yet the wild beauty of the landscape and those mountains casting their shadow over the land had a way of reminding me how small I was in comparison, and in the grand scheme of things, so were my problems. While I told myself this and had an "I am a blip on the radar of time" moment, I could still feel the knot of tension lingering in my stomach, and the sense of unease that had followed me since I boarded this bus was still ever-present.

No matter how beautiful it was, I still wanted to know if

the man at the station was waiting for me or if I truly just had an overactive imagination.

All too soon, I was picking up my stuff and getting ready to disembark. I needed to catch one more bus to get to Kettlebridge.

I followed the limited directions to get a local service, half expecting a rickshaw or something to be waiting to take me to the next stop. Instead, I saw the familiar shape of someone I knew.

"Doc?"

He looked up from the newspaper he was reading, checking his watch before getting to his feet. "You're early?"

Glancing at my own watch, I saw that I was. "Oh." The bus I was on was supposed to be more scenic, which it had been, but I thought I got in later. "I must have read the timetable wrong."

Doc took my backpack off me, without asking, and the feminist in me wanted to protest, but I was also relieved as it was heavy, so I decided that I could let it slide this time.

"Why is this so light?" Doc asked, hefting it over his shoulder. "Is there another bag?"

He thought it was *light*? "Um, it's heavy. No, there's no other bag."

Doc smiled. "Okay, you ready?"

"Yup." I followed him to a truck, and I shouldn't have been surprised to see Ned waiting, but I was. "Oh, hi?"

Ned was wearing shades, and I had to say, he looked very appealing in his dark khaki jacket, denims, and black boots. He had that whole bad boy vibe. Which I hadn't appreciated before, and now, knowing he was probably watching me check him out, I wished I hadn't appreciated it at all.

"Hey," he greeted with one of those slight dips of his head, all cool-like and hip. "You got any sketchbooks you need to show us?"

"Right in there, eh?" I murmured, saying thanks to Doc, who opened the truck's back door for me.

Ned wasn't fazed by my remark. "Do you?"

Pulling on my seat belt, I opened the backpack and handed the whole thing to Ned, who was in the passenger seat. Doc was already signaling to pull out. "A few of them are new." I was going to explain about the guy from the station, but Ned was ahead of me.

"When did you meet him?" He was twisted around in his seat, looking at me, his sunglasses in his hand, maybe so I could see how pissed he was in case his tone of voice hadn't been a huge indicator.

"It's a bit weird—"

"Explain weird."

I gave him a look as irritated as his own. "If you let me speak, I'd be happy to."

Ned held my look for a moment longer before he gestured for me to continue. I caught Doc's look in the rearview and bit back my snappy retort. Quickly, I ran through the events at the bus station, noting that Ned became stiller and stiller until it was quite unnerving, and I couldn't help but think of Caleb confronting the wolf in the middle of the road.

Doc pulled over, the engine idling as I finished. They exchanged a look, and with a low curse, Ned was out of the truck, striding away from it, a phone pressed to his ear.

"What just happened?"

"Tell me again," Doc instructed gently.

I fidgeted with the seat belt, looking over my shoulder to see if I could see where Ned had gone. "There was a guy on the platform at the bus station. He was huge, like them." I jerked my head to the way that Ned had gone. "He was standing off to one side, and he was just...staring at me. I thought I was being paranoid, but then I thought about everything I know now, and I don't know. I didn't like it."

"Staring at you?" Doc's voice was low, but there was an edge to it, and I wasn't sure if it was aimed at me or not, but regardless, it made me sit up straighter. "Did he follow you? Say anything?"

"No, he didn't speak. He wasn't close to me. It's why I was able to get the other bus." I thought about him standing there, scratching his head when I tricked him. "I think I surprised both of us when I jumped onto the other bus." Glancing over my shoulder one more time, I looked for Ned. "I felt it was weird, I take it you agree?"

"I think it's not normal," he told me with a grim smile, "but then, nothing rarely is." Doc leaned back in his seat. "You sure he didn't follow you?"

"I don't think so," I told him uneasily, "but I don't know. He didn't seem like the kind of guy who caught a bus, know what I mean?"

Doc was nodding, "So, he could be in a car behind the bus?"

"I don't know."

His fingers drummed off the steering wheel as we waited

for Ned to return. "If someone's watching you, we need to find out who and why. A shifter rarely stalks human prey."

"Human *prey*?" I asked. The high pitch of my voice could have broken glass.

Doc winced. "Poor word choice," he said with a sheepish shrug.

"Is this something I need to be worried about now?" I demanded.

"Probably not." *Probably?* "We'll see," he added with another apologetic smile.

Silence fell between us as we waited for Ned to return, but the silence and the previous conversation were making the truck feel claustrophobic. "Is he connected to Caleb? To the pack?"

"I don't know."

I watched the clock as the time passed slowly. I had so many questions, but it was unlikely that Doc knew the answers. Between my racing heart, gulps of air, and already overcrowded mind, I was sure I was going to snap under the mounting tension.

Looking out the back window again, I was relieved to see Ned coming back. He looked grim and serious, and I already hated whatever he was going to say.

Reaching the truck, he stooped to look through the open window at us. "We've got more to do here," he told Doc. I was pretty certain he wouldn't tell me anything.

"Like what?" I asked him, my voice tight.

"Cannon isn't sure who it was," he said with barely a glance at me. "He'll look into it." He swept his gaze over me. "The break-ins and now this," he said, turning back to Doc. "Someone's interested in her."

"Who?" I asked, jumping in before Doc spoke.

Ned shook his head, stepping back, and then with a sigh, opened the door and got in. "We'll figure it out."

"We going to the Peak?" Doc asked him casually, almost indifferently, ignoring my silent back seat meltdown.

"No." Ned turned to look at me. "Cannon wants you close, but we don't know if this guy"—his finger jabbed at the portrait of the man from the station—"is friend or foe, so until we know, we keep you close."

I waited, and when he said nothing further, I gawked at him. "Is that your pep talk? Am I supposed to be reassured?"

Ned sighed, running a hand through his hair. "Look, you're tied to Caleb. People may know more than we thought. The link between you two is dangerous. It could have gotten out."

"Caleb on that mountain is dangerous," Doc grumbled.

My anxiety levels were possibly at their peak. That's what it felt like. "Why would anyone care if I was tied to Caleb? I'm just me. Plain and simple."

"Who has a mind link to an alpha," Ned reminded me as if I needed it.

I was just a regular person, or at least I had been until Caleb came crashing into my world.

"We won't leave you alone," Doc assured me.

I nodded, though the reassurance didn't settle my nerves. I didn't sign up for this. Drawing a few innocent sketches of a hot guy shouldn't have led me here. I felt like I was drowning, and the water was so deep I wasn't sure if I'd ever make it back to the surface.

"We need to stay here tonight," Ned told Doc. "See if she's followed."

Doc looked back at me. "You okay?"

"Does it matter?" Neither of them answered and I think that pretty much summed it up.

Doc merged with traffic, and as I buckled my seat belt, the weight of everything pressed down on me. Whoever the man at the platform was, it was clear this wasn't over.

And I didn't know what to do with that revelation.

THIRTEEN

Willow

WE WERE IN A MOTEL, IN ADJOINING ROOMS. DOC WAS IN one, I was in the other, and Ned was "patrolling." I assumed, though no one confirmed, that he had shifted into a wolf. Which they seemed to think was better, and I couldn't help but wonder if they had ever considered *who* it was better for. I knew if it was me—*and not just because it was me*—seeing a wolf lurking around the edge of my motel would freak me the hell out. It wouldn't make me feel safe or protected even if there was a solid wall between me and it. I would scream, lock myself in the room, and call Animal Control or something, to bring their attention to it.

And I was a pretty level-headed person. I could already see Lily's reaction. She would have things pushed up against doors and be demanding boards over the window just in case. How they could think a wolf wouldn't draw more attention than a guy, was perhaps a demonstration of how out of touch they were with actual humans. A wolf, especially in a place like this, would only stand out, not blend in. People noticed that kind of thing. "Oh, did you see the wolf?" From there, it would escalate, and if they wanted to stay under the radar, this was the complete opposite of doing that.

Or maybe I was overthinking it and the people using this motel were weary, blurry-eyed travelers who only saw the bed waiting for them.

Doc currently had the interconnecting door open, not open fully in an inviting manner but in an "if you want to come in, you can" manner. He knew I had questions, and I did want to ask all of them, but I didn't want to ask *him*. I knew it was to my detriment, but the only person I wanted to tell me all about shifters was the one man I wanted to track down.

My fingers brushed along the cover of my sketchbook. Biting my lip, I looked between the door and the book. I wanted to draw, and I had a strong desire to do so, but I wasn't sure if it was rude to sit down and lose myself in a sketch. I didn't feel any other compulsion like I sometimes did when I drew Caleb. I just wanted to unwind and lose myself in some pretty landscapes inspired by my bus journey here.

"You want anything to eat?" Doc asked, startling me. I hadn't noticed him come into view from his room. His eyes dropped to my hand and the sketch pad, but he said nothing as he waited for me to answer.

"Um..." I didn't know. Was I hungry? "Maybe?"

He nodded, walking further into my room but not far. I think he was trying to let me know there were boundaries. A fact I appreciated.

"Same. I could eat, but *do I want to* is pretty much how I'm feeling."

"Exactly." He was a relaxing guy. He would have been

perfect in a hospital or a GP's practice. He just had a smooth manner. "Why aren't you a doctor somewhere?" I blurted without thinking.

Doc chuckled at my embarrassment when I stumbled over an apology for my rudeness. "It's fine, Willow. I *am* a doctor somewhere," he reminded me. "My patients are just more specialized than others."

"So...what kind of ailments do you treat them for?" I asked as I sat on the bed, and Doc took the unspoken invitation to come into the room. He looked at the one chair in the corner, and I nodded. "Please, sit."

"Well, to be honest," he began, "they don't really need me for day-to-day things. If they get a bruise or a cut, they can shift, and the magic of the shift heals them."

"Magic?" I could hear the skepticism in my voice, even though I *knew* they had to have something supernatural about them to be able to turn into wolves to start with.

Doc watched me with understanding. "I get it, I do," he assured me. "There are words and terms in our vocabulary that we're so familiar with we don't even question them anymore. Words like *magic* or *shifter*. They roll off the tongue so easily, but when you think of the actual definition in reality? That's a lot harder to accept in our general day-to-day. It's all very well to read about magic in books or see it in a TV show or movie, but when you're faced with it, in *your* reality, in your own life, then it stops being a *concept* and becomes truth, and it's a truth that you *can't* ignore. That's when the veil between reality and make-believe comes down and the real challenge begins. How do you adjust to that? How do you accept something into your every day that was once nothing more than fantasy?"

"I'm ready to be given the walkthrough," I joked lightly, holding my hand out. "Cheat sheet please?"

Doc laughed, shaking his head. "I don't have one, but I can let you know how I coped when I found out I was...different."

"If you don't mind sharing?" I asked, getting comfortable on the bed.

"My mother is human," he told me with no preamble. "My father is not." He didn't let me ask questions, moving on swiftly. "I don't know who he is, but my mom assures me that their relationship was consensual, and he took off when she learned she was pregnant."

His words were sure, well-practiced, and I wondered how many times he had told this story and how many times he had practiced it to remove the emotion from the retelling. "Sorry," I murmured.

"Nothing for you to be sorry for. I wasn't the first guy to have a deadbeat dad, and I won't be the last." This time, there was a hint of anger, but he recovered quickly. "Mom never knew Dad had something more in his DNA, and it wasn't until I met Cannon that I knew I was different. I was twenty-eight."

My eyes widened in shock, and his lips twitched with a smile.

"Yeah, I pretty much had that look too. Cannon knew I was more than human but not enough to be a shifter. From my understanding, it's not something that happens a lot. Shifters like to keep to themselves, and for most, a relationship with a human is frowned upon. It risks exposure. So the more they populate the world with half-breeds—" He held up his hand at my reaction to the term. "It's not a slur in *this* context; it's an accepted term in our society. And it's a truth. I am half of one type of species and half of another completely different."

"Doesn't mean I have to like it," I grumbled.

"True." He gave a quick smile and continued. "I didn't take the news well. I was an educated man—I was a *doctor* for God's sake—but it's very hard to deny the facts when the guy in front of you strips down and shifts into a big black wolf."

"I can imagine."

"Scared the shit out of me. I ran every test possible for where I was." He saw my look of confusion. "I was a medic in the army. Cannon was a soldier. We served together."

"The *army* army?"

"From adolescence to early twenties, male wolves have anger issues," he told me easily. "They need to expel all that pent-up energy, and many of them join one form of armed service or another. They learn discipline and training, and since they can't be too badly harmed because of the ability to shift, they do well in the military."

"I'm thinking scary super soldiers," I admitted with a shudder.

"No, they don't abuse it. They don't draw unnecessary attention to themselves. The whole existence of shifters is to stay *under* the radar. They don't want human attention. At all."

"Because?"

"Because we're human, Willow. And we're the most destructive, vile species that ever lived. We'd swoop into their packlands and take them and experiment on them, cut them open, try to breed them. It would be a horror story."

It was a horrible picture he painted, but I also couldn't defend it. "So, what did you do when you accepted it?"

Doc rubbed his cheek, reddening slightly. "Exactly what I just shamed humanity for. I experimented." He winced at my reaction. "Yeah, I'm a hypocrite, but I wanted to know what *my* limitations were. I knew I couldn't shift, but could I heal? Would I stop aging? Was I as susceptible to illness as my fellow man?"

"And?"

"I can't heal, not completely, not like them. I can heal faster. A broken leg on my body takes maybe two weeks to be as good as new instead of the four to six weeks for the rest of us. I definitely age," he added ruefully, "but slower. Like them, but not as slow as they do. Illness, it depends. I wasn't really sick as a child, and it wasn't until I met Cannon that I knew why. But I can still get sick. I test the pack regularly with diseases and always test myself too." He grimaced. "Had some pretty bad experiences, I have to say."

"And the terminal illnesses? How can you test for that?" I was completely caught up in his story.

"I can't and shifters aren't immune to all diseases. The big C is as much a curse word to them as it is to us, but rarer in them. I've come across only one case of leukemia. No MS, no Parkinsons, but I haven't met them all yet."

"You like this research," I realized aloud, "don't you?"

"Love it," he told me truthfully. "I have near-perfect specimens to compare against"—he pointed at himself—"and me."

"Sounds dangerous," I cautioned him. "So, where do I come into this? I don't have mixed DNA. What makes me different?"

Doc sat back in his seat. "I don't know," he admitted. "I know there is magic in the world. I live with it, so I can't rule out it's just one of those things, but I am also a doctor, and science rules my life," he said with a self-deprecating laugh. "But I also know the shaman, and I've seen the gift of Luna in his workings."

"Like what?" I wanted to learn everything.

"Well, when he licked your blood, remember?" Seeing me nod, he continued. "The analysis he did with a simple taste, I would need a petri dish, a microscope, and several machines."

"Bummer."

Doc grinned widely. "Thank you, you truly appreciate how frustrating that is for me." He smoothed his palm over his jeans. "I tried to explain that to my friends, and they did not get it at all."

"I guess their reality is that some doctor can replicate what their shaman can do."

Doc looked thoughtful. "I don't think I ever thought of it that way."

"So, the new reality for me is that I have to accept they can heal themselves, they are ageless, and they are all really big and strong?"

"Yup."

"And I can see them?"

"Both physically and non-physically."

"And if I was to guess, the latter freaks them out as much as it freaks me out?"

"Pretty much," he confirmed.

"And how do we stop it?"

Doc's look was assessing. "Do you want it stopped?"

"Yes."

"So quick to answer."

Puffing my cheeks out, I blew out a breath. "Yes." I broke eye contact with him. "I can feel his pain," I admitted softly. "When I draw or paint him, I can feel him. It's not my place to do that. I hardly know Caleb, and I'm pretty sure he doesn't even like me." Doc cleared his throat but said nothing. "Even the guy from the platform, I can feel his frustration from me evading him. And I spent the better part of my journey trying to convince myself that I didn't, but this is our safe space," I joked. "We can share here without judgment, right?"

"Of course."

"Well, I can feel it *all*," I admitted, saying it out loud for the first time and accepting it as *my* reality. "The emotion, the... *weirdness* of knowing that they're real-life...people?"

"Still people," Doc confirmed.

"The places I paint, I can feel the difference. I know something, um, what's the word, otherworldly?" It felt right. "Yeah, otherworldly is happening there. I don't mean aliens and shit, just, more—"

"Magic."

We looked at each other, and I slowly shook my head. "It seems so contradictory for a man of science to say that word so easily."

"Oh, trust me, it didn't come easily, not until very recently."

"What changed?" I asked curiously.

"Cannon's wife is very persuasive."

The emphasis on *wife* piqued my curiosity. "You didn't want to say *wife*? Why?"

"They're mates," he told me after a moment of consideration. "It's a magical pull. They are mated to each other."

"Like fated?" I thought about it. "That usually has negative connotations in books and things."

"It's a good thing," he assured me. "They share a bond that only Luna can give them."

I thought about it. "Is this what..."

"No," Doc corrected me. "You're human. You aren't his mate. You couldn't be." I didn't know what he saw in my face, but he looked sympathetic. "I'm sorry."

I was already riding the train to denial as I waved his comment off, brushing it aside with a forced laugh. "No, no need to be sorry. I don't want to be anyone's fated mate. Especially Caleb's."

The words felt too flippant, too casual, like saying them out loud would make me feel as if they were true. But as I spoke them, there was that nagging part of me that knew the truth. Denying it didn't make it any less real—it just made it easier to pretend that I wasn't disappointed.

Because maybe I *was*.

And I wasn't ready to explore that. Not yet.

"I wonder..." I began hesitantly. "I get what you're saying, I do, and you know better, I get that too. But if Luna, your Goddess, is hands-off humans and that, then why is she sending *me* visions? A human?"

Doc grimaced. "I don't know." His look was assessing. "The shaman has a theory."

"I'm listening."

"He believes that with Caleb being distant from his home, his pack, and the way of pack life, that he would have been more open to a human than a shifter."

"Open?" I gave him a dubious look. "Caleb?" Doc nodded

once. "I don't think that man knows what it means to be open," I added skeptically.

Doc sighed, leaning back in his chair. "I admit, I think that may be the truth, but..." He paused, his look one of consideration, judging what to say next. "But, he has responded to you better than with others."

"Has he?" I grunted, looking down at my hands, which were clasped in my lap.

"Caleb's spent ten years away from his packlands. He's lived among humans, hiding his nature, suppressing it. He's been a loner for a long time. And that's dangerous."

"Why?"

"Lone wolves don't survive for long."

"He's been alone for ten years." I heard the defensive tone in my voice and cursed myself for sticking up for him when he hadn't stuck up for me.

"Wolves are pack animals," Doc said smoothly. "They thrive in a family environment. They are *social* animals."

Social? Caleb? The thought was funny. "Someone needs to tell him," I cracked the joke, expecting a laugh, a smile at least.

"I think that's what you're doing," Doc said casually, his eyes watchful. "We think, well, the shaman thinks, that your visions, sketches, they're a reminder of what he's lost." He sucked his teeth. "And that your artwork is reminding him of what he needs to survive."

"Why can't he be left alone?" I felt like I was too demanding when I said that.

"Because a lone wolf turns."

"Turns?"

"We call them rogues." Doc was watching me with an

intensity that made me realize how important this was, and I paid closer attention. "No pack, no accountability, no anchor to pack life." He considered his next words carefully. "They spend more time as their wolf, and as they do, they lose their humanity. Turning wild. Dangerous."

"Caleb isn't like that."

"Not yet." The empathy he'd displayed earlier was gone. The look was hard. The belief he was right was evident in the set of his shoulders, the focus of his stare. "He's an alpha, Willow. His destiny isn't to be living alone, it's to provide for a pack. It's to keep the bloodline alive."

The stab of jealousy I felt was unexpected, but what did I expect? I may care for Caleb, but I never thought of him as my future. Christ, we didn't have a present, never mind anything else. I was being silly.

But hearing that Caleb's destiny, his *fate*, was to be head of some extended family and impregnate a *mate* to produce babies for his bloodline to continue, made me sad.

"If his Goddess only wants for him to be a domesticated man, she chose the wrong shifter." Pushing myself to my feet, I tugged my sweater down. "I don't know him well, and I never knew what he was like before, but I can tell you that she's gonna need a helluva lot more than me and a sketchbook to convince that man to be *sociable* or conform to anything that he doesn't want to."

"The shaman could be wrong," Doc conceded after a moment's silence.

I don't think he believed that though, and I didn't like that a part of me didn't believe it either.

"Why me?" It was the fundamental question after all. "I'm

not his mate. I'm not his pack. I'm not a shifter. Why has Luna picked me? You don't believe that explanation of me showing him what he's missing out on any more than I do."

"We don't know."

"Shouldn't you?" I challenged, causing Doc to smile.

"We're trying."

Well, try harder.

Being told so emphatically that I had no future in his life cut deeper than I wanted to admit. It was like a punch to the gut I hadn't seen coming or ever expected. The sharp sting of reality gnawed at me, taking root under my skin, and it didn't make it easier to accept.

Denial had its limits, and I was already way past the city line. Every word, every dismissal, only pushed me closer to having to confront the mess of my emotions that I'd been avoiding looking too closely at.

But pretending that this didn't hurt didn't make it any less real, and I was running out of places to hide from the truth.

FOURTEEN

Willow

WE WENT OUT TO GET DINNER. DOC WAS VERY CASUAL IN his approach to protecting me. I was sure Ned would have preferred me to be locked in the room, but Doc was more of a "let's see what happens" kind of guy.

It was a little bit freeing and also slightly terrifying. I knew Caleb would disapprove, and it was probably for that reason that I was sitting in Doc's truck, eating my weight in drive-thru burgers.

"Should we get Ned something?"

"He'll eat on his own." Doc didn't look up from his fries. "You don't need to worry about him."

Was it wrong to say I wasn't? I hadn't given one thought to Ned until now. Opting for silence as the best answer, I ate my meal.

"So, apart from your ME," Doc started, glancing over at me, "what else should I know about?"

I paused, my fry halfway to my mouth. "You mean like allergies?"

"Sure."

His casual indifference made me frown at him, and I saw him hide his smile as he sipped his soda.

"You're a terrible interrogator," I chided him, causing him to chuckle. "Not much to know about me, I'm afraid. Family history, I can't tell you, I don't know them. I was pretty healthy as a child." Popping a fry into my mouth, I chewed quickly. "Medically speaking, I'm allergic to penicillin."

"Inconvenient," he murmured.

"Well, thankfully, I've never had to test it." Picking up a fry, I dropped it again. "I'm O-negative, but I am sure you knew that."

"Also inconvenient," he said with a grin.

"Other than that, I'm normal." I waggled my eyebrows at him, and he laughed.

"Any food intolerances, hay fever, shellfish?"

"Isn't shellfish a food?" I teased.

"Accepted." He rolled his wrapper up, his food finished. "Nothing alarming," he agreed. "Not sure I would say normal though." He winked playfully.

"True." I finished my meal, and we gathered our trash into the bag. "I'll drop this in the trash," I told him, reaching for the door handle.

"I'll do it. You stay in the truck."

So maybe he's not as casual with my safety as I thought. I watched him stride with confidence to the trash can, and then he lingered in front of a small jewelry store. He idled for a few minutes, and with a glance at the truck, he looked like he remembered I was there.

"See something you like?" I asked him when he got back in.

"I'm out of touch with some things," he admitted. "I saw a necklace that an old friend would have liked." He didn't hide his wistfulness as he spoke.

"You're no longer friends?" I guessed that's what he meant by "out of touch."

"No, I'm very much off the grid now."

"Oh." The atmosphere had changed slightly. "I'm sorry." Curiosity pushed me to ask the next question. "What was it?"

"An amethyst silver necklace." Doc pulled away from the sidewalk.

"Pretty," I murmured. Tugging at my thin gold chain, I looked at the store as we passed. "I don't wear silver," I told him, wanting to lighten the mood to before. "I'm a gold girl myself."

"Expensive," he joked.

"Yeah, I know, I'm so high maintenance." I laughed. "Plus, I prefer not to have the red itchy skin and blisters, you know." I caught him staring at me. "I'm allergic to silver jewelry," I explained. "Makes my skin break out." He was still paying more attention to me and not the road. "Why are you staring? Are you trying to crash the truck?"

"Nothing," Doc told me hastily, looking away.

Weird.

Back at the motel, we kept the door open again, and Doc asked me if I was comfortable with it open during the night, to which I said yes. I didn't go on to tell him I felt safer like that, and I didn't think I needed to. He was a pretty intuitive guy.

I was in bed, jammies on, sketchbook on my lap, when I heard Doc's door open. The low murmuring of voices was still loud enough to identify Ned. When the interconnecting door got pulled closed with no explanation other than the unspoken message of them wanting privacy, I put my sketchbook aside and, like any other person would, went over to the door to listen.

I couldn't hear anything, which annoyed me, and then I remembered they would hear *me*, and I hurried back to the bed. I sat and waited for one of them to come to me, but neither of them did, and the unmistakable sound of the main door closing had me hurrying out of bed again to go to the window and peer outside into the night.

"Go to bed, Willow."

I yelped in surprise, turning to face Doc. "What happened? Why did he come back?"

Doc was at my bed, my sketchbook in his hands. "What's this?" he asked me instead.

I flushed guiltily. "It's just a doodle."

Looking at me with raised eyebrows, he held the pad up. "This full-blown scene of a pack gathering is *just* a doodle?"

"I got carried away," I told him, crossing the distance and taking the artist pad off him. "You gave me the idea earlier with the whole social gatherings. I was bored," I added defensively. "I doodle when I'm bored."

He didn't say anything for a moment, and then with a shake of his head, he went to the adjoining door. "Remind me never to show you my *doodles*." He looked at me over his shoulder. "Get some sleep."

It took a lot longer to sleep after Ned had left, but I did drift off eventually.

Waking up with a hand over my mouth, struggling to breathe was terrifying. My heart was racing as panic took over, and I fought for breath. It took me a moment to register where I was. The shadows of the unfamiliar room merged, adding to the sudden suffocating darkness. The weight of the hand against my mouth was too heavy, too constricting, and as I started to struggle, I felt another hand press into my shoulder.

"Shh, it's me," Ned whispered urgently. I instantly stopped fighting, but he kept his hand over my mouth. "You need to do everything I say," he spoke into my ear. "No questions, no hesitation. Okay?" I nodded, and I felt the answering squeeze of my shoulder. "There's no time to dress," he added.

He removed his hand, and I felt him move away. Quickly I pushed back the covers, getting to my feet and stumbling over my sneakers, which he had placed as close as possible to the bed. I felt his hand grab me and steady me, the unspoken warning to be more careful communicated by the tight squeeze of my elbow. Slipping my sneakers on, I felt something soft being pushed into my hands. Recognizing it for my sweater, I pulled it hastily over my head.

I took a brief moment to take a deep inhale, pushing the last vestiges of sleep from me. Ned reached for me—I assumed it was him—and he led me away from the main door, keeping a firm hold of me.

I recognized the smell of the bathroom, and a thin sliver of moonlight seeped through the high window. A high window Ned was now pushing wide open. When I realized his intent, I was backing away, but he yanked me closer.

"I lift you up, you go through, you drop, land in a crouch. Brace yourself for impact, and try not to scream."

Wait...what? Try not to scream? Brace myself? What the fuck?

I had no chance to ask, because I was picked up and soon, I was grabbing for the thin window ledge. I wanted to scream at him that I was never going to fit through this, and how far was *down* on the other side, but he said to do what he asked, and I was too scared of whatever was out there to stop now.

The little air I had in my lungs left me with a whoosh as I was manhandled to the position that allowed me to wiggle through the window. It was a bit bigger than I'd thought, but I had no time to be thankful. A firm hand landed on my butt for a shove, and then I felt his hands on my sneakers, and I was practically pushed through the window.

Headfirst.

I swallowed my scream as I fell.

Land in a crouch? Was he joking? The fact I never broke my neck was a miracle as I clambered to my feet. A hand grabbed for me, and I yelped in fear, but a warm hand over my mouth and a flat palm between my shoulder blades let me know Ned was right behind me.

With a gentle shove, I started to run. We ran around the back of the motel, and I was confused as we ran *away* from where the truck was parked, but as promised, I never said a word. I needed my breath to do the sudden sprinting that was expected of me and to hold back the fear that was robbing me of every deep breath possible.

When I heard the footsteps behind us, I didn't need Ned pulling my arm out of its socket to encourage me to run faster. My feet found their second wind easily.

The lights of a truck caught my attention, and I said nothing as I was scooped up, the door open, and then I was being bundled into the back seat of Doc's truck. Doc already had the engine running and had the truck in reverse before Ned had closed the door.

"Hang on," he told me.

The tyres screeched, screaming against the asphalt as they spun at the speed Doc used to reverse. The sharp smell of burning rubber surrounded us, and my body jolted forward as the car lurched into drive. I gasped against the tight pull of the seat belt against my chest.

"Seat belts work," I grumbled through clenched teeth, but he ignored me.

Doc put his foot down, his hands gripping the wheel tightly, his eyes on the rearview more than the road in front of him. Every nerve in my body was on edge, and my heart felt like it was in my head with the pounding in my ears so loud.

We raced out of town, and from the tension of Doc's shoulders, I kept my questions to myself, peering out into the darkness to see if I could see if we were being pursued.

The tension eased from him gradually, and it was only when his white-knuckled grip on the steering wheel lessened that I dared ask my first question.

"Where's Ned?"

"Behind us," he answered, the tone of his voice tight. "Your backpack is on the floor. Check you have everything?"

I hadn't even seen it, that's how high my adrenaline had been. Pulling it onto the seat beside me, I didn't ask why my backpack was fully packed, including my toiletries. I rifled through my sketchbooks, and when I looked up, Doc was watching me in the rearview.

"I left one," I whispered, and I saw his eyes close briefly. "It was on the bed."

"I'll let him know." He had the phone at his ear, and I heard a man's voice answer, too low for me to identify. "One's behind. She says it's on the bed." He paused. "*Yes*, we checked the bed, but if we missed it, we missed it." Another pause. "I understand." He hung up and dropped the phone beside him, turning to look at me. "You okay?"

"Not at all."

That made him smile. "Yeah, I get that." His next look was assessing.

"It had a new sketch of Caleb," I told him before he asked. "It was generic. Just Caleb in jeans, boots, a shirt, and a jacket."

"Dressed?" Doc asked me, and my cheeks flared with heat. Did he know that I spent far too long admiring Caleb's abs?

"Yeah." I cleared my throat. "Why?"

"Where was he?"

I shook my head. "It doesn't work like that. I don't know."

"Forest, mountain, town?"

I thought about my sketch before bed. "Trees...thinner than usual. Not as dense."

Doc cursed and picked up the phone again. "He's on the move," he told the person who answered. "She left a sketchbook. The most recent drawing is of Caleb, fully dressed." He listened to the person, nodding along. "Sure." He reached behind him, the phone in his hand. "Cannon needs to ask a few questions."

Taking the phone with trembling fingers, I put it to my ear. "Hello?"

"How are you holding up?" His voice was low and steady. It soothed me instantly.

"Freaking out?" I admitted.

"I bet. You're unharmed though?"

"We left Ned behind!" I blurted in panic.

"He'll be fine. Worry about yourself, Willow." Such a simple request that wouldn't be that simple to carry out. "The sketchbook?"

"Not much in it. It's smaller, maybe A5 in size. It was a quick sketch. We'd been talking about Caleb, and he must have been in my mind. It says nothing," I added defensively. "It's very generic."

"It's a sketch of a man you shouldn't know," Cannon reminded me gruffly. "I've sent Ned back to see if they found it. Hopefully, the way you got out confused them."

My stomach roiled with anxiety. *"Them?"*

I heard his slight hesitation, and then he spoke with the same authority I was used to from him. "Yes, them. I'm sure you were aware there was more than one of them. It looks like we're dealing with a pack." Cannon let that sink in. "You're on their radar, and I think it's safe to say that it's no longer an accident."

The heavy realization of his words weighed on me, making me feel so much smaller than I was. Weaker. Hearing it said made all my attempts at denial futile. "Is it the same pack that trashed my store and my home?"

"Likely."

Breathing was difficult. My breath was too shallow. "Right. Likely," I repeated stupidly.

"She's having a panic attack," Doc said, sounding very far away. I felt a shudder, and when a cool hand rested against my forehead, I jolted with surprise. "Okay, Willow, it's just me," Doc said soothingly. I was being maneuvered, and the fresh night air made me take a deep breath. "Head between your legs, girlie." His hand was on my head, gently pushing me down. "Just keep breathing steadily until the world stops moving, okay?"

I nodded, because he was right. The world was spinning. But I also knew we didn't have time for me to be freaking out. I felt him move away from me, his voice low as he spoke to Cannon. When he came back, I was sitting straight, my knees drawn to my chest.

"Seat belt on?" Doc asked, getting back in the truck.

"Yes."

"We've got a few miles to go until the next stop. Will you manage?"

"I'm literally in the back of a truck," I said, hating how emotionless my voice sounded. "What can I not manage about that?"

"You'd be surprised." The roar of the truck starting cut off my reply.

We didn't speak. The only sound was the truck as it drove along the quiet road. The night outside was a seemingly black void, broken only by the truck's headlights as it cut its way through the darkness. Staring out of the window, I hated the eerie silence.

It was too quiet. Too still.

A deafening thud caused the truck to jerk violently, just as the truck was lit up with lights from the vehicle behind us that seemed to come from nowhere. Twisting in my seat, I saw the black shadow of a truck behind us, dropping back and then speeding up to ram us again.

"Doc!" I screamed just as the truck hit us again, and I heard the screech of metal as they drove into us, pushing us along, suddenly dropping back. I heard Doc yell, and then I heard the hiss all around us as the truck's tyres blew, and then we were spinning in circles. My body slammed into the door, my seat belt constricting my movement as my hands clutched at the empty air.

"Hold on!" Doc shouted above the noise, and I knew he was fighting to control the vehicle, but between the impact of the hit and the tyres blowing, I knew he was as useless as I was in the back seat. The truck hit something hard, making us lurch off the road, and then the windows exploded, glass raining all around as the world flipped.

My head banged against the roof as we rolled, gravity pulling at everything all at once. My screams were lost in the mix of metal crunching as we tumbled down a ravine.

As suddenly as it started, the truck came to a sudden staggering stop. My body tried to jerk forward, but the seat belt held tightly on, and I felt it burn against my neck from the force of the jolt.

My hair hung around me, my body felt broken, and I felt a wetness running down my face, knowing it was blood as it dripped onto the roof.

I was upside down. There was nothing to be heard except my own strangled breathing, and I was being strangled by the seat belt that had saved me from being thrown from the truck.

"Doc?" I didn't recognize the hoarse whisper that came from me. Dizziness swamped me. "Doc?"

Silence answered.

FIFTEEN

Caleb

I'D TRAVELED FAST. ALTERNATING BETWEEN WOLF AND man, I'd stolen more clothes in a few days than I had in my entire life. I'd almost reached Whispering Pines when I'd stopped.

The connection between Willow and me had never been this visceral. But I was a few miles from her home when I pulled the stolen car over and got out, inhaling deeply.

My eyes narrowed on the road I'd just been on. Wetting my lips, I forced myself to concentrate and focus.

"Son of a dick," I cursed, hurrying into the thicket. Stripping off my clothes, I changed to my wolf, relying on the wolf's sense of smell more than mine. I'd passed a bus on the road. The fact that she was likely to have been on it pissed me off. Where the hell was she going? Did she know she was in danger? Flooring it, I raced after a bus I passed a few hours ago.

I didn't even know the destination, but I would find her.

I checked three bus stops before I caught the scent of her. I made the change from man to wolf. I was in packlands now. I couldn't remember the shifters of this territory, and they lived further up the mountain, but still, it was easier to deal with patrols in my wolf form.

I never met any, and I made a note of where I had been, because even though I was a drifter, there was *always* pack border patrol to talk around while you passed through. The fact that there wasn't any here was noticeable.

After deciding to not go on to Whispering Pines, I stood in a wrecked motel room. The jeans I wore were too short, the shirt too big, and the boots fit but they were old and worn. I'd grabbed the jacket from the back of someone's truck at a drive-thru. It had been hard to detect her scent over the smell of fast food, trash, and fumes, but I got a brief hint of her.

"You her boyfriend?" Turning my attention to the night receptionist who was looking at me with interest, I nodded once. "You know she was with *two* other guys, right?"

I'd scented Doc, but the shifter was fainter. Confirmation that Willow was traveling with two people made more sense.

"So, she cheating on you?"

Bending down, I grabbed the edge of the bed and lifted it, the frame creaking under the strain. With a quick jerk of my head, I motioned for her to look. "Anything under there?" I asked, my voice low but tense.

Her hesitation and look of wariness lasted but a moment before she crouched down, then with another look at me, she ducked her head to see if there was anything hidden.

"You see anything?" I asked, but she was stretching under the bed.

"Only this?" She straightened, holding a notebook in

between her finger and thumb like it was diseased. "You interested in this?"

Snatching it off her, I flicked through it, recognizing the familiar pencil strokes, hesitating briefly when I saw how much I featured on the pages. Closing it, I shoved it in my back pocket.

"Thanks."

"That it?" she asked indignantly.

"That's it." I walked out of the room, ignoring her muttered curses about being too lousy to tip. I walked around the back of the motel, and from the ground, I could tell that Willow and the shifter had come out the window.

Which meant they were being chased.

"Damn it." I needed to get to her, fast, because time was slipping away. I would need to use both human and wolf forms to be most efficient. The wolf could cut across the mountains for speed, but I would also need to use the efficiency of human transport.

If Doc was with her, then they'd be heading to Blackridge Peak. The last place that I wanted to be. I didn't want to be around Cannon or his pack, but I didn't have much choice.

Looking at the Rockies, I decided to take a car as far as I could, and then the wolf would take me across the ridge. I needed another car. I wasn't particularly proud of how easy I found it to steal. But picking pockets was one of the ways I'd gotten by for years when I needed money or transport.

I ended up with a hybrid that had a small engine, but it was clean, had a full tank of gas, and I'd heard the owner discussing going to the movie theater with a date, so they wouldn't miss the car for hours.

Driving out of town, I once again felt a surge of resentment towards Cannon's pack. Yet I couldn't avoid him or his pack. Willow was heading there, and I knew I wasn't the only one following her.

The thought sobered me. Who else would be tracking her? What did they want with her? Was it me? Were they out to get me and thinking they could use Willow to do it?

As I sat in a stolen car, heading to a pack I didn't want to see, the irony that it was working wasn't lost on me. But the thought that if I didn't reach her first, that if they got to her before I did...

Pressing my foot down on the pedal, the little hybrid roared in response, echoing my frustration that I couldn't let anything happen to her. I'd destroyed the cell phone when I left Cannon's house that day, and I hadn't replaced it. The only number in it had been Royce's, and I no longer remembered it. I wanted to talk to one of them and find out if she was safe, but I also didn't want to trust any of them.

I was still sure they were trying to trick me, but I knew in my bones that Willow being in danger wasn't their fault.

It was mine.

NICHT FELL QUICKLY. THE ROAD WAS EERILY QUIET, THE moon hardly a sliver in the sky. As the car ate up the miles, the feeling of urgency began to ride me harder. Tension settled within me, and I couldn't shake the feeling that something was wrong.

Something was really fucking wrong.

With frustration, I opened the windows, letting the night air saturate around me as I hoped to catch a trail of her scent. Blue and red lights shone in the distance, and I pushed the car even faster, slowing down as I approached but wanting to run into the thick of it.

Getting out of the car, I edged closer. No one noticed me as I slipped into the trees. The smell hit me before I saw anything.

Blood.

My breath caught in my throat, the coppery tang of spilled blood burning my nostrils, making my mouth dry. Up ahead of me, I saw police and EMTs looking downwards. I was already aware that something rested at the bottom of the slight valley.

My feet slowed when I caught a glimpse of the overturned truck that lay on its roof. All the windows were shattered, and two of the doors were missing completely. The smell of gasoline, burnt rubber, and blood was a lot for my senses, but it didn't stop me from getting closer, my eyes narrowing as I searched the scene for any signs of her. I could feel my wolf close to the surface, and I tried to control my emotions, but the scent of blood was messing with my head.

Her blood.

So much blood.

Ignoring the humans, I got closer to the truck, taking in the blood-covered leather seats. Blood on the dashboard, on the roof of the truck, I took it all in. Seeing the torn seat belt, my anger surged.

There were so many scents. Doc, I could identify, his shifter blood coming through. Willow's scent was everywhere, but not strong enough to indicate she was nearby. I tried to sift through the other scents, trying to distinguish between first responders and anyone other.

Stepping back, I saw her backpack, recognizing items of clothing strewn among the wreckage as hers.

But one thing was clear. She was gone.

Circling the truck, I looked for any other signs of her or who took her. I knew she wasn't in an ambulance. The nearest hospital was behind us, and they would have passed me on the road.

My wolf grumbled in my chest, a low growl sounding from me, hinting at how restless and angry I was.

Had someone taken her? Did they have her? Searching the ground, I looked for tracks. Where the fuck was she?

Crouching down, I dipped my fingers into the blood as I struggled to keep the wolf contained. The blood was still wet, and my instincts were telling me she was alive.

But for how long?

Why would they take Willow? My fingers curled. The need to swipe my claws across this truck and release my frustration was building.

I saw her backpack again, and at the same time, a human saw me.

"Hey! You! Get away from there!"

Snatching her backpack, I ran to the trees, the dense forest hiding me from their sight, and I knew woods much better than any of my pursuers.

Still, I moved carefully, hoping to find a trace of Willow. My nostrils flared as I caught a faint hint of fresh blood. My head whipped in the opposite direction of where the wreck was. I was running towards it, barely taking a moment to consider if it was a trap.

The scent of another had me slow down and start to move with caution. Resting against a tree, I forced myself to quiet down and listen. Pushing past the sounds of the emergency services at the wreckage, I drilled into the sounds of what *else* I could hear.

Footsteps? Straining, I concentrated. Two sets and...*there.* Willow.

I was running again. I had her scent now. It was faint, and I knew she was in trouble because I wasn't the only shifter in the woods honing in on her.

He came at me from the side, catching me unawares. The force of his impact took both of us off our feet, and we hit the ground hard. I didn't recognize him, but he was definitely a shifter. His punch to my gut winded me, but I didn't have time for a fistfight. I caught his neck with my teeth, my fangs elongating, sinking deep right over his jugular, and I bit down. His blows fell across my body, but with a quick jerk of my head, I ripped his throat out. Blood poured over me, and I cursed as I pushed the lifeless body off me.

Wiping my face of the blood, I resumed my search for Willow.

She was on her hands and knees, her hair wild and bloody. She was swaying, and I guessed it was because she hadn't consciously fallen. She was so out of it. From my position, I could see the glazed, vacant look. She was hurt and in danger of passing out.

But I couldn't run to her because of the shifter who was across from me. We stared at each other, and a quick inhale told me it was only me, him, and Willow, who was currently in the middle of us.

Which one would get to her first?

We had the same thought as we both rushed forward at the same time. Only, he made the mistake of thinking she was my target.

She wasn't.

He was.

So, when I jumped over her body, my body shifting to my wolf, claws and fangs ready, he wasn't ready for the savagery of the attack.

The fight was over before it began, and I shifted back to human, turning to see she was lying on the ground, her eyes closed. Crouching down beside her, I placed my hand on her neck, checking for a pulse.

"Willow?" I whispered, my fear closing around me. "Willow, can you hear me?"

She didn't move, didn't stir. My heart lurched, my pulse throbbing with how fast my heart was beating. Hovering over her, I laid my head on her chest. Faint, so faint. She needed a hospital.

"Willow..." I tried again, but my voice sounded raw.

Nothing. No movement. No response.

I stripped the dead shifter of his pants, his boots, and the shirt he'd been wearing, and hurriedly dressed. I didn't care what I looked like; I needed to get her to the EMTs. My eyes fell on the backpack across the other side of the underbrush, and I knew I couldn't take it. I could only hope that there was nothing discriminating in it, and it was for that reason that I sprinted across to it, grabbed it, and stashed it as far as I could from sight.

Picking her up gently, I rushed back the way I'd come, encouraged when I saw the red and blue lights of the ambulance still there.

"Help!" I yelled. "She needs help!" Men surged into action, and when I ran up the embankment, there was a gurney waiting. They took her from me, my fingers digging into her soft skin before I relinquished my hold of her.

Questions were fired at me as they buzzed around her like bees. A mask was placed over her mouth, and somehow, not long after, I was in the back of an ambulance with her while being told I was lucky I wasn't in worse shape.

They assumed the blood that covered me was hers and mine. I didn't correct them. The scratches and cuts I had from the bushes where I put her backpack and the run back to the road served me well. I willed my body not to heal too quickly so I wouldn't look even more suspicious. Not that it would work, but maybe there was a chance that Luna was listening to me.

"We'll check you out at the hospital," the male told me.

"Just focus on her."

"We are." He reached over and patted my knee, and I almost ripped his hand off for trying to console me when he should have been paying attention to her. "She needs blood and a lot of it." He didn't notice my anger as he returned his focus to Willow. "It's a nasty cut on her forehead, but nothing seems broken. We'll know more when we get her to a hospital." He continued to check her when he looked up again. "You were the driver?"

"No."

"Her?" He looked confused, and I suddenly remembered Doc.

"Our friend, he was driving, did you find him?"

He shook his head, and using his phone, he told someone there was another body out there.

Body.

I remembered the two I had killed. I didn't need them to find them. With sudden clarity, I remembered Royce's number.

"I need your phone," I told the medic. "Please."

He thought about it, and then he handed it over. Quickly punching Royce's number in, I waited for him to answer.

"Who is this?"

"Caleb." I sensed his stillness. "They ran them off the road, not sure if it was intentional, think it was. She's in an ambulance with me to the hospital, two behind, not sure where our driver is."

The responder was pretending not to listen, but he kept shooting me worried glances as I gave a very emotionless, detail-less account. Like I had something to hide.

"You got it?" I asked as the silence stretched.

"We have an idea of your location," Royce confirmed. "We'll find him."

I heard movement in the background and hung up. I took a moment to delete the call history, handing the phone back. It wouldn't stop him from searching his phone record to know, if he wanted, but not many people were that invested.

"How much farther?" I asked, reaching out to take hold of her hand.

"Almost there."

My finger traced her vein, feeling the throb of her pulse,

not trusting the machine that they'd hooked her up to. Her pulse was faint. I clutched her hand tighter.

"This shouldn't have happened to you," I whispered hoarsely, my voice heavy with regret. I leaned forward, gently raising her hand to my lips, and pressed a soft kiss to her bruised knuckles. The kiss lingered for longer than it should have, but I couldn't pull away. My hand trembled as I held hers, wanting to protect her, but I was too late.

Willow lay unmoving, but the machine told me she was alive, though her chest barely rose, her breathing shallow. The sight of her, lying like this, twisted inside of me, the ache of regret and guilt.

I'd failed her.

"I'm so sorry," I murmured against her skin. "I won't let you die," I told her.

Her fingers moved slightly, barely a movement, so subtle I could have imagined it, but I held her hand tighter. "That's it, fight, Willow." I looked at the EMT and he nodded. Had he seen it too?

"We're here," he announced.

I stayed out of the way as they unloaded her, and the surge of doctors and nurses swallowed her up, rushing her to the ER.

"I'll fix this," I promised the cold night. "I'll make this right."

It wasn't an empty promise, because the thought of her suffering more than she had, because of me, was more than I could bear.

Whoever had attacked them, I'd find out.

Then...I would kill them all.

SIXTEEN

Willow

Everything hurt.

Everything hurt and it was very loud. Machines were whirring, and a strange sound like an air pump kept hissing.

It was dark.

Where was I?

Panic seized me as I remembered the accident. I'd been in a truck, and I remembered the terror as the truck rolled.

Beeping sounded all around me.

The air pump was hissing louder.

Oh God, where was I?

Something was holding my eyes closed. Is that why it was dark? I couldn't move. I couldn't see.

Panic overtook me, and I struggled to fight against my restraints. Shaking my head from side to side, I fought to see. Voices penetrated my panic, and then warm fingers curled around my arms, a familiar touch.

"Sir, you must stand back!"

"Willow!" The sharp voice was so familiar to me, and I

stopped struggling as I felt his warmth envelop me. "Willow, calm down. You're in a hospital. Open your eyes."

How could I tell him I couldn't? Something was in my throat; were they trying to choke me? Panicked once more, I shook free of his hold, and my hands reached for my mouth, finding something plastic over it.

"No, no, *no*! Willow, *no*, leave the tube, you need to breathe through it," Caleb scolded me. I felt his hands take mine, and I clutched onto his strong hands. "That's it, I've got you, you're safe."

I was safe. Caleb had me. I tried to squeeze his hands to let him know I was okay.

"Open your eyes."

It took so much effort to do that. It felt like they would never open. Was he sure I could open them? Slowly, so slowly, they lifted and instantly shut against the bright lights. A hand cupped the side of my face.

"Try again, I'm blocking the lights now," he spoke gently. My eyes opened quicker this time, and the blurriness took shape, and I saw his deep chocolate brown eyes filled with concern. I started to cry, and he smiled. "I didn't think I was that bad to look at," he teased gently, wiping away a tear with his thumb.

I tried to speak and felt the pain of the tube in my throat. Caleb understood and stood back, taking my hand when I grabbed for him.

"Take the tube out of her," he commanded tersely. "She can breathe on her own."

"We'll wait for the doctor," came the equally curt reply.

"And when will he be here?"

"Soon." She didn't sound convinced.

"Fuck that."

My eyes widened in alarm when he came back into my line of vision with that determined look on his face. He reached up and I felt the sharp tug of tape being removed from my mouth.

"Sir!" The nurse sounded exasperated and furious, and it amused me how he seemed to get most people to react to him like that. "Oh for goodness sake," she muttered, and then I saw her too. She was older than us, pretty, with warm blue eyes that looked down at me. "When I tell you to, push out a big breath, okay?"

I didn't understand, but then before I knew what was happening, the tube was being pulled out of me, and I struggled to breathe as it was pulled from my esophagus. As I was coughing and spluttering, Caleb was there with a cup of water with a straw, encouraging me to drink. The nurse took over, checking me and instructing me through the wheezing.

"You're okay," she assured me gently. "Can you breathe?"

Tears streamed down my face, but I could, I could breathe. "Yes." The frog voice was not unexpected, but still, it was enough of a shock to make me stop speaking.

"Drink more water," Caleb commanded from his perch on the side of my bed, ignoring the nurse's command for him to get off, and I saw the nurse's eyes narrow with impatience.

"Let's just let your wife catch her breath first," she told him in a no-nonsense tone.

It took a few minutes, but I was helped to sit up. She checked my vitals, whatever they were, and also let me sip water. The whole time, Caleb waited impatiently at the side, and the whole time, I kept my gaze fixed on him.

"Right." With a sigh, she finally stood back. "I'll go get the doctor and leave you two." She spoke to him more than me. "Do not overexert her. Understand?" The look he gave her would have made lesser men falter; she barely blinked. "Glad we cleared that up."

When the door closed behind her, he was beside me, his hand curling around mine. "Tell me how you feel. What hurts?"

"Everything hurts," I said honestly, wincing as I tried to sit up more. "Wife? Again?"

Strong capable hands hooked under my armpits, and I was gently but effortlessly pulled up to sit straighter. "It keeps me in the room, no questions," he explained.

Made sense. "Nothing broken?" I asked in surprise, looking down at myself.

"Truck looks like shit," he told me. "It's definitely broken."

"Doc?" I was almost too scared to ask.

"Cannon and his pack have him."

"Ned got to him?" I was confused. Why would they take Doc and not take me?

"Sure."

It was his tone of voice, the fact he looked away from me when he said it. "You have no idea, do you?" I accused him.

Caleb met my look, and instead of answering, he picked up the cup of water. "Drink. You're making my throat dry with how hoarse you sound."

I didn't get the chance to tell him it was because I had a breathing tube down my throat—he was already placing the straw between my lips. I sucked water, maintaining eye contact, so I saw his eyes dip to my mouth. His eyes flared, and he quickly looked away.

What the heck was *that?*

Pulling my head back, I wiped my mouth with a shaky hand. "Do you know where Doc is? Ned?"

"They're not here," he told me, too casually. "I assume that's a good thing."

"You assume?" I didn't bother hiding my irritation. "How can you not care?"

His look turned hard. "I killed two shifters to get to you," he told me bluntly. "Two who I assume were the reason your truck rolled to start with. I carried you back to the road, bleeding and almost dead, and then I rode with you here. I haven't left your side, so I don't know where they are. All I cared about was that *you* lived. Now that I know you will, I can find out what happened to them. Happy?"

I was speechless. Caleb's matter-of-fact way of delivering harsh truths was something that always took a moment to process. It had been a while since I'd last seen him, and I'd almost forgotten how incredibly jarring his bluntness could be. He was such a strange contradiction—unapologetically honest yet cloaked in a veil of deception that left you unsure of what to believe. I'd never met anyone like him. How could he be so forthright, but you still felt like he was hiding something?

"What? Nothing to say?" His tone was mocking, and I reached out to punch him for it. That was about as effective as a feather hitting a wall.

"You're still a contrary A-hole then?" I grumbled as he looked at me in amusement.

"What you see is what you get."

"Is it though?" I challenged him. "I don't think it is. I never know what to expect from you," I told him truthfully. With a sigh, I dropped my head back against the pillows. "I'm exhausted," I admitted. "And I hurt, and shouldn't they be giving me, like, nice lovely drugs that make me not hurt?"

Caleb broke eye contact with me, his eyes on the door instead. "I told them you were anti-pain medication."

I knew I was gaping at him. "*Why?*" My mouth opened and closed a few times in disbelief. "I was in a truck that rolled over *a lot*. I was pretty much the human equivalent of a cat in a washing machine. Why wouldn't you let me get drugs?"

"Painkillers," he corrected absently, his voice lacking any warmth. His deep brown eyes, so rich and delicious, were closed off and unyielding. I hated that look—the way it had become so familiar, like a wall I could never break through. "I needed you coherent when you woke up," he continued brusquely. "I need you awake and alert because I can't be here with you twenty-four seven."

The last part caught my attention first. "What? Why? You *just* said you told them I was your wife for that very reason!" My voice was sharper than I wanted it to be, but the panic I was feeling at his statement was real. The idea that he would leave me now, of all times, was making my heart pound. "Tell me you aren't leaving?"

The unspoken *again* lingered between us like a weight, pulling the air tight between us.

His jaw clenched, his gaze shifting away from mine for a moment, betraying an emotion I couldn't quite put my finger on. Guilt? Weariness? Frustration? With Caleb, it was impossible to tell.

"I have to leave," he told me, the words labored as if saying them was against his will. "Things are happening, things I need to understand."

My heart was sinking with every word that he spoke, and I swallowed past the lump in my throat. "And what about me? What if they come for me again?"

His eyes flicked back to mine, softer now, still guarded but gentler. "Nothing will happen to you again. I won't be far." He reached out, his hand hovering in the space between us before he pulled it back to his side. "Blackridge Peak Pack will be close. Cannon won't be far away."

"You don't know that," I protested. "You don't even know where he is."

Caleb didn't answer that, brushing it off as he spoke. "You'll be safe, Willow."

Safe. The word was losing any connotation of what it was supposed to mean. It felt hollow now. An empty promise spoken to keep me grounded and stop me from spiraling, no doubt.

"You keep saying that," I grumbled, crossing my arms over my chest, an act more of self-defense than defiance. "But it doesn't feel like I am. It hasn't for a long time, not since you left."

Caleb was silent and I was sure that may have been worse than arguing. It was like he was agreeing with me without saying the words.

"They broke into my store," I told him, watching him closely. "And my home, Caleb. My *home*."

"Done that a few times myself." He heard my gasp of outrage, and his head dipped. "That came out wrong, honest."

My eyebrows must have been climbing into my hairline, because I heard his sigh. "I know they broke in, and I know you're scared, and I know we need—*I* need—to put a stop to it."

"Wait until I get out. I was coming to find *you*. Now you're here, please wait for me to get out."

Caleb looked me over, and I hated to think how bad I looked in the hospital bed. What did he see, a weak and broken woman who didn't have an ounce of strength?

"I can't keep you safe if I'm dragging you into danger with me." He stood from the bed. "And I can't fight if I'm standing still."

"Fine." My voice was sharp. Angry. "Go. Do what you want. You're going to anyway."

"I'll check back with you. Stay alert."

I heard him move, but I refused to look at him. I couldn't. I knew I was going to cry, and I refused to let him see me even weaker than he already thought.

I felt the bed dip, and strong fingers caressed my jaw, turning my head. Caleb looked down at me, a hint of affection in his gaze that warmed the chill of his earlier words. "So stubborn," he murmured, a teasing tone to his voice that didn't echo the tension between us of only a moment ago.

Dipping his head, his lips brushed mine—gently, tenderly—causing a flutter of warmth low in my belly. The uneasiness between us faded, and the anger and unresolved feelings melted away as he kissed me again, a little deeper. His mouth caught mine so easily, claiming it as his. He nipped my bottom lip before he pulled back.

As he broke the kiss, reality returned, and I struggled to regain my composure and control my racing heart. "Caleb?"

He looked so conflicted, his eyes closing briefly, and I wondered if he needed to take a beat too. "I shouldn't have done that; it wasn't fair."

"Why? Because you're leaving anyway?"

"Yeah."

"Then why kiss me?" I itched to reach out to him, but I kept my hands on the bed linen.

"It felt like the right thing to do."

There was that honesty again, truth laced with something else. "Or an easy play to make me shut up, you mean?"

"I'm not playing." His voice was stronger, steadier. "You mean something to me, but I can't stay here with you when I know I need to be out *there* finding out who wants to hurt you, and why."

"And if something happens while you're gone? If something happens to *you*, how will I know, how—"

"Willow." His voice was firm but gentler. "You are stronger than you think, and you need to trust me."

Trust? It tasted as bitter as the word *safe*. But I couldn't deny the look in his eyes, the commitment he had to protect me, and hadn't he just said I meant something? Surely *that* meant something? Maybe there *was* something here, between us, that I could hold onto. Something that I could drive myself insane over when he wasn't here and my brain overthought every word and look between us.

"Okay," I finally relented. I didn't miss how his shoulders dropped slightly as he relaxed at my acceptance. "Don't do anything reckless," I warned him. "Don't leave again without coming back to tell me."

"I won't." He turned swiftly, and his footsteps sounded

loud as he walked to the door. He didn't look back, and I didn't call out for him to stay, because he wouldn't, and I knew that.

The door clicked shut, and I sat in the sudden stillness of the room, thinking of everything that had been said. He was gone, but the link between us, I knew it was still there. I could feel it. A fragile thread that tied us together no matter the distance.

Looking around the hospital room, I was suddenly faced with my reality. Someone had run us off the road.

They'd tried to kill us.

They were following me.

I had no idea if Doc was okay, if Ned had him, or even if either of them was alive. I'd been so focused on Caleb and him being here I hadn't demanded he go and find out if they were okay. He said he would, but what good did that do if he wasn't coming back right away?

Were they safe?

There was that word again. How long had it been since I was safe? It felt like such a distant memory. A past life, before Caleb, before shifters, before their world crashed into mine.

Each time someone told me I was safe, it felt less convincing, and now I was sure it was just a lie. No one believed we were safe, because it was just something you said but held little reassurance.

My home and my store had been broken into. I'd been followed. I'd run from a motel in the middle of the night as we got chased. I'd been run off the road. Caleb had killed two shifters who tried to get me.

Now, I was alone in a hospital room, while the people who

were after me were out there somewhere, probably waiting for their next opportunity. The one person I trusted most to keep them away had just walked out the door. I don't even know *why* I trusted him either.

The room was suffocatingly quiet. I could hear activity outside, nurses and doctors going about their business and other patients, but no one was coming to me. Had Caleb pissed the nurse off so much? I smiled despite myself at the thought. He probably did. He was abrasive at the best of times.

Pushing the sheet down, I inspected my body. Huge bruises on my legs, bandages, and gauze everywhere, I looked like a patchwork quilt. Pulling the gown away from my chest, I winced at the color of the bruising across my chest and abdomen. My back felt equally battered and bruised.

Maybe I looked worse than I was. The doctor hadn't come, so I guessed that was a good thing. My quick check over had revealed the catheter, and I resigned myself to waiting for someone to come check on me.

My head was thumping, and I tried to scoot down on the bed to get more comfortable. As I lay in the silence, I tried not to think of how vulnerable I was. But I couldn't shake the feeling of unease, and I wanted Caleb to come back.

You mean something to me.

I knew that would come back when I had nothing else to distract me. Did I mean something to him? The kiss would suggest I did, or I was fooling myself. Because if I *meant* something, surely he would stay when I needed him?

He left to keep you safe.

That freaking word was mocking me now.

Looking down at my bruised body, the thumping in my head intensifying, I had the rogue thought, if this was their idea of safety...I wasn't sure how much more I could handle.

SEVENTEEN

Caleb

I FELT LIKE CRAP LEAVING HER ALONE. SHE LOOKED LIKE... well, she looked like she'd been bounced around a truck that rolled. Seeing her open her eyes hadn't quelled the rage in my heart. Knowing she could breathe on her own hadn't soothed my anger. Tasting her lips hadn't tampered my fury.

She was in a fucking hospital bed.

They put her in a hospital, and they would know what retribution felt like before they took their final breath.

My pace was quick and sure as I exited the hospital, heading to the parking lot, but movement to the right caught my eye, and I stopped suddenly, my attention on the man who approached me.

My eyes narrowed as I recognized the dark hair and build. Cannon moved with a confidence that came from someone who knew his power—and wasn't afraid to use it. His every step was deliberate. Calculated. The predator surveying his territory. I sensed no hesitation from him, dominance radiated from him, and I saw more than just me watch him as he crossed the lot.

It was hard not to admire his strong build, the kind that came from years of fighting. Surviving. The hard line of his jaw, the gleam in his eyes, he was an alpha through and through.

"Cannon?" My eyes darted around the parking lot. "Where's Doc, and the other one?"

"Doc's on his way back to the pack," he told me, stopping as he reached me. "Pretty banged up, but he'll heal. *Ned* is around." He then jerked his head towards the hospital doors. "Willow?"

"Will be fine." I looked past his shoulder. "Around where?"

"Hunting."

We held each other's stare. "He has their scent?" I asked eventually.

"You left a pretty bloody trail."

I squinted at him as I considered his words. "You're judging me?"

"Two bodies with their throats ripped out?" Cannon's voice had been low, I thought so he wouldn't be overheard. Now I realized it was anger that he was keeping a tight hold of. "Yes, I'm fucking judging you. Do you want the humans to take them to their morgues? Two *shifters*?"

I felt myself straighten under his judgmental gaze. "I don't give a fuck where they take them."

"You...are a liability," he seethed at me.

I stepped closer to him, ignoring the interested stares of passersby. "She's in a hospital." My jaw clenched. "She had a tube down her throat, to *help her breathe. A tube,* Cannon. I don't care what happens to the ones I killed. I would quite happily kill them again."

"Lower your voice."

"Fuck you." The tension between us built, and I knew if he made a move, I wouldn't hold back.

"I am not your enemy." Cannon watched me. Assessed me. I didn't like it.

"No? You should try harder to convince me of that."

Cannon let out a snort and I heard his frustration as he stepped back. "I'm here to make sure Willow, the *human* girl who is connected to you through our Goddess *Luna*, is okay."

"Right." I heard what he didn't say. "The shaman sent you."

"I would have come anyway," he said with conviction, and I was surprised at myself when I believed him. "How is she?"

"In a hospital." I saw his barely concealed irritation at my non-answer. "What happened?"

"She was followed. She thought she could shake them by getting a different bus, but she doesn't realize how futile that is for people like us."

"Why was she on a bus?" I asked in bewilderment and then remembered Willow couldn't drive. "Where was she going?"

"To us." Cannon motioned for me to move further from the hospital entrance, and I followed him. "The visions are chang-ing. They are showing some...disturbing things."

"Me?" I guessed.

"The longer you remain alone, Caleb, the quicker the dark-ness can consume you."

Gritting my teeth, I shook my head in denial. "I'm not a rogue."

"Aren't you?" His steady stare challenged me once more. "You sure about that, Caleb? Willow's drawings say different."

"Her sketches tell you that I'm a rogue?" Disdain dripped from my tone as I looked the alpha over. "Or maybe that's what you *want* to believe. Huh?"

"What I *want* to believe is that someone whose father was such a strong alpha, a *good* alpha, who led a loyal pack, would never be so weak to fall to the blackness like you seem to be doing, Caleb. What I *want* to believe is that you are a stronger alpha than you've shown me so far."

"Strong alpha like my father?" I asked him with a sneer. "You mean the one who was murdered by his *loyal* pack? That alpha?"

Cannon looked at me with sympathy, which made me want to wipe the look from his face. "You blame them," he said with understanding.

I'd stepped forward, my finger in his chest, not even realizing my anger had made me move. "The fact that you don't is why there's no point talking to you about it."

Cannon glanced down at my finger, an eyebrow quirked as he raised his head to meet my glare. "If you want to keep it, I suggest you remove it."

With a scoff, I stepped back, not from his threat but because I was done with him. "Go back to your pack, *Alpha*. I'll handle this."

He was silent as he considered me. "The link that ties you together needs to be severed. It's too dangerous for her, and the longer she is exposed to us, the danger to *us* increases. Willow is human, and you know Pack Law, though you don't always adhere to it." His tone was scathing. "The shaman believes the link can be severed—"

"If you harm her, I will kill you all."

Cannon's look was one of contempt. "We are not suggesting anyone hurts her. For fuck's sake, Caleb, are you so far gone in the madness you've forgotten what you are?"

"I am not mad."

"Yet."

We were in a stand-off and quite possibly heading to the place where neither of us cared who saw us. We were close to exchanging blows. Cannon obviously felt the same way as he moved away from me, because he was more level-headed than me, it seemed.

"I cannot help you if you refuse to help yourself," he told me. "I cannot help Willow if you refuse to face the past. There are others of our kind out there who are not happy with her tie to you. To the packs."

"You think this is why she's targeted?" I asked incredulously. "There have been humans before who knew about us."

He nodded. "I know that. Willow is...more."

She was. I knew that, and I didn't like him saying it.

"And..." He considered his next words. "There have been revelations over the last few months that we didn't know, which put us *all* in danger."

"Like what?"

"We aren't as unknown to some as we thought."

It was a diplomatic, careful way of saying humans knew about us. More than they should.

"How bad?"

Cannon looked away. "Very."

"I'm going to need more details," I snapped at him, our frustrations bubbling once more.

"When I trust you, and you trust me, we'll talk." Cannon looked past me. "You shouldn't leave her unprotected."

"I need to know who is hunting her." Running my fingers through my hair, I looked to the hospital entrance. "Once I know that, I'll return."

"Or, you stay where you are. You stay *with* her, and when she can, you take her to us." Cannon's voice was firm. "She can't do this alone. Neither can you... I don't think you're in the right place to face this without..."

"Without *pack*?" I almost growled at the suggestion, but I held it back. Cannon watched me control my temper, and I changed the subject back to Willow. "She's stronger than you think," I told him, though I knew that wasn't good enough, not for this. Staying with her, I wanted to, I did, but I thought of the kiss I'd given her. I hadn't meant to. She just pulled me in.

"I don't think she's weak," Cannon responded calmly, interrupting my thoughts. "But strong willpower isn't enough for what's after her. You know that as well as I do."

Feeling restless, I started to pace. My instinct was to move. Act. Chase. Waiting here? That went against everything in my nature. Yet, I didn't know *who* my enemy was. Or what they wanted with Willow. While I wanted to act, I also wanted to know more.

I'd thought Cannon and his pack would know, and I was disappointed they didn't. My fingers flexed at my sides, the fighter in me wanting me to do something other than just *sit* helplessly in a hospital room.

"Caleb?" Cannon was waiting patiently while I wrestled

with the choice. "You've lost too much already. I think Willow means more to you than some human you need to protect. Doesn't she?"

Tilting my head back, I looked at the sky, bright blue and hardly a cloud to be seen. The sun shone brightly so many thousands of miles away, as out of reach as perhaps my answer to that question. My gut churned. I wanted to run, hunt, and kill whoever came after her. But the image in my head of her body, practically lifeless, on the forest floor was seared into my mind.

She was all alone in that room. She had no one to call for help. Except me.

I should stay.

I didn't have to like it. I didn't have to be comfortable with the decision. It didn't mean I was listening to Cannon. It didn't mean I cared for her more than I should.

It just meant I was the best choice to protect her right now.

With a resigned exhale, I looked back at the alpha in front of me, the weight of my decision clear on my face as I saw Cannon give a nod of approval. "Fine," I grunted. "But only because I'm the best choice. The minute I know who's responsible for this...I take them down."

"Agreed." Cannon's jaw tightened. "I'll be right beside you."

"I need a phone." Wordlessly Cannon handed me one, and I took it with increased suspicion. "You knew I would stay?"

"It was a fifty-fifty chance."

Ignoring him, I turned toward the hospital entrance. "I want updates," I called over my shoulder.

"You'll get them." He was already walking back to wherever the hell he came from. "I want updates too."

"If I don't lose your number."

I didn't hear his reply; I was already inside. I took the stairs to Willow's room. Pushing open the door to the hall, I paused. What was that smell? Shifter?

The door opened with more force than I intended, banging off the wall. My muscles tensed as I ran down the hall. The scent grew stronger as I neared Willow's room. Too strong.

Someone had been here.

Pushing the door open, I looked around the room, the scent of the intruder one I wouldn't forget. My nostrils flared, and my fists clenched in anger as I searched for anything out of place.

The room was empty.

Where was she? The bed was still unmade, the cup of water with the straw was overturned on the floor, and I focused on it longer as I forced myself to remain calm. Panic could come later. I didn't have time for that right now.

I could still smell Willow, her vanilla scent faint but here. I couldn't scent fear. Was that a good thing?

Crossing the room to the window, I brushed the short drapes aside. There was no sign that anyone had come through, which was a relief since she was four stories up. A shifter wouldn't blink at the drop, but Willow would.

My attention switched to the bathroom door, and I opened it. My teeth ground together when I saw it was empty. The sound of footsteps caught my attention. They were coming closer.

Poised, ready to pounce, I waited. The door pushed open, and I caught myself from attacking as the nurse from before backed into the room, pulling Willow with her as she sat in a wheelchair. The nurse turned them around, jumping in fright when she saw me.

"Lord above, are you trying to kill me?" she berated me, her hand on her heart.

My gaze roved over Willow, checking her, avoiding her curious stare. "Where were you?"

"X-ray," the nurse told me, recovered from her shock. "Your wife said you left for the afternoon." She didn't hold back the judgment from her tone. I didn't answer, but I did help get Willow out of the chair by simply lifting her and placing her on the bed. The nurse looked at me. "You do that twenty more times for me today, I might forgive you," she murmured.

Willow said nothing as the nurse fussed over her, telling her she'd be back soon. I got an almost nod as she left the room.

We both spoke at the same time.

"Who else has been here?"

"Why are you back?"

"*Willow*, who else has been here since me?"

Her brow furrowed and she shook her head. "You and the nurse are the only two people I've seen since you woke me up."

"No doctor?"

"No, the nurse said there's been a huge pile up on the highway, and all doctors are in the ER or operating rooms." Willow looked at me nervously. "Why? What do you know?"

"Someone's been here." I looked around the room. "I wasn't gone that long. Where's the X-ray?"

"She came for me a few minutes after you left. X-ray is just at the end of the corridor." Willow licked her lips. "This hospital is more than my insurance will like."

"You feel okay?" I asked as I looked out the window again, searching the parking lot, looking to see if where Cannon and I had stood could be seen from this angle. Had they seen us, had that spooked them?

"Why are you back?"

Turning to her, I raised an eyebrow. "Want me to leave?"

"Seems to be what you do." Willow's voice was laced with a bitterness that hit harder than I expected.

So she was still feeling feisty. I got it. I hurt her earlier. She was physically hurt because of her involvement with me, but still...hearing it laid out so plainly, so unguarded, I fought the urge to look away. My jaw clenched as she watched me. Was she waiting for an apology?

She wouldn't get one. I'd come back. *For* her.

Cannon made you come back.

I ignored the reminder. "I realized I was the best person to make sure you were safe." Her sneer was ugly, and her body tensed. "What is it?"

"I hate that word. *Safe.* I never knew I could hate a word so much."

I had nothing to say to that, so I let it drop. "How long were you gone?"

"How long were *you* gone?" she snapped at me.

"Is there a reason you're being so unreasonable?" I asked her calmly, watching her eyes widen in surprise.

And here it comes.

"Are you serious? I mean, are you freaking *serious* right now?" Her eyes were full of anger, and I heard the barely controlled fury in her voice.

"I thought leaving would be best, but then I realized you needed me, and I had no choice but to come back."

Willow scoffed, her arms crossing over her chest. "You *always* have a choice, Caleb."

And my first choice had been to leave her, that's what she wasn't saying. She didn't need to.

Silence hung thick between us, the air charged with unspoken tension. I stepped forward, the urgency to find who was in her room pushed to the side as I focused on her. Willow turned her head as I bent to look at her.

"Look at me," I encouraged her. I didn't touch her. We both knew what happened the last time I touched her.

Willow half turned her head back in my direction.

"You think I don't know you're pissed at me? For going? For coming back?" I asked her. "You think it is an easy choice for me to walk away from you?"

Her lip trembled, but she remained steadfast. "Then stop making really stupid decisions." Finally, she made eye contact, her voice low. "Stop running away from me. We're *connected*. Whoever is out for me, is out for you."

Those pale green eyes saw past every defense I had. For a moment, I was spellbound, caught in her stare. I wasn't used to this feeling of...vulnerability.

"I won't do it again." I didn't mean to say that, but the words were heavy with promise. One I wasn't sure I could keep. Reaching out, I brushed the stray lock of hair from her face. My fingers lingered on her cheek for a second longer than necessary, the connection between us tightening.

Willow swallowed hard, her gaze searching mine as she

processed my words. She didn't pull away, and for now, that was enough. "I'll hold you to that."

"I expect you will."

Her smile was quick, and the faint flush of her cheeks made her look even more delicate. She was so fragile-looking, but I'd seen how strong she could be.

Maybe even stronger than me.

As I took a seat beside her, settling my body into the curve of the chair, ready for a long stay, I forced the wolf in me down. It wanted to hunt, find the shifter who had come into her room, and rip their throat out.

But I had told her I wasn't going to leave again, and I was starting that promise tonight.

Let them come for her; I was waiting.

EIGHTEEN

Willow

I KNEW I SLEPT, BECAUSE IT WAS DAYLIGHT WHEN I NEXT opened my eyes. I knew Caleb *hadn't* slept, because I felt exhausted just by looking at him. For someone with my illness, I knew what exhaustion looked like.

"You didn't sleep."

His attention had been on the door, but I saw the small curve of his lips as I'd spoken. "You slept, and that's all that matters." He turned to look at me, and I tried not to grin like an idiot.

He had no idea how good it was to see him. Aside from all the other stuff between us, seeing him well and *here* made me happy.

Really happy.

"How can you protect me if you're too exhausted to fight?" I teased him, pushing myself up in my bed and fighting the urge to check my hair. "Shouldn't you be saving up your energy in case you need to go all Caleb on them?"

"Caleb on them?" His eyebrow quirked as he watched me. "What's that supposed to mean?"

I knew he wasn't pissed off. His tone had a teasing lilt to it, and I laughed as I looked away. "You know, all..." I looked back at him, curling my fingers into claws in front of me. "*Grrr.*" I fake growled.

Caleb's eyes widened with mirth. "What the actual hell is that supposed to be?" He imitated my pose. "*Grr?*" His hands dropped. "Is that me?"

I shrugged, my cheeks flaming. "Maybe with less *grrr* and more *Grrraw.*"

"Please stop," he deadpanned.

"You know, I feel like I should." Biting my lip, I tried to keep the laughter contained.

We shared a look of amusement. Caleb checked me over and his levity faded. "Your bruises look worse in daylight."

"Definitely feel worse," I admitted, shooting him a look. "Of course, if I had painkillers, I may feel better."

"Masks the way the body feels," he told me smoothly. "You're not an advocate of masking pain. I've been in your bathroom cabinet," he reminded me with a twinkle in his eye that shouldn't make him look delectable when he was reminding me of an unforgivable act of breaking into my house.

Asshat.

"You know that isn't even remotely comparable, don't you?"

"Do I?" He cocked his head, and I hated how quickly we went from being playful to me wanting to slap him.

"You can shift into a wolf, and all your aches and pains disappear," I retorted sharply. "Don't even begin to think you have any experience of physical pain."

His eyes were somber as he watched me. "Oh, I've felt pain, the kind that you can't hide from, trust me."

I immediately felt guilty as I remembered all the drawings I had done. "Your family?"

Caleb turned his attention back to the door, breaking eye contact. "You don't know what you're talking about."

The reprimand was probably warranted, but also screw that. "I know you don't like talking about it," I told him, trying to be firm. "But I've seen more than you know—"

"You know nothing." His jaw clenched as he turned his head away. His voice was low and edged with frustration when he next spoke. "You know nothing about my past, Willow. You think you do, but trust me, you don't."

"I—"

"You've seen what? Pieces? Fragments?" He turned back to look at me, anger brimming in his eyes. "You haven't seen the whole story."

I felt my own anger building, and I refused to back down. "I've *seen* it, Caleb." I heard the unevenness of my voice and hoped he didn't notice. "I've seen the pain, the loss, the blood. All of it. I've seen the way it haunts you. You may not want to admit it, but *don't* tell me I don't know."

Caleb was on his feet, his glare fierce, his hands curled into fists at his sides. "You've seen what? A few visions of dead wolves? A couple of nightmares of slaughter? That's *nothing* compared to the reality of it." His voice shook with temper. I watched as he took a step back, running a hand over his forehead. "You see a reflection of a memory," he told me bitterly. "You didn't live it. You didn't feel it."

"Didn't I?" I challenged him, wrapping my arms around

myself, suddenly cold in the tension-filled room. "I feel you. I felt you each and every time I drew it. I've seen the weight you carry every single day. I don't need to have been there and seen it as it happened. I see it *in* you. I see the darkness inside you, and I see how badly you're losing in the fight against it."

His sharp exhale and look of disbelief made me inwardly curse. I hadn't meant to say that much, reveal that much. We'd only just gotten back to being civil to each other.

Caleb looked down at his boots, and for the first time, I realized that none of the clothes he was wearing fit him properly. Were they even his?

"You don't know me." His voice sounded rough, and for the first time, I heard the raw emotion of his past. "You don't understand, you can't. You don't know what it's like to have this in your past."

"Help me understand," I whispered pleadingly. "You're not alone, Caleb. Don't shut me out. I've seen it, and maybe I don't understand it, and maybe I will never feel it like you do, I know that. But if you let me in, I can understand it with you."

For a long moment, he stared at me, those dark eyes unreadable. The silence stretched, and I began to hope that he heard me, that maybe the wall he surrounded himself with was slowly coming down.

Caleb broke the silence, and any hope that I had was shattered. "I can't. I won't." His look was almost tender. "It's better this way, trust me."

I was already shaking my head in annoyance. "No. You're wrong."

He blew out a frustrated breath and walked to the door. "I'm going for a coffee, want one?"

"Caleb?"

He glanced back at me. "Drop it. We won't ever agree on this."

"It's not that simple. It's not your choice to make."

"Make it that simple." He stepped out of the room, and I hated that he knew I couldn't follow him.

Slumping against my pillow, I eyed the door with so much animosity that when the nurse walked in to check on me, she stopped and looked over her shoulder.

"You good?" she asked hesitantly. She was a different nurse from the one I had last night.

"Yeah." I immediately changed my answer. "Actually, I hurt. A lot. I know my...husband...said I was anti-meds, but is there any chance I can get some painkillers? Please?"

Picking up my chart, she scanned it and nodded. "No problem. You have pain meds on the chart signed off by the doctor. I'll check your blood pressure and temperature first, then go get them. Okay?"

"Sounds perfect."

When she left, I was alone and ready to cry with frustration. Caleb hadn't come back, and I just knew the asshole was sitting outside in the hall rather than coming back into the room.

When the nurse came back with a little cup, I didn't care what people thought of us, and I asked the question. "He's out there, isn't he?" I didn't make eye contact, but when she was silent for so long, I looked up.

Her look was full of sympathy and understanding. "It can be a huge shock for our loved ones to see us wounded and in pain," she told me compassionately. "Give him a moment to adjust. It's not easy for either of you."

I said nothing, merely nodded and suffered the consoling pat on the shoulder as I swallowed the pills. I didn't ask what they were, and she didn't tell me.

When I woke up, I knew without opening my eyes that Caleb was gone.

LOOKING UP FROM MY CHOCOLATE PUDDING, I MADE EYE contact with Ned, who was also finishing his own cup. He winked at me as he licked his spoon.

"Honestly, if they told us that we would get this if we were sick, more of us would line up at Doc's testing room."

I giggled despite the fact I was sure he was deadly serious. "It's not even good pudding," I told him and enjoyed his look of dismay that there was better out there and he didn't have it.

Ned had been in the room since Caleb left. I'd jumped to the conclusion that he had left because of our talk and that he had been a chicken shit again. Instead, it seemed their pack authority had called for him and he had no choice but to go. I'd taken the painkillers and been in a happy no-pain sleep, and he didn't want to wake me to explain.

So, there was the fact that I felt guilty for thinking the worst, and there was the further complication that I confessed what I thought to Ned in a moment of weakness, and he had told Cannon, who I was sure would tell Caleb.

Awkward.

So now I wasn't sure if Caleb hadn't come back because of me...or yeah...because of me.

"I'll miss these," Ned told me, dropping his cup into the trash.

"I won't," I said emphatically, making him laugh. Looking down at the jeans and sweater I was wearing, I couldn't stop the smile. "I am so looking forward to leaving this room and going home."

I'd been in the hospital for four days. Despite being very lucky and not breaking anything or rupturing anything, I'd suffered a head injury. Although I was concussion-free, I had stitches in my head I hadn't even known about, and they kept me in for observation. Then I caught an infection and that added a couple of days onto my stay.

But today, *today*, I got to leave.

My *brother-in-law*, Ned, hadn't left. I was sure at first that I was the subject of many a nurse's speculation over the water fountain, but that was quashed once they'd been in my hospital room. Ned and I had reached an amicable, almost friendly, relationship, but a secret affair with my husband's "brother" was definitely not in the cards.

"Not home," he reminded me smoothly, the way he had every time I mentioned leaving.

"Yes, yes, I know," I grumbled. "I get to go to the underground test center again."

"I told you they moved you into a bigger room."

Because that's what I needed, a bigger windowless room to relax in.

"Has he been yet?"

My casual indifference was shot down when Ned hooted

with laughter. "You're not subtle," he teased, standing and stretching. He shrugged. "I haven't checked in today, but I don't think so."

I said nothing. My whole agitation at the man that was Caleb Foster would wait until he was in front of me.

Because while he had been told to go, and he had left, he had, of course, being Caleb, not turned up.

Cannon was pissed, and I couldn't decide whether Caleb was truly brave or truly reckless, because *that* alpha was not one I would piss off.

"Have they checked the mountain?" I asked curiously.

Ned lost his humor. "Shadowridge Peak is a difficult mountain at the best of times."

"But it's not unreachable."

"Difficult."

That was as much as he had told me. Caleb had been summoned, left to go, and then not arrived. They'd checked the mountain, but Caleb was not on it. Or if he was, they couldn't find him.

My questions of *Where was he? Where else would he go? Is he okay?* went unanswered no matter how many times I asked them.

"Is it a mountain I can climb?"

Ned cut his burst of laughter short by slapping his hand over his mouth. Clearing his throat loudly, he added insult to injury when he turned away to regain his composure.

"Jesus. Really, Ned?" I muttered, heat flooding my cheeks.

"I'm sorry," he said, clearing the gruffness from his throat. "I wasn't expecting it."

This was what's wrong with shifters. They're all big, tall,

muscular, ripped abs, and all attractive and pretty. I hadn't met any of the women, but I was sure they were all drop-dead gorgeous. Luna blessed them with good looks as well as their other *gifts* because that's what was fair. Slow to age. Able to heal. Super strength and speed. And being freaking models to boot.

And, in my opinion, all of *that* made them egotistical asshats.

"I can hike."

"Can you?" Ned looked me over, and I wished that punching him wouldn't hurt my hand, because we both knew it was the only thing that would hurt if I tried.

And my pride.

Nah. My pride plummeted into oblivion a long time ago.

Ned's phone rang before he could say anything to make it worse, and he turned away to answer it. "Yeah?"

I could hear a voice, but it was too low to make out who.

"Just waiting for the okay to go. She needs a doctor to sign her out or something."

"Discharged," I mumbled. "It's called discharged."

"And insurance paperwork," he reminded me, looking over his shoulder.

"I did it when you were raiding the lunch carts for chocolate pudding."

He grinned at me. "Good times." He listened to who was on the phone. "I thought Royce was coming?" he asked. "Doc's good. He has a good relationship with her."

"I can hear you." He flashed me a thumbs-up.

Lord, give me strength.

Turning away to check that I had everything, I tried not to

listen to him in case my water pitcher *pitched* itself off his head. I'd come in with nothing. But after a few days in the hospital, with a shifter for a companion who listened to requests, I had some toiletries, a few magazines, and the all-important blank sheet sketchbook. He'd also turned up with clothes. I decided I didn't want to know where they came from. They weren't mine, and that was all I needed to know.

"Willow?" I turned to Ned, who was facing me now. "Alpha wants to know what you drew today."

"Two portraits of Caleb, and the death scene." It was my nickname for the scene outside that cabin with the dead and dying pack of Caleb's family.

"Get that?" Ned asked Cannon. "Yeah, same old, same old." He ignored my flat look and put his hand over the receiver. "Wants to know if you've seen anything and not drawn it."

"No."

"She says no," he said, and I saw his eyes narrow as he listened to his alpha. "I don't know." He stilled, and I saw him look at me with what could only be described as guilt. "Yes. If I had to bet on it, then yes, I think she's lying."

My gasp of outrage fell on deaf ears. It didn't matter he was spot on, that wasn't the point.

"Yup, see you soon." Ned hung up. He held his hands up automatically in supplication. "You can't ask me to lie to him; he's my alpha."

"I wasn't lying!"

His look was one that clearly said *don't bullshit me.* "Your heart rate speeds up when you lie. You get sweaty palms, you shuffle your feet, and you push your hair behind your ear." He let out an exaggerated sigh. "Your body language is easy to read."

Right, because he was a shifter with heightened senses. "Shut up."

He grinned at me again, and both of us turned when the nurse came in with my discharge papers. Ned was keen to leave, and on this, we agreed.

I had to go out in a wheelchair, which made no sense, but it was hospital policy, another thing that amused Ned. But it was hard not to giggle as he ran down the hospital corridors, pushing me at almost dangerous speeds, ignoring all shouts of protest and warning.

He scooped me up out of the seat at the door and carried me bridal style outside. As we burst through the doors, my laughter faded when I saw him waiting for me, and hope surged within me as Ned lowered me to the ground.

"Caleb?"

Caleb looked at how close Ned stood to me, his face unreadable, but when he stepped forward, his hand closing over my arm, he tugged me gently towards him. His hand rested on my lower back.

"Thanks, I've got her from here."

NINETEEN

Caleb

The shifter, Ned, watched me, his eyes flicking between me and Willow with uncertainty. My palm rested on her lower back, my fingertips pressing lightly against her sweater.

Willow looked up at me, her eyes a combination of relief and wariness, searching my face as though trying to decide if it was good to see me or not. Her lips quirked into a small, hesitant smile, but it didn't mask the concern that lingered beneath the surface.

"You look better," I murmured, my thumb brushing small circles against the fabric of her sweater. It was the slightest of touches. I doubted she would even feel it, but it grounded me—kept me focused—and I needed that right now.

"I think I still pretty much look like I got rolled in a truck," she said with a careless shrug, contradicting her soft-spoken tone.

I looked down at her in amusement. "I said you looked better; I didn't say you were catwalk-worthy."

"So that's it? You just come back and don't do what the alpha told you to?" Ned's gruff voice held a note of challenge in it that I didn't appreciate.

"I don't need to." My stare was hard and full of warning. "Remember your place, pup."

Ned's low growl caused Willow to press into my side. I didn't think she was even aware that she'd done it, but Ned saw, and that was all that mattered. He reined in his temper and straightened his spine, squaring his shoulders.

"I'm phoning Cannon."

"Tell him I said hi."

Sliding my hand down Willow's arm, I laced our fingers together. "Come on, let's go."

"We're going?" She looked between me and Ned, torn. "I'm supposed to go to Black—"

"Change of plan," I told her easily. "I'll tell you on the way." I took two steps away, but Willow, stubborn and frustrating as always, hesitated. "Willow?"

"Ned's been here for the last few days," she said, looking back at him. "It's really rude to just leave with no warning."

Sweet stubborn girl.

The slight squeeze on her fingers made her step towards me, and I felt more open to listening to her concerns when there was more distance between him and her. Why was I acting like a jealous idiot? I would analyze that later, but seeing him holding her in his arms, it had rubbed me the wrong way.

"Ned," I said with a sigh, and I watched his eyes narrow suspiciously. "While I do not have to explain myself to you, for Willow's sake, I will. I'm heading to see a shaman. I need Willow with me. Do we have a problem with that?"

His look was shrewd and assessing. "Which shaman?"

I gave a tight smile. "That's not your concern."

"The one who licks blood?" Willow asked, looking at me with doubt.

I saw Ned hide his smile at her innocence. Leaning into her as if divulging a secret, I whispered, "I hate to break it to you, but they all do that."

Her nose was wrinkled in distaste. "I'm sure you're all half vampires," she muttered. "It's not normal behavior."

"You coming anyway?" I asked her, my tone teasing.

Biting her lip, she looked back at Ned, and I thought I would have to outright kidnap her, but instead, she surprised me. "Is it okay if I go with Caleb?" She didn't know her hand tightened in mine, but I felt it, and I felt insanely smug that she did.

"Is that what you want?" Ned asked doubtfully. "He has a habit of leaving you stranded."

"Watch your words," I warned him again. "That's twice I've warned you now. There won't be a third."

I felt my wolf rise, and Ned saw it in my eyes as they changed color. "Alpha." He dipped his head in supplication. He pissed me off by asking Willow again. "You want this?"

Willow stepped into my body, her sweater warm against my arm. "We need to figure this out, and everyone keeps saying we need me where Caleb is, right? So...shouldn't I go where he's going?"

Ned had no comeback for that. "I'll tell Alpha Cannon to expect your call?"

I merely held his gaze as Willow thanked him for staying

with her, and he had no choice but to break the stare as she prattled on nervously until a slight squeeze of her fingers encouraged her to just say goodbye.

Ned handed over the small bag with her stuff in it, and as we walked away from him, I had no doubt he waited to see where we were going, and I was pleased I had the foresight to park the stolen car out of sight.

Willow slowed as we neared the car. "Whose is this?"

"A friend's."

"You don't have friends."

Looking down at her, I saw her face flush as she looked away. "A few days in the hospital, and you become brutal in your observations."

"Sorry."

"Don't be," I assured her, opening the car door. "You're right, I stole it." Willow froze in a half-in-half-out position, and I laughed at her uncertainty. "If they want to leave their doors unlocked and the spare key in the glove box, they deserve to get their car stolen."

She considered the validity of my argument before she nodded and got in the car.

Opening the back passenger door, I pulled out her backpack. "Thought you may want this?"

Willow grabbed it with a happy squeal, and while I drove us out of the lot, she rummaged through her pack. "My wallet! Two notebooks!" she declared triumphantly, holding them aloft like prizes. "I've lost one, but it's better than losing three, right?"

"Right." I cleared my throat. "I also have the third one, you left it in the motel." I jerked to the pack. "It's in the back."

She flicked through them, not asking me if I'd looked because she knew better than that by now.

"My phone!" She fiddled with it and then looked over at me in disappointment. "Dead."

"It's been a few days since you last saw it," I reminded her. "Batteries don't last forever."

"So reasonable," she grumbled, stuffing everything she'd pulled out back in. "Thank you for bringing this."

"I stashed it the night of your crash. I was glad no one had returned for it."

"Good thinking."

She was chewing her lip, shooting furtive glances at me until I put her out of her misery. "Speak, Willow. Let it out."

"Was I too obvious?" she asked with a sheepish smile.

"Bulls in a china shop had more finesse."

It was nice to hear her laugh, though I saw her wince and hold her side when she did, and I knew she hadn't recovered yet from the accident.

"Careful," I said softly, looking over at her with concern. "You just got out. We don't need you going back in."

Willow watched me, her smile fading. "You left again."

I nodded, knowing she'd bring it up. "I had to go. When you get the summons I got, you have no choice."

"But you *didn't* go." The cuffs of her sweater hung over her knuckles, and I wondered who had gotten clothes for her. Was it Ned? I wouldn't say I liked how I felt about him doing something so personal for her. "So why did you leave?"

"I attended to what I needed to." It was a half answer, and she knew it, and she also knew she would get little else from me. That latter knowledge, I didn't feel so good about.

"Where are we going now, then?" Willow asked. "I can't believe you pulled rank on Ned."

"Pulled rank?" I asked her with amusement. "We're not in the military."

"But you were?" She had turned even more in her seat to focus on me. "Doc told me that some of you join the armed forces."

"Doc told you more than you maybe needed to know," I murmured. Glancing over at her once more, I took a good long look at her. Willow held my stare, and for a moment, I almost forgot I was driving. "You look tired," I said, turning away, focusing back on the road. She'd already been in one car accident, and I didn't need to put her in another.

"I'm managing," she told me, her head dipping down. "It's been a lot, but I'm doing okay."

"I'm sorry for what's happening to you."

"Are you?" Reaching over, Willow looked like she would touch me and then thought better of it, letting her hand drop to her lap.

"What's that supposed to mean?" I asked her, hating the feeling of uncertainty when she didn't answer immediately.

The silence hung heavy between us, and I saw her fingers twist together in her lap, her knuckles whitening as she clasped them tightly, as though she was trying to physically hold back whatever she wanted to say. I heard her exhale, and with a glance, I saw her lips part like she was ready to speak, but instead, she turned her head away.

"Willow? What's that supposed to mean?" I repeated, my voice sharper than I intended.

Out of the corner of my eye, I saw her shake her head, the

faintest, almost imperceptible movement before she finally turned back to meet my gaze.

"It means... I don't know what it means, Caleb." Fingers pushed her hair behind her ear. "Are you sorry that our lives are seemingly linked, or are you just saying it because you think you *should* be sorry and it's what you think I *expect* you to say?"

"So...you think I'm lying?"

Biting her bottom lip, she looked away again. "Isn't that what you do? Lie?"

"Willow..."

She let out a deep breath. "Yeah, you're right. That was mean." She sounded bitter. "Unkind. And no, I don't actually think you're lying." Her chin dropped as she raised her hands to rub her eyes tiredly. "I think you maybe feel guilty...but..."

"But?"

Raising her head, she regarded me with a weariness I knew in my soul. "I don't think it's for me."

Nodding, I pressed my lips together in case I blurted out something harsh. She didn't deserve harsh. "Maybe you're right," I admitted slowly. "I don't think I am responsible for what's happening to you." Tapping my index finger off my temple, I spoke clearly. "I have nothing to do with what's happening inside your head—"

"I know that!" Her tone was as sharp as the spark of anger that flashed in her eyes. "I'm not blaming you for the visions, or whatever they are, but there *is* more to this story—our story, if you will—and you know what it is."

"Do I?" I hated how hard I sounded.

"Yes! You say you're sorry, but you can fill in the blanks for me, and maybe if I know more, I can do more."

"You mean my past," I spoke flatly.

"Yes, I—"

"Don't need to know," I snapped, shoving my hand through my hair, frustration building. "You don't *need* to know everything. You think you do, but you don't."

Twisting in her seat, she glared at me, her eyes narrowing to slits. "Yes, I do." She spoke over me, cutting me off before I could start. "And it *is* your fault that I don't know. This world I've been thrown into? This whole other living *species* that I didn't even know existed, yes, I think we both know if I didn't see *you*, then I wouldn't see any of it." Her breathing was shallow as she struggled to keep her temper. "If you stopped shutting me out or leaving, then maybe, *maybe* we could figure this shit out."

"That's not fair," I protested, a warning tone in my voice not to push it. Not to try to get me to talk about things that weren't any of her concern.

"Isn't it?" Willow's gaze locked on mine, the challenge clear in her eyes. "Caleb—" She broke off, taking in a deep breath to calm herself down. "Look, you know I've seen things, and we can't go on like this—"

"Like what?" I snapped, signaling and pulling the car over on the road. Switching the engine off, I turned in my seat, looking at her full-on. "Can't go on like what?"

"Forget it," she muttered, turning her head away.

Reaching over, I cupped her jaw, turning her head to mine. "What have you seen, Willow?" My voice was quiet, coaxing, the tension an undercurrent that she didn't miss.

"I've seen enough." Her gaze dipped to my lips and back again. "Enough to know there's a lot that you need to tell me and some things you need to never share." Her eyes softened as she looked into my eyes, trying so hard to get past the barriers. "I've seen your past, I've seen the pain, I feel the loneliness..." Tears welled in her eyes. "You can't hide from me."

Her words hit like a blow. Each word was a punch in the gut, and I had to break our stare so she couldn't see how much she affected me. I'd buried so much for so long; she didn't get to come into my life and demand answers.

I was damaged, I knew that. The last weeks on the mountain, with only the company of the spirits of the dead, highlighted how screwed up I was.

"I'm not hiding," I told her gruffly, pulling away from her. "I faced my shit a long time ago."

"Liar."

I looked at her, trying to keep a hold of my temper. "Willow—"

"No." She shook her head. "Just...no."

"Just no?" I asked, my voice low, my whole attention on her, knowing she didn't have a fucking clue how close she was to me losing control.

Willow swallowed hard, sensing that maybe she'd pushed too far. But, dear Goddess, she was a stubborn woman. I saw it in the realization that she was on dangerous ground. I saw her accept it, and I saw her raise her chin in defiance as she held my stare.

Held my stare like Ned couldn't earlier.

She was so brave.

Or reckless.

At the moment, I wasn't sure which.

"No." She wet her lips, her fingers curling into her thighs as she faced me down. "Your bullshit stops today. Right here. Right now."

"Is that right?" I felt the sneer and couldn't stop it. "Who the fuck do you think you are, little girl?"

Willow's heart rate sped up as fury lit up her eyes, her cheeks flushing despite the fact she was squaring her shoulders. "I'm the *little girl* that's been drawing your *misery* for months. So stop with your macho bullshit, and tell me what the hell I need to know."

Dear Luna, she was stunning. Did she know how sexy she looked as she openly challenged me?

Reaching out, I heard Willow's breath hitch as I tugged her closer, the fabric of her sweater bunching in my hand. Her lips parted in a small gasp, so close to mine that I could feel the warmth of her breath against my skin. Her eyes were wide with surprise and something else—something that echoed inside me —and I wanted to explore it further, but I knew I couldn't.

"You don't need to know everything. Do *not* ask again."

Her chest rose and fell with shallow breaths, but she didn't pull away. Her gaze flickered between mine, and I could feel the tension between us.

Electric.

Dangerous.

She was as pissed off as I was, but beneath her anger, there was something raw, and it matched the fire in me.

"Maybe I don't need to know it all," she whispered, the tremble in her voice not from fear. I could sense her arousal, and I almost wished I couldn't. "But I've seen enough, and I need it to make sense." Her fingers curled lightly around my wrist gently. "You don't need to carry it alone."

My grip on her sweater tightened, and I was clenching my jaw so hard it hurt. She was too close. Too close to me, too close to the truth, and yet I was the one holding onto her. I wanted to push her away, but my fist remained tight in her shirt.

I felt her fingers caress my wrist. "Let me in, Caleb."

TWENTY

Caleb

IT WAS MY PULSE THAT I HEARD POUNDING IN MY EARS. IT was my instincts that told me to retreat. It was my inner voice screaming at me to let go before I dragged her into my darkness. But still, I held on, resisting the urge to run from this connection, this bond between us, even as I knew it was getting stronger.

I hated it as much as I needed it.

"You don't want this, Willow," I murmured, my lips brushing hers as I spoke. "You don't know what I've done. If you did, you would never let me this close to you again."

I felt her other hand rest against my chest, her palm flattening over my heart. "I know that it's not evil." Her lips were so close I could taste them. "I know this darkness you fight can't take you. I won't let it."

"Willow..."

"I'm here, Caleb." She pulled back slightly, her stare steady and strong. "I'm still here."

Her words broke through my defenses.

Fuck.

I closed the distance between us, my hand pulling her flush against me. My other hand cupped the back of her neck, fingers lacing into her hair, just enough pressure to make her tilt her head up towards me.

There was a heartbeat where we both seemed to stop, the tension so thick it felt almost unbearable. Her eyes searched mine, and I knew she felt the same, the same force dragging us together and both of us were done fighting it.

I kissed her.

It wasn't gentle. It wasn't soft. It wasn't an apology. It was hard and unrelenting. It was filled with every unspoken truth, every frustration, every emotion we'd been ignoring. Our mouths collided, and the world outside of the car didn't matter. It was just me and her and the fire that burned between us.

Willow responded instantly, her fingers fisting into my shirt as she kissed me back with equal intensity. Her hunger matched mine. Her desperation to be closer was as much as my own. I could taste her, feel the way her body pressed into mine, and I knew there wasn't an inch of space between us.

My hand in her hair tugging her head back more, I deepened the kiss as my tongue slid against hers, drawing out a moan from her that sent a shiver down my spine. It felt as if every nerve in my body was on fire, every part of me was alive with the feel of her. The taste of her was addictive, and I knew I would never have enough of her.

Willow's hands slid upwards, smoothing over my shoulders, then higher, curling into my hair, pulling me down to her, as though she needed this as much as I did.

The kiss grew more urgent and more intense as our connection became raw and unconstrained, causing a flood of desire to well within me.

A car horn sounded, causing us to break apart as the sounds of the outside world rushed back in between us. Resting my forehead against hers, our breathing heavy, we both tried to understand what had just happened.

Drawing my head back, I took in her swollen lips, her eyes half-lidded and shining with excitement.

"Luna, forgive me," I murmured, dipping my head and catching Willow's lips with mine once more, gentler this time, taking my time to explore.

Pulling back, I dropped a kiss on the tip of her nose. I knew what I had to do. Starting the car, I pulled out back into the traffic.

"Caleb?" she still sounded breathless, and my cock twitched at hearing it.

"You want to know?" I asked, facing forward, trying to pretend I wasn't as affected as she was and failing.

"Yes." I heard her apology as she answered honestly. It was who she was—unapologetically real.

"If you want to know, then you need to see."

"See?"

Glancing at her, I nodded. "You up for a hike?"

Willow's eyes widened in understanding. "You're taking me to your home?"

"It's not been my home for a long time." I heard my regret and anger. Reaching over, I took her hand in mine.

This was right. I knew it now. As I felt her fingers grip mine with unspoken support, I squeezed back, knowing I would need her strength in the coming days.

When we were clear of the town, Willow didn't look as we passed the crash site, and I wished I could pull her closer to soothe her discomfort.

We'd been silent for a while, both of us trying to process what had happened, but her hand was still in mine, and she hadn't pulled away, and I hadn't let go.

What did that mean? I was driving us to the foot of Shadowridge Peak. What was I planning? Did I really intend to make Willow hike up my mountain?

I remembered being convinced as I stood on the ridge looking down only a few weeks ago that they were trying to trick me. Now, in a few hours, was I really, willingly, escorting her up the cliff face?

"It's not like Blackridge Peak," I spoke suddenly, startling her. Willow turned to look at me. "Shadowridge Peak," I explained gruffly. "It's a bitch to climb."

I saw her look down at her clothes dubiously.

"Yeah, you'll need new clothes," I confirmed. "Boots, too." Unclasping our hands, I rubbed the back of my neck. "I won't be able to carry you like last time, not all the way."

"I'll manage."

Puffing out my cheeks, I struggled with how to word it, to make her understand.

Willow gave a light laugh. "Okay, from the coronary you're having, I assume I won't manage, I'll struggle?"

"*I* struggle," I told her bluntly. "And it's my mountain."

"Your mountain?" Willow's tone had a teasing lilt. "Can a mountain be yours?"

"Yes." My answer was flat. My doubt about her real intentions once more crept in.

"Oh." I could practically feel her thinking. "Is it, like...a pack thing?"

Clearing my throat, I checked my side mirror, hiding from her curious gaze. "It is." Shifting in my seat uncomfortably, I cleared my throat again. "And it's...it's a me thing."

How the hell was I going to get her up Shadowridge and explain all the shit if I couldn't even say the word *alpha* to her?

"I'm sorry," Willow spoke quietly. "I don't understand."

"It's an alpha thing." The knot in my gut tightened as I told her things that humans need never know. "The mountain, Shadowridge Peak, is mine."

"Did you buy it?" she asked, not trying to hide her confusion. She wasn't being sarcastic or a smart-ass, she was genuine.

"You think of ownership as something you bought and paid for. Something you get a receipt for," I scoffed. "Not everything is about money."

"Okay." Willow moved in her seat so I could see her more clearly without having to take my eyes off the road as much. "Not everything is about money, but how do you *own* something if you don't pay for it? Was it a gift?"

"Of sorts." I pointed to the roof of the truck. "Luna gave it to us, technically."

"Us?"

"Pack." Even now, with her in the car, and only her, I still struggled to say the word. "Each pack, or group, who forms has the right to claim somewhere they feel is their home."

"Is it one pack per mountain?" Willow sat forward, peering out of the windshield to take in the mountain range that looked closer than it was.

Her question was naive, but I reminded myself she was still

clueless about so much regarding shifters, and up until now, that had been the way I wanted it.

"Not all shifters pick the mountains for their homes. We're fairly spread out, and still so close together."

She settled back in her seat, her attention back on me. "You sound disappointed."

I gave her a tight smile. "What can I say, I like my own company."

Willow cocked her head, studying me with those intelligent eyes of hers, seeing far more than I wanted to admit. "You say that, but I don't think it's company you avoid."

"And what do you think it is?" My voice was as dry as my sense of humor, given the topic.

"Memories."

The word hung suspended between us, filling the car with a feeling of discomfort, the kind you get when something cuts too close to the bone. I tried to keep my expression neutral, unwilling to give anything away.

"Or, maybe I like the comfort that comes with solitude," I answered, keeping my voice smooth.

Willow snorted, folding her arms across her chest. "So, what are you saying? It's the mountain that keeps you away from everyone?" She tsked. "It would be less insulting if you remembered I *know* that you *just* went back to it." Willow had a shit poker face, so I could see her anger.

My jaw clenched. "I'm not insulting you. Just because I haven't been on the mountain doesn't mean I'm sociable."

"The shaman says that being alone is dangerous for you."

"The shaman told you that?" I asked her doubtfully.

"Okay, Cannon told me the shaman told him that." She

hesitated for a moment, considering her next words carefully. "They said that without a pack, you go mad."

"Superstition."

"Really?" I understood why she sounded so doubtful. "The spirit guide and the alpha are superstitious?" Willow shook her head as she looked away. "You are either delusional or you're avoiding whatever is going on with you and you've become an idiot."

"I'm not avoiding anything."

"Then why do you keep running away?"

Looking over at her, I saw the determined look in her eyes, unflinching when she saw how pissed off I was.

"Sometimes, being alone is the safer option."

"For who?"

"Everyone."

Willow hesitated, studying me once more. "You can't believe that."

"Does it matter to you if I do? You're still wanting to follow me up a mountain."

The punch to my arm was uncalled for. "To *help* you, jackass."

I let out a short laugh, seeing her rubbing her knuckles after she punched me. "Is that you also helping me?"

"Shut up." She didn't try to hide the small smile as she shoved her hands under her thighs and more or less sat on her hands. "And yes, by the way, I am helping. Hopefully, seeing it with my own eyes can stop my dreams or visions from showing me."

"I hope you know what you're getting into."

Willow gave me a flat stare. "Or you can prepare me?" She rolled her eyes at my blank look. "Tell me, stop stalling."

"I can't." Licking my bottom lip, I saw her disappointment as she started to protest. "I will tell you, but not when I am driving. My story will start when we start climbing Shadowridge Peak."

"Okay."

We settled back into silence, and the miles between the car and the mountain slowly disappeared while the quiet stretched longer between Willow and me.

We'd been driving for a long time, the steady hum of the engine and the quiet all around us lulling us into a comfortable silence. We could do that, I found, sit with each other in silence and not feel the need to speak. Willow spent most of her time taking in the scenery, and I knew she was probably itching to draw.

The sun had started to dip behind the mountains, casting long shadows across the landscape, showcasing the beauty of the autumnal scenery. I kept my eyes on the road, keeping a lookout for any cop cars in case they tagged my plates and got an alert for a stolen car. Every now and then, I glanced at Willow from the corner of my eye, waiting for or expecting a conversation about the line we crossed earlier.

Kissing her had changed things. Had it? Fuck, I was useless at this kind of thing. She wasn't the first person I kissed, not even the first human, but this felt different. I didn't know if I trusted it.

Trusted her.

Then why are you taking her to Shadowridge Peak?

I didn't have an answer for that either.

Suddenly, she broke the silence, her voice catching me off guard.

"You said that there are other places shifters live," she said, looking over at me. She looked out the window again. "I can't think of wolves anywhere but mountains."

"Wolves inhabit forests, tundra, grasslands, and of course, mountains."

"And are shifters there too?"

"Why? Do you think we cohabit with them?" I asked her only half-seriously.

Willow made a face at me, causing me to smile. "No, silly. I was just thinking how difficult it must be for you to blend, but if your kind picks remote places, then maybe you're harder to detect?"

"We're careful," I acknowledged. "Many of my kind live on outskirts of towns and cities, usually where there is access to large areas of land."

"For crops?" she asked, and I could see my answer had confused her.

"To run."

"To run? Oh...you mean when you shift."

"Yeah." Rubbing my cheek, I looked over at her. "I wasn't suggesting a 5K regular route."

Leaning over, she swatted my arm playfully. "Meanie." She digested what I had told her. "So...there's more of you than just in the Rockies."

"Lots more."

"And you haven't been in communication with any of them?"

Frowning, I looked over at her. "What makes you think that?"

"The others," she admitted. Her gaze shifted from me to the window, and I knew she was struggling to find the words. "They are worried that you are too alone, so I assumed that you had no contact with anyone of your kind? Isn't that why they think you're dangerous?"

I let out a breath, my jaw tightening. She had no idea how close to the truth she was, how much I had isolated myself after my pack was destroyed. It wasn't until Willow, in her innocence, asked questions I'd been avoiding answers to for a long time, that I realized why the shaman was letting her know things she ordinarily wouldn't be allowed to know.

But did my self-imposed isolation mean I was dangerous?

"I'm not—"

"You are," she interrupted. "My drawings, they're loaded with violence." Her voice was a low whisper, and if I didn't have shifter hearing, I may not have heard her.

"Shifters run a bit more violent than most," I said casually. "We're men, but we have a natural instinct of the wolf, the hunter. We tend to lean towards bloody a lot."

"Bollocks."

Her expletive made me look over at her. "Bollocks? Not your everyday curse word." Thinking about it, I remembered the way she'd date stamped one of her drawings. "Your foster parents, one of them was British?"

Willow looked over at me, a thin frown line showing as she studied me. "Yeah, Jan. You got that from *bollocks*?"

"You date stamp wrong."

"One could say I date stamp *right*."

"One could, but one would be wrong." Fighting my smile, I heard her giggle and was pleased that the tension had eased once more, knowing the next thing I said would probably make it worse. "You need to sleep." Placing my hand on her leg, I squeezed lightly, cutting off her protest. "You just got out of the hospital, remember?"

"I'm painfully aware." Willow's dry tone made me smile.

"Then sleep, because you're going to need your strength."

"Are you going to Vulcan death grip me?" She saw my confusion and made a claw with her hand. "You know, the pressure point thing you do."

"I was hoping you would just sleep?" I offered openly, hearing the tiredness in my voice. "With no argument."

She started to say something and then changed her mind. "Okay, can we pull over so I can lie down in the back?"

"You're hurting?" I asked, kicking myself for not stopping sooner and letting her walk off her stiffness.

"I was in a truck that rolled," she deadpanned. "Pretty sure I'll hurt for a long time yet."

"And you want to climb a mountain," I scoffed.

"And you're going to help me," she shot back, wearing that determined look I was too familiar with.

Pulling over, I helped her move from the front seat to the back. It took her a few tries to find a somewhat comfortable position, but when she did, I knew that she'd be sleeping as soon as I was back in the driver's seat. She'd been holding it off too long, and I'd been too self-involved to notice.

"When I wake up, will we be there?" Willow asked from her curled position behind me.

"Probably."

"You okay?" Her voice was heavy with fatigue, but I could still hear her genuine concern.

"Not sure."

"It's okay, Caleb. I'm here."

The fact that she immediately fell asleep after her declaration didn't take away the fact that those five words gave me the strength to keep driving and take her to the mountain where she'd learn about my darkness.

Yet, I didn't turn around. I kept driving.

There was no going back now.

TWENTY-ONE

Willow

Caleb had been generous in his estimation of how long I'd be asleep for. I lay in the back, curled into a ball, trying to ignore the pains in my legs from not being stretched out, but I was content to lie as I was for as long as possible.

The sky was still dark, a deep indigo that blurred against the horizon. The faintest hint of dawn lingered beneath the clouds, and the world felt still. From my position, my view was limited, but I imagined the landscape was much different for Caleb, who was silent as he drove.

"I'll pull over," he spoke suddenly, causing me to jump. "You need to stretch and a bathroom break."

How long had he known I was awake? I could ask him, but I doubted he'd tell me because he would think it irrelevant.

When I was finished, I emerged from a clump of bushes on the side of the road and found Caleb standing with his arms folded across his chest, his eyes on the mountain range now much closer than it had been.

"It doesn't get easier peeing in nature," I joked, even though

221

I was deadly serious. I saw his lips twitch and dutifully held out my hands when he offered me hand sanitizer. "It also doesn't get easier knowing you're on the other side."

"This is a human hang-up," he told me smoothly, capping the bottle and fighting the smile as I vigorously sanitized my hands. "Shifters don't care."

"So, what, you're all nudists squatting to pee here, there, and everywhere?"

The look I got was one of astonishment, confusion, and general bewilderment.

"Yeah, okay, I'd ignore that too," I muttered, climbing into the passenger seat. "Let's forget I woke up?"

"But you're so delightful in the morning," he murmured as he got in the car.

"Ha." Looking pointedly at the still-dark sky, I settled back in my seat. "It's not morning yet."

"Then go back to sleep."

It was a command, not a suggestion, and I decided it was too early in the morning to argue with him. The headlights of the car lit up the gloom, illuminating the road ahead as it curved through the open landscape. The Rockies' jagged silhouette beckoned us forward, and I worried about how in the heck I was going to climb a mountain.

Again.

Caleb flicked the heater on for me, and I murmured my thanks as warm air fell on my feet.

Leaning against the window, I felt the cold of the outside air as I watched the passing landscape. Pine trees that had been sparse were growing denser, their towering height blocking the view at times.

Caleb was silent, focused on the road, his hands firm on the steering wheel, and I felt the weight of all the things we hadn't said yet. I couldn't help but wonder what waited for me, for us, in the mountains. We rounded another curve in the road, and the Rockies rose in front of us, like a promise, an untold truth waiting to be told.

Dawn broke through from the cloud cover, the first light touching the mountain peaks, casting a faint purple glow over snow-capped summits.

"Snow?" I squinted at the top of the peaks.

Caleb leaned forward and gave a non-committal grunt.

"It's still only October."

"Down here, it is." He pointed out the window. "Snow hit the peaks a couple of weeks ago."

"Is it snowing where you are? I haven't drawn anything with snow."

Caleb glanced at me, and his smirk was bitter. "Well, that must make it right," he muttered, "if you haven't drawn it."

"Don't be testy," I scolded. "How much further?" I asked, forcing myself to shake free the sleep that lingered in my brain.

"A few hours. Sleep some more," he encouraged. When he saw me sitting up straighter, I saw his jaw clench, but he kept his thoughts to himself.

"Do you have any idea who broke into my house?" I asked him suddenly. It wasn't something we had spoken about. Actually, most of what we spoke about wasn't about anything at all. Who would have thought Caleb was so good at small talk without *actually* being good at small talk?

He looked over at me, his look questioning. "Diversion tactics?"

His bemusement made me laugh out loud. "What? Hardly." The look he gave me made me lose my smile. "I thought you may have found something out by now." His frown deepened and I looked away. "Or not, it's okay, sorry I asked."

"Hey." His hand landed on my thigh. "Don't do that. *I* thought perhaps Cannon or Ned would have told you, that's all."

"Told me what?"

Caleb shrugged. "I killed two of the ones who ran you off the road. I left the bodies behind. Ned and whoever—I don't keep count of the names." His eyes flicked to mine, almost apologetically. "There's always another one," he added slightly defensively, and I hid my smile before he saw it and stopped talking.

"You killed two men, right?" I suddenly realized the seriousness of it, and I lost any humor I had.

Caleb sniffed derisively. "Shifters. I killed two shifters who would have killed me." His look was hard when he glanced at me. "Who *tried* to kill you."

"Yeah, I know, you told me before, but I don't think they wanted to kill me." I spoke without thinking and should have been prepared for the sharp jerk of the car as Caleb pulled over. "Caleb!" Trying to soothe my rapidly beating heart, I glared at him. "I was *just* in a car crash."

"I'm not Doc." He shrugged off my concerns easily, his tone dismissive but his eyes sharp, focusing on me with that penetrating gaze of his, making me feel like there was nowhere to hide. "What do you mean you don't think they wanted to kill you? What have you seen?"

There was so much I wanted to say to him, but his hard,

demanding, *expectant* stare made me blurt out the truth. "Nothing."

He waited and when it was clear I wasn't going to say anything else, he widened his eyes slightly, urging me to speak.

I hesitated, my mind replaying the images that had haunted me since the break-in. "It's kind of hard to explain." I saw his carry-on motion and wanted to kick him. "They came in when they knew I wasn't there—I mean the store—they did that in the time it took me to walk home and see what they'd done to the house."

"It's not something to praise them for," he growled.

"Will you quit it?" I snipped at him. "What I mean is they had the chance to hurt me, if they wanted. Probably more than once, if you think about it. And they didn't. So..."

"So?" His voice was gruff and hard, and I felt like I did when I used to go to confession. Guilty but no idea why.

"So...doesn't it feel more like a test?"

"A test?" His voice was flat. Unimpressed.

"Yeah, like they did what they did, the break-ins and that, and then kind of sat back to see what would happen. Like they were testing the waters."

His brow furrowed, his teeth grinding as he stared off into the distance. "Testing?" His hands tightened on the steering wheel, although we were stationary. "That's a hell of a jump to make, Willow. People like that don't waste their time *testing*. They go in, get what they need, and leave."

"But they didn't get what they needed," I said, ignoring his piercing stare. I pressed on, desperate to get it out now without any more interruptions. "I don't know how to describe how I know, but...but I don't think it was me they were trying to get the attention of." Clearing my throat, I looked away. "It felt too…"

"Calculated."

We shared a look, and Caleb ran his tongue over his bottom lip as he considered my argument. "They broke into your home, they wrecked your store, they basically destroyed your life, and you're telling me that it wasn't about you?" I nodded. He sucked his teeth. "So what then? They didn't run you off the road to kill you? Is that what you're saying?"

His presence could be very overwhelming in a small space, and I pressed the switch to lower the power window so I could breathe, ignoring the chill from the morning air.

But I'd never been a quitter, so I met his gaze, refusing to be silent. He asked, I was talking. "I'm saying, I don't think they came to *kill* me specifically. I don't know what they wanted, but I don't think it was my life. I think—I *feel*," I corrected myself quickly, "I feel like it was a test to see what happened."

"Are you serious?"

Could he sound any flatter? "Yes."

His eyes flashed with something I couldn't place—fear, anger, maybe both, maybe neither.

"*Why* are you only telling me this now?" His hands were curled into fists, his jawline tight, his eyes narrow and fierce, and I felt a thin sliver of anxiety that suddenly this car wasn't big enough for his anger.

"Caleb—"

"Are you out of your mind?" he growled at me. "I'm genuinely curious." His tone suggested the complete opposite.

I held his gaze, refusing to back down. "I didn't have a lot of time to tell you anything. I was in a hospital bed and then you left!"

Caleb let out an explosive breath, running his hand through his hair, frustration evident in every line of his body as he watched me, his expression closed off. "This changes things," he mumbled under his breath, his fingers tapping the steering wheel as he thought about things. "If they weren't after you, if they were *testing,* who the hell was their target? Cannon?"

"You." I looked at him like he was an idiot. "Isn't that obvious?"

"No. It isn't obvious at all." He shook his head. "I left Whispering Pines months ago. You may have left with me, but you didn't come back with me. I've not been near you in weeks." He turned his head towards me. "Cannon ever come back in those weeks I was gone?"

"No. Only Royce, Ned, or Doc."

"Still, they see you with shifters," he mused, returning his attention to the mountains in front of us. "Right?"

"I guess. I don't know. You think that matters?" My voice was small as the weight of the mess of my life pressed down on me.

He locked eyes with me again, the look more intense than before, and I hadn't thought that possible. "What have you seen? What else, Willow? What else haven't you told me?"

"Unfair," I grumbled as I faltered under the intensity of his stare. I hesitated, adrenaline coursing through my veins. I could lie and say I hadn't had more visions, scenes of things that made no sense, things that I couldn't explain, but I knew Caleb wouldn't let this go. Not now.

"I've had a few dreams," I admitted, avoiding looking at

him. "Visions, I guess. Maybe. Of the ones..." I cleared my throat. "Of them."

Caleb's stare was punishing, his face a tight mask of control. "And did you mention this to any of your babysitters?"

I winced at the term but shook my head. "You told me you killed them! I didn't think they were relevant!" I snapped back, feeling frustration rise in me too.

"You need to tell me *everything* you see," he ground out, and I was sure he was speaking through clenched teeth.

"Do you think I was right? Was it a test?" I swallowed hard, feeling the weight of his words and my own reality. He gave a sharp nod of his head, and it didn't soothe me like I hoped it would. "What does this mean, Caleb? Am I right that it's not me they want?"

"I don't know yet," he admitted. "But something isn't adding up, and we need to know what we're missing."

"Okay."

We sat in silence for a few minutes, each lost in our own thoughts. "Do we do that before or after we climb the unclimbable mountain?"

His huff of amusement eased the tension in his shoulders. "Not unclimbable, just difficult."

"Like you." It popped out, and I felt my eyes widen at what I'd said and saw his humor fade, his eyes darkening as he watched me. "Which I like," I rambled on stupidly, wishing I could shut up. "You. I like you. No, wait, you know...the tall, dark, mysterious, and difficult type, it's fine, it's all good. Um, why can't I stop talking?" I took a deep breath. "Shut *up*, Willow."

Caleb's eyebrow quirked and I cursed under my breath. He

leaned over, his hand slipping around to cup the back of my neck. His lips covered mine briefly, a hint of a taste of what I hadn't asked for yet. But I knew I would soon. One of us, both of us, would lose control soon.

Or now.

He pulled back, and I felt a stab of disappointment when he did, but I acted without thinking, and my hand caught him and pulled him back down to my lips. My mouth opened under his, tasting him, learning the feel of his mouth on mine. I felt Caleb grip me tighter, and then his hand was moving down, unclipping my seat belt, lifting me out of my seat. Our lips parted briefly as he maneuvered me into position, and I settled over his hips, aware of the feeling of the steering wheel at my back.

Caleb's hands rested on my thighs, digging in slightly, his grip tightening, and in one swift motion, he pulled me closer, pressing me firmly against him. My breath hitched, my heart pounding as I felt his strength and heat radiate through my body. Caleb's hand slid upward, his fingers slipping under my sweater, his touch rough but deliberate as his fingers skimmed my skin, sending shivers down my spine as he traced a path slowly up my back. My hips moved, and my thighs parted wider, causing me to settle over him better, aligning with him, and I began to rock in a slow grind against him as our bodies fit together.

The tautness between us was thickening, and I could feel his body responding to mine as he took control of the kiss. There was something raw and undeniable between us, and I moaned into his mouth as his hands began to move over my body with confidence and precision. He knew exactly where to touch me to get me to respond.

I couldn't breathe. The air between us was heavy, and I pulled away to catch my breath. Looking down at him, I saw his eyes dark with desire as he looked up at me, his control teetering on the edge.

I knew exactly how he felt.

Studying me, as if expecting me to stop him, he moved one hand to cup my breast, his thumb circling my nipple, and his other hand moved to my waist, guiding my movements as my hips rolled against him again, slower this time, more deliberate. Caleb groaned softly, his eyes tightening with restraint as he watched me, but he didn't stop me. Instead, he pulled me closer, his breath hot against my skin as his lips brushed against me. I felt his tongue slick over the pulse in my neck, and my thighs clenched against him.

My hands curled into his shoulders, fisting his shirt, clutching him desperately for support as I moved against him. The car was loud with our breathing, thick and ragged as we gave into our desire. I felt my wetness between my legs, and I chased the release only he could give me. His hands dug into my ass, gripping me possessively, pulling me down harder as his hips rose to meet mine.

We were unraveling, and I knew my control was gone when it came to this man. His touch was everywhere, *he* was everywhere, and I needed him *there*. "Caleb." My moan was pleading, desperate with want. "Please."

"Tell me what you want." His voice was low and rough, his lips barely touching mine, ghosting over my lips, teasing me. "Say it, Willow."

"You. I want you."

TWENTY-TWO
Willow

I closed the gap between us, our mouths crashing together as my desperate need became unbearable, our kiss hot and full. His lips were as demanding, his control gone. My jeans were unsnapped and I moaned with appreciation as his rough fingers caressed over the bare skin of my ass before slipping lower. My head tilted backward, exposing my neck when he found my wetness, a finger, then two, sliding between my thighs, caressing me exactly where I needed.

In an inhuman show of strength and speed, I was lifted off his thighs, and my jeans were yanked down my legs, my foot helping to push one leg free. Caleb pulled me down over him, and the feeling of only his jeans and my panties between us had me almost seeing stars as our bodies were now fully locked into a rhythm that neither of us wanted to stop.

I felt the sting and heard the rip of fabric as he tore my panties, but it was a secondary feeling, dull compared to the heady feel of his finger pushing into me. My fingers tangled in his hair. "Caleb." My whisper was swallowed as he claimed my mouth once more.

"Ride my hand." He sounded guttural, exposed, wild.

He watched me with an intensity that only made my need for him grow. His thumb traced over my clit, rubbing circles with gentle pressure, while his other finger moved inside me. My eyes were fixed on his, silently begging him not to stop, and the burn of another finger sinking into me had my eyes rolling back in my head as I pumped my hips over him.

"Fuck, Willow, I want you. You're so fucking beautiful like this." Caleb's voice was low and rough, a confession that seemed to be dragged from deep within. His teeth nipped at my exposed neck, and I felt my blood soar as he continued to rub just right.

My hands were desperately reaching for the button of his jeans. I moved off him slightly, giving him time to shove them down while I had him in my hand. Our moans were mixed as I started to stroke him. Caleb pulled me back into him, his length sliding between my legs, my wetness lubricating us both.

My hands wrapped around him, relishing in his ragged breathing as I took control. Placing him at my opening, I held his stare and hesitated. Caleb's eyes were black with desire, his breathing short and tortured, my fingers flexed around his heavy cock, and he gave a throaty groan that made my insides clench.

"Okay?" My whisper sounded loud in the silence of the car, and it was my turn to moan when Caleb's hips rose slightly, pushing the tip of him inside. "Caleb?"

"Yes," he growled, "Goddess, yes." His hands on my hips pulled me down over him as he slipped inside. My eyes widened as I felt him stretching me, and I tried not to cry out. My own wetness helped him, but it still made me gasp as my body adjusted to accept him. Caleb's thumb was back on my clit as our bodies started to move together, and I completely forgot where we were.

Our mouths fought against each other as we set a hard and unrelenting pace. Caleb's fingers on his left hand would leave bruises on my hip, I was sure, but I didn't care. This was everything. Having him inside me, filling me, it was addictive. I needed more. So much more.

"I need more," I groaned into his mouth.

"Greedy," he teased, pulling my sweater aside and kissing along my collarbone. Sitting straighter, holding me tighter to him, he pushed the button that lowered his seat back. The flat of his palm rested between my breasts. "Lean back."

I did so, my back hitting the steering wheel, but it was an insignificant pain as my body took more of Caleb's cock into me. Seeing him lying out under me made me want to touch all of him. From this angle, he took over, pulling and pushing me over his hips, my back arched as he delivered infinite pleasure, and all I could feel was him moving inside me.

"Oh shit," I breathed as my core coiled in anticipation. "Caleb!" I sounded like a stranger, my voice hoarse and broken, and when his thumb dropped back to press lightly against my clit, I cried out as I came undone around him. He let me ride out my orgasm, and then he pulled me forward. My hands fell to his abs, supporting myself shakily as I leaned over him. His hands on my hips were tight as he moved me over him at a relentless pace, his hips thrusting upwards as he chased his own release.

Caleb's head tipped back, his eyes heavy-lidded with desire as he watched me, and I watched him as his movements became more and more urgent until I saw him reach his peak. With a roar, he came inside me, his body sitting up smoothly, arms slipping around my waist and sliding up my back, gripping onto my shoulders as he pulled me down, pumping into me with a heady groan. Teeth grazed against my throat, nipping and sucking as my thighs clenched against his hips. Seeing him come undone had triggered another release for me, and I shuddered around him once more.

We stayed like that for a long moment until the sound of passing traffic penetrated our bubble, and I realized I'd just had sex in a car in the bright morning sunlight at the side of the road.

Caleb realized the same thing at the same time. "Shit." My sweater was pulled over my ass, and while I dropped my head to hide in the crook of his neck, Caleb was making sure we hadn't been seen. "The windows are fogged," he assured me. "No one would see inside."

He didn't mention that it wouldn't take a rocket scientist to know what we had been doing, and as we shuffled off each other and fumbled to get dressed, my cheeks burned with embarrassment.

I avoided looking at him while I tried to pull my jeans on, quickly coming to the uncomfortable realization that I had no underwear and was full of Caleb.

"Shifters don't have STDs right?"

Well, that's how you make the moment awkward.

"We don't." His voice was low, his breathing still uneven like mine, and that made me feel better. "You doing okay?"

"Just got screwed at the side of the road, and now have no underwear, and I am full of..."

"Cum."

Swallowing hard, I nodded. I felt him move and then he was bringing a pack into the front seat. I heard him rummage through it and was handed some napkins from a fast-food restaurant and a used shirt.

"Best I got," he told me apologetically. "Use them to clean yourself up. You have clothes in your backpack?"

Nodding, I twisted in my seat and, after a quick search, secured a clean pair of underwear. "And how do I do this?"

"I'll open the front and back door, and I'll stand in front of the car so no one can see through," he assured me.

I had nothing to offer, so I simply did what he told me, and using his shirt as a towel, all the napkins, and some hand sanitizer as carefully as I could, I cleaned myself as much as possible and then pulled on clean panties and tried not to think negative thoughts about my being a wanton hussy.

When I was done, I stood up and tried to work out the knots in my body. Caleb came around to stand beside me, and with no hesitation, he reached out for me, tugging me into his body, and kissed me soundly.

"I'm sorry that got awkward," he said softly against my lips. "If we ever do that again, I'll make sure it's in better surroundings."

I was finding it hard to speak. What did he mean *if*, shouldn't it be *when*? "No audience would be better," I said instead of demanding answers. I couldn't be *that* girl who thought a fumble at the side of the road meant more than it was.

Actually, screw that. "If? What do you mean *if?*"

Caleb's smile was slow and sinful. "Good girl," he murmured before pressing a light kiss to my lips. "You ready to move?" he asked, pulling back.

"Yup. Bring on the mountain."

His smile was infectious, and with another quick peck, he waited for me to get back in the car, quickly following me.

"You need to sleep?" Caleb asked as he started the car.

"You said a few hours before..." My cheeks were red again.

"Yup. Sleep if you can, you'll need it."

"You don't need to sleep?"

Caleb's grin was wicked. "Nope, I have a sudden burst of energy this morning."

Laughing at his playfulness, I shoved at his arm. "Shut up." As I settled in the seat, we fell into an easy silence while Caleb drove. I tried not to look at him all the time as I replayed every touch of his on my body. Eventually, the excitement of the morning caught up with me, and I fell asleep.

"Hey, Willow, wake up." The gentle touch on my shoulder was interrupting my lovely dream. A dream where I was wrapped up in the cocoon of Caleb.

"Go away, I'm still sleeping," I mumbled.

"Yes, you are, but you need to wake up."

I knew that voice. That amused lilt in his tone, which I never knew if he was laughing *at* me or *with* me. Opening an eye, I saw Caleb leaning over me. "Hey?"

"Hey," he greeted. "You can wake up now." Stepping back,

I saw the high mountains surrounding us, and a streetlight, and looking past him, I saw a store and more. "Thought you might want to eat?"

My tummy rumbled at the thought, and within a few minutes of waking up, I was brushing my teeth in a diner's bathroom with my toiletry bag from my backpack open beside me. I'd also taken the opportunity to do a better job of cleaning up. I still wasn't shower clean, but it was better.

When I eventually came out, Caleb was seated and eating his breakfast sandwich. Men had it so easy.

"Took your time," he commented as I slid into the booth.

"See you didn't wait for me," I replied, but whatever he was going to say was cut off when a plate of food was placed in front of me.

"There you go. We kept it warm for you," the waitress told me. "Your man get it right?" she teased with a smile at Caleb.

Looking down at my breakfast, I nodded. "Looks good."

"Your tea's just coming," she told me.

"Thanks." I looked at my plate and back to Caleb. "Should it surprise me that you ordered for me?"

He took a bite of his sandwich. "Anything I got wrong?" he asked with a smirk.

He knew he hadn't, and for that reason, I picked up a slice of toast and began buttering it without replying, ignoring his wide grin as he ate.

He watched me intently as I focused on the toast, his smile lingering as if he was savoring more than just his breakfast. I could feel Caleb's eyes on me, waiting for me to react, but I refused to give him the satisfaction of knowing he was right.

Instead, I slowly buttered my toast, pretending I wasn't noticing him at all.

"That's how you want to play?" he asked with genuine amusement. "Nothing to say?"

I kept my attention on the task, not allowing myself to meet his gaze. The warm buttery toast did little to distract me from the heat in my cheeks. He knew how to get under my skin, and that smirk he was wearing, while charming, was infuriating.

"You missed something," I finally said, setting the toast down on my plate and scooping up some eggs.

"Did I?" I could hear his amusement, and I knew he was laughing at me. "Enlighten me."

The waitress placed a pot of tea and a cup down on the table, and I murmured my thanks through a mouthful of eggs. When I met his gaze, he was watching me in that cocky, expectant way he had.

"Well?" Caleb gestured to my plate with what was left of his breakfast. "Tell me."

Swallowing, I met his stare. "You forgot to mention how obnoxious you can be."

His low, rough laugh did something to my insides that I didn't want to explore so quickly after what we had just done at the side of the road only hours before.

Caleb leaned back in his seat with a wide smile as he watched me. "Maybe it's part of my charm?"

Picking up a piece of bacon, I bit into it. "Maybe you need to learn the definition of charm."

"Maybe you like my charm just fine." Reaching over, he snagged a piece of bacon, avoiding the swat of my hand with ease.

"Ass."

Caleb chuckled and I realized I'd so rarely seen this lighter side of him. Maybe he needed to get laid more often? Maybe I could help with that? My cheeks flared as images flashed through my mind, and I pressed my thighs together reflexively. Berating myself for being foolish, I didn't notice his hands were still on the table, his smile faded.

"Whatever you're thinking about," he spoke to me, an undercurrent of strain marking his tone, "and if you don't want a replay of this morning in the diner's lot, can you stop?"

Looking up, I knew my eyes were wide with surprise, and when I saw the heated look he gave me, my mouth was suddenly dry. "I... What?"

"I can smell you," he told me, his voice low. "And my scent is still on you." His hands gripped the table. "And it's taking a *lot* not to drag you out of here, press you up against a wall, and slide right back inside."

Holy *shit*.

"Um..." I saw his pupils dilate, and I cursed myself for reacting to his lusty threat. "Don't make promises like that, and I won't react." My rushed whisper had him pushing himself out of the booth. "Caleb?"

"I need to walk it off," he muttered. He hesitated for a moment more, then dipping down, he caught my chin and delivered a punishing kiss. "Eat quickly."

It wasn't until he had left me that I saw he'd stolen all my bacon.

"You complete ass," I grumbled, stabbing my eggs with my fork.

I was finishing my cup of tea when he came back. Sliding in across from me, the earlier playfulness was gone.

"What happened?" I asked, instantly looking around.

"Need to find a new method of transport."

"Have the police...you know."

"No, I noticed a tag on the car. I should have seen it earlier. Stupid." He glared at the outside, and I reached over, taking his hand.

"You can't see everything," I told him. Trying to lighten his mood, I made a joke. "Isn't that what I'm supposed to do?"

He grunted but said nothing.

With a sigh, I withdrew my hand, but his hand snapped out, catching mine and pulling my arm back across to his side of the table. "No."

Good grief, I was melting like butter here. "What does the tag do?"

"Tracks us."

Oh. Well, now I knew why he was so pissed. "Then we ditch the car?" His grunt was one I roughly translated into *obviously*. "Is it far to walk? You know, to the...place."

His eyes flicked to mine, the corners crinkling with amusement. "We'll take the bus."

"You have a bus stop?"

This time, he laughed. "No, we'll get off at the closest point." He raised my hand to his mouth, placing a warm kiss on the tips of my fingers. "I'll help you, okay?"

I nodded, letting the warmth of his words settle in, the simple reassurance easing the tension in my chest.

"Who is it?" I asked softly. "Who's after us?"

"I don't know," he admitted, his eyes darkening with unreleased anger. "But I'll find out."

"I'm scared."

Caleb gave me a look of understanding that made me want to reach out to him. "I'll keep you safe," he assured me.

We paid for breakfast, I didn't want to ask where the money came from and Caleb led me outside, unpacking the car quickly, leaving the keys inside, telling me that's how he found it.

We started to walk into the town, Caleb's arm brushing mine, giving me some comfort.

But I could sense the storm building around us. Something was happening, and I had the feeling that it was much bigger than either of us fully understood.

And I didn't know if we were ready for it.

TWENTY-THREE

Willow

THE BUS HISSED AS THE DOORS CLOSED AND LEFT US standing at the side of the road. The driver had grumbled, but Caleb was persuasive, and he'd let us off in the middle of nowhere.

Well, not in the middle of nowhere, Caleb knew exactly where we were. We were at the base of Shadowridge Peak, and I'd been dreading this almost as much as Caleb, I think, though probably for entirely different reasons.

The air had too much bite to it, and I was glad of the coat I'd picked up in the town where we had breakfast. I was decked out in new clothes. Hiking boots, thick weatherproof pants, a long-sleeved thermal shirt under a fleecy hoodie, and then the new padded jacket on top. I felt a bit like a marshmallow, but as I felt the crisp air sting my cheeks, I wondered if I had time to pull another layer on.

The late afternoon sun cast long shadows, and as the fresh mountain air swirled around us, I noticed the sky remained a sharp, cloudless blue. It was the kind of day where you could see everything laid out in front of you, including the climb that lay ahead.

Standing next to Caleb, I saw him looking up at the trail that was partially hidden in the dense forest ahead. Shadowridge Peak loomed large, almost too large, and I felt incredibly small as I stood staring up at it. My stomach was in knots as I considered the insanity of climbing this thing. But with another glance at Caleb, I knew I couldn't back out.

"It's really big," I said stupidly.

"That's what she said," he quipped, and I grinned as I heard him grunt when my elbow dug into his ribs. Caleb looked over at me, his eyes betraying his uncertainty. "You ready?"

"No."

He nodded, and I knew he had been expecting that. Quietly, he adjusted the straps of my pack, which he carried over his broad shoulders. He didn't look towards the peak that was his home. If anything, he looked like he was avoiding looking at it. "I'll be right beside you," he reminded me.

"Yeah, I know." I looked back up at the imposing mountain. "It's just...steeper than I thought it would be."

I saw him fight the almost-smile, and his eyes held an amusement that warned me that I wouldn't like what he said next. "It gets steeper before it gets easier."

"Great. Of course it does," I grumbled sarcastically. Taking a deep breath, I wondered if the shaking in my legs was adrenaline or fear. A sudden thought popped into my head. "It *does* get easier, right?"

"Sure."

It was a lie and we both knew it. Whatever dismay he saw on my face made him reach forward and brush a soft kiss across my lips. "You ready, or do you want to turn back?"

He wasn't challenging me, but there was something behind his words. It was like he was testing whether I would keep pushing forward—to find out all his secrets if I carried on. Was he hoping that I turned back so he would never have to tell me about his past? After what we did this morning, after all the little kisses and touches since? He was delusional if he thought I was backing down now. Shaking my head, I looked him square in the eye. "I'm not turning back."

Caleb considered me, seeing more than I probably wanted to share, but he nodded, and it was almost as if it was with approval. He stepped forward, his hand resting lightly on my lower back as he guided us across the road and towards the trail. Even through three layers of clothing, I could feel his touch easily. His hand was steady and firm like him, and as I was beginning to realize, being close to Caleb anchored me. He settled something deep inside me, and even though I didn't understand it, he made me feel stronger.

The beginning of the path was easy. The trail was relatively flat and clear, but it didn't take long before the incline started to challenge my legs. Like before when we had climbed to get to Cannon and his pack, the trees grew denser, the canopy above heavier, cutting off most of the sunlight and encasing us in an eerie shadow. Faint sounds from the road traveled to us, but they were being replaced by the sound of dirt being crushed underfoot and the occasional call of birds that nested high in the branches above us.

"You want my story?" Caleb asked suddenly, and I was ashamed that I'd almost forgotten that's the whole reason we were here.

"Always."

Caleb glanced at me but kept walking, his steps sure and confident. "So quick to answer," he murmured.

"It's why we're here," I reminded him and saw his head dip. "We can wait until we're there if you want."

But he was shaking his head. "No point, they're already listening."

They? Looking around, I felt the anxiety start to bubble in the pit of my stomach as I followed him. I felt a shiver run through me, and it wasn't from the cold. "What do you mean, they?"

Caleb hesitated, his brow furrowing as though he was considering how much to reveal to me too soon. "The dead live on this mountain," he said, keeping his voice low. "They're waiting for me to come back to them." He glanced at me. "I warned you," he added almost accusingly.

"Is that why you don't want to come back here?" I asked, but he shook his head. And I knew what he didn't want to say. "It's why you don't want *me* here." I swallowed past the sudden lump in my throat, but too bad, I *was* here, and he just had to accept it. "I'm right here, Caleb," I assured him, like I had before. "I'm going nowhere." Where did this confidence come from? I didn't know, but I did know I believed every word of it, and seeing his look, I knew he did too. "Talk to me, I'm listening."

I watched him as he gritted his teeth, and I waited when he

didn't answer immediately. Caleb's gaze was fixed ahead, seeing something that wasn't visible to me.

"I hate this mountain," he started, his steps still steady and sure, and I worked hard to keep up with him. "There are ghosts up here. Memories." He sighed heavily. "So many fucking memories." His voice was bitter, the pain a strong undercurrent as he spoke. "Memories that are better off left alone. I avoid here because..."

"Some things are easier to bury?"

His head jerked in a sharp nod, and I didn't push. I knew enough to know how hard it was for him to talk about this, but as we walked the trail, I knew that here, he couldn't hide from whatever haunted him.

We walked for a while in silence, the incline becoming steeper, and my body started to protest. My legs burned, but I kept moving, refusing to give into my weakness. The path narrowed and the way Caleb led me, it soon disappeared completely, and I had to concentrate on avoiding rocks on the uneven ground. I stumbled more than once, but he was there, catching my arm, steadying me as I struggled onwards.

We came to a small clearing, and Caleb stopped, turning to face me, his eyes dark and unreadable. "We'll stop here for tonight."

My body screamed its thanks at the thought of a break, but I was worried stopping meant we wouldn't go any further at all. "Here? I can keep going," I told him stubbornly.

His look told me he knew that was a load of bull, and with a sigh, I sank onto a tree stump.

"Drink your water," he told me, looking around. I watched as his eyes closed. Taking in a deep inhale, he opened them to see me watching him. "Drink as much as you need. There's a stream a little further up; you can refill there."

I almost asked him how he knew but shut my mouth when I realized it was a stupid question.

Caleb dropped my pack. He'd amalgamated both of our belongings earlier, and almost absently, he handed me a sketchbook and my tin of pencils. "Just in case," he murmured. He pulled out a blanket and then untied my sleeping bag. When I'd asked him where his was, he'd laughed like I was genuinely funny.

"We sleep here?" I guessed, snuggling deeper into my thick jacket, wondering if I would manage to sleep in a place so cold.

"Yes, the next clearing isn't for a few hours yet, and I would rather do the trek in the daylight."

He meant he would rather *I* do the trek in the daylight. I was pretty sure Caleb would already be at his packlands if it wasn't for me. "Okay." I hesitated. "Thank you."

He nodded, turning to face me. His look was guarded, his eyes wary. "Before we go any further, I need to know something."

My heart sounded loud in my ears, but my voice was steady. "What is it?"

"Are you ready to hear it all?" His voice was low, intense. "Because when it's out and you know, it's a long way down on your own."

My mouth was suddenly dry, and I sipped the water from my flask as I considered the weight of his question. The challenge was more than me physically climbing the mountain, it was the deeper trial of learning who Caleb really was. Whatever was waiting for me was more than learning about his past and his pack. It was about *me* too.

And that realization sent a ripple of dread through me.

But then I thought about everything that had happened—the danger, the break-ins, the crash, the hospital bed, the continuing uncertainty every time I drew something I shouldn't know or see. The cloud of fog that swirled around my life like a storm, could be cleared when I learned about him. I'd been running from it just as Caleb had. I wanted answers, and while I knew he may not have them all, he had more than I did.

We were linked and I didn't understand it. I may never understand it, but I knew I needed to know everything about him. Even if it was ugly, it wouldn't change how I felt about him. I knew that now. Looking up at the mountain, partially hidden by trees and the darkness, I felt my determination harden.

"I'm ready," I told him, my voice sure, and I knew it was true.

Caleb watched me. I saw his expression soften a fraction before he pulled that hard mask back over him, guarding himself. Protecting himself from me. I hated it, and I wanted to reach out, but I knew now wasn't the time. He didn't want my comfort.

Not yet. Maybe not ever again, but I would worry about that later.

He rolled out my sleeping bag, fussing over it, and I was just about to tell him to stop when he started to talk.

"We were a small pack," he told me, his hands quick and sure as he set up a small camp for us. "My father, Amos, was alpha. A good one and a good man." His voice sounded wistful.

"He believed a happy pack was a healthy pack," he told me as he pulled out the food we had bought in town.

I watched as he deftly got my meal ready, a simple pre-made sandwich and chips, but I hadn't realized how hungry I was until he handed it to me. My murmured thanks went unnoticed as he put the other food away. I didn't ask why he wasn't eating.

"My mother was his mate." He glanced at me. "Mates are chosen by Luna. An alpha needs a mate for balance to counter him." His voice was clipped and clinical. "My father was a good alpha, strong and stern, and my mother was just as strong but gentler." He looked away, the pain etched in his face. "Shadowridge Pack was a powerful pack," he continued, his voice rougher. "The pack was respected in the region, maybe even further. Amos commanded respect and he got it." Caleb sat on my sleeping bag. I don't think he noticed as he plucked at a loose thread. "I was his only son." He swallowed hard, his fingers stilling. "To become alpha, you challenge for leadership, or the death of an alpha means he needs to be replaced."

"Challenge?" My sandwich lay forgotten in my lap.

Caleb noticed. "Eat, Willow. Your ME needs you to look after yourself." He waited until I took a bite, and then he continued. "Cannon's pack, his father was a mean bastard who trod his pack to the ground. Cannon challenged him, they fought, one died, one didn't."

Oh my God. He made that sound so normal. "Cannon killed his dad?" I knew I sounded as shocked as I felt.

"He wasn't a good alpha. He deserved to die." Caleb didn't look bothered at all.

"But your dad was good?"

"I didn't challenge my father," he told me bluntly. "But I was groomed early in my life by my mother and father to take over leadership when Amos stepped down."

"Oh. Like royalty?"

Caleb snorted but he didn't deny it. "I was trained in combat, strategy, and leadership skills. Amos wanted to make sure I was the best I could be. He used to spend hours with me, training me himself, telling me how much *promise* I held. How much *strength*." The bitterness was hard to hear as he spoke, but I dared not interrupt him. "My father believed that the pack seeing me training with him meant I would earn their respect and trust as he had."

I was almost scared to ask questions. I wanted to know if it worked, but I had a feeling I would soon learn if it had.

"Not every shifter born of an alpha becomes an alpha," he explained, looking up at me and frowning when he saw I still wasn't eating. "If you don't eat, I won't continue."

I took a bite and chewed furiously as he watched me swallow and take another bite. "Didn't realize blackmail was in your resume," I mumbled between bites. "I'm eating, tell me more," I demanded.

He grinned, but he continued with his story. "Rarely, it happens, but some sons of alphas don't become alphas. The gene..." He paused. "I don't actually know if it is a gene," he mused. "Anyway, the signs become evident when we hit our twenties. You know some of us join the human military?" When I nodded, he continued. "Female shifters hit their heat around their mid to late teens. It's Luna's sign they are ready to enter maturity and start families."

My nose crinkled in distaste at the very misogynistic view

of their Goddess. I didn't expect a *female* deity to want the women of their species to set up a home and pop out babies.

"Don't look at me like that," Caleb scolded, a smile playing around his lips. "We are few. It's an animal's nature to reproduce and ensure the continuation of the species."

"It's archaic," I grumbled.

"You want to hear more, or should I stop so you can burn your bra in protest?"

"Ass." Caleb grinned at me. "Tell me more," I insisted.

"Females, or shes, as we sometimes call them, enter maturity when they experience their first heat. Males don't have a heat, but we get very aggressive and very destructive, and our elders discovered a long time ago that discipline and control are best learned in an environment where we *must* blend. Where if we do not learn to control ourselves, we expose more than just a bad temper."

"The army does that?"

"Yes, any military service really. Some of us prefer to enter college sports and get out the aggression there, but for me, it was the army." He lost some of his lingering humor. "Every pack has an alpha, or pack leader, and each leader has at least two betas." He looked over at me. "Royce is a beta to Cannon."

"Ned too?"

He shook his head. "I don't think so, but I don't know. I am not overly familiar with the Blackridge Peak hierarchy." He looked down at the thread in his hands as he continued. "My father had two betas, and one of their sons, Jonah, was my best friend. We grew up together, we served together, we lost our virginity together." When he saw my surprised look, he laughed. "Not like that. We were in the same room, different shes."

"Right." I looked away, embarrassed. "You were close, I get it."

Silence descended, and I wanted to push, but Caleb was lost in thought, his memories pulling at him.

"He was a good friend?" I eventually asked.

"No. He was a traitor."

TWENTY-FOUR

Caleb

I KNEW SHE WAS BURSTING TO ASK ME QUESTIONS, BUT when it came to this, I couldn't answer quickly. Familiar rage welled within me as I thought of Jonah.

"Pack life isn't always easy," I said to her. "Like any culture, I suppose, we have our rivalries and feuds. Mostly about territory," I explained. "You asked if it was one mountain per pack, and in a way, it can be." Looking up at the mountain's shadow, I felt it tug at me, wanting its alpha on its peak. "Some share the mountain, especially the smaller packs." Looking at her, I saw the question. "Amos didn't like to share," I told her bluntly. "We were small, but we were a strong pack, and this mountain was ours."

"That caused problems?" she guessed.

"It's only a problem if the other packs don't get the message." I felt the need to explain as she frowned at me. "That peak?" I pointed up. "It's Shadowridge. It's my father's peak, and his father before him, and his before him."

"Not yours?"

I looked away, not ready to answer that. "Our rival pack, the Cristone Pack, was a forest pack. They kept to the trees and the pines, but their leader had his eyes set on heights his pack did not deserve. We'd had a few skirmishes with them, and every time, we sent them back to the lowlands with their tails between their legs." I grunted in recollection. "I left my pack," I spoke softly, the weight of remembrance pressing down on me. "I was an alpha coming into my power. My Will was strong, and I knew, *we* knew, I was too strong, too soon." Swallowing hard, I looked towards the peak. "I left to do one more tour, to learn my control better."

"They attacked when you weren't there?" Willow guessed, her voice soft in what she thought was understanding.

"They didn't attack," I told her, my hands clenching into fists. "They slipped into their home, while my parents slept in their bed, and they slit their throats before they were even awake."

"Oh my God, Caleb!"

"Cannon has no guard on his door," I told her, "but his pack patrols. Their pack can sleep at night, as their border is protected. All packs do the same." I scrubbed my hand over my eyes as I remembered getting the call. "There was no patrol the night they killed my parents. My pack was not at fault. A simple miscommunication. Those who thought they were on duty were changed. It happened, Amos did it a lot to keep us on our toes." Anger burned inside me. "But that night, the ones who thought they were changed for another were simply not replaced. Our packlands were left exposed. Vulnerable."

"It was a mistake?" Willow asked softly.

"No. One shifter stood guard at my parents' door that

night." I felt the lump in my throat. "And when they came for them, *Jonah* stood aside." Pushing myself to my feet, I started to pace. "*Jonah* fed the patrol the wrong information. *Jonah* opened the door to their home. *Jonah* showed them where my parents slept."

"Caleb..." Her voice was heavy with unshed tears.

"I felt the power shift into me as soon as my father left this earth," I spoke on. "Luna showed me his last moments as the power of the alpha transferred to me. I saw my best friend invite the enemy into his alpha's house, and I saw him shake the hand of the man who slit my father's throat." I could still see it so clearly. "His hand was still wet with my father's blood."

"I'm so sorry." She wept for me. But her tears were shed too soon.

"You should save your sorrow," I told her, more harshly than I should. "You don't know all of it." My eyes flicked to hers, but I couldn't hold her look. She was so innocent, and I hated that soon she would look at me like I was a stranger. "I left my post. I rushed to return to here." The peak was hidden in the darkness of the night, but I knew every line of that mountain. "Driven by my desire for revenge, I returned to a decimated pack. It wasn't just my father and mother that died that night."

We fell into silence, and I could hear her sniffling, trying not to make too much noise as she fought her emotions.

"How long did it take you to return?"

"Three days." I blew out a breath, the memories hard to speak. "Cristone Pack were in my packlands. In our homes."

"What did you do?" Her voice was filled with trepidation.

I met her look. I would not hide from her, not for this. "I

waited until they were all in our hall. They were celebrating their *win*. Their defeat of an unprotected pack." I took in a shaky breath. "They celebrated the murder of my parents." I held her wide-eyed stare. "And while they cheered for their *leader*, I went into the hall and I served my revenge."

Willow licked her lips. "What did you do?"

"I killed them."

I saw her swallow, her eyes wide. "How many?"

"All of them."

She looked as pale as I'd ever seen her. "How?"

"You mean how did I kill them?" I knew my voice echoed my surprise that she wanted details.

"Yes. You were alone. I don't understand."

"I'm an alpha." I held her gaze, seeing the horror in her eyes. "Cristone Pack had a pack leader, not an alpha."

"You compelled them?" she asked with understanding. "You made them...what? What did you do?"

"I told them to stay where they were. Using my Will, I kept them there. I used my Will to make sure they would not move, and then I slit their throats. One...by...one."

"Caleb." She was on her feet, like the gruesomeness of what I told her was too much to take sitting down. "That's...that's..."

I knew this was coming. I knew her revulsion at my actions would come. I hardened myself against her disgust. "That's who I am," I told her, my lip curling into a sneer. "They took my family, my pack, so I took theirs."

"That is *so* much more than an eye for an eye," she said with despair. "How could you? How much hate was in you that you could do that?"

I laughed. I full-out laughed at her. My head tilted back,

and my laughter sounded as jaded and bitter as I felt. "How much hate was in me?" I asked as she watched me with wide eyes, confusion written all over her face. "You speak as if the hate *left*. It didn't, I carry it with me every day."

"Well, *that's* healthy," she snapped, her hands on her hips. "No wonder you're all messed up. Mass murder tends to do that to a person!"

We stared at each other across the small space. Her anger was evident, but it was insignificant to my own. The only difference was that Willow was mad at *me*; I wasn't angry at her.

I knew she'd be like this. It was understandable. She didn't understand. I doubted anyone would ever understand.

"Did you get them all?" she asked suddenly. "The pack? Jonah?"

Why would she ask that? "Why?"

"Because if there are survivors, or people holding a grudge, they could be, you know...after you."

Wait...she was concerned? Seriously? "You're *worried* about me?"

"Of *course* I'm worried about you!" She stamped her foot against the ground, and I fought the urge to laugh at how adorable she looked. "You can't kill all those people and expect there not to be consequences! Their families, their loved ones, *someone* is going to come after you!"

Her purity and overall *goodness* continued to amaze me. "I don't have that problem," I told her gruffly.

Willow rolled her eyes, her hands thrown up in frustration. "How can you even know that?"

"Apart from the fact that it's been ten years?" I asked flatly.

"Ten years is nothing. Have you never read *The Count of Monte Cristo*?"

"No. I haven't."

"Well, you should, it's really good." She drew a deep breath. "Anyway, you don't know that what's happening now is not someone looking for revenge."

"I killed them. *All* of them." She stilled as I spoke, whether she finally listened to what I was saying or my tone conveyed my seriousness. "The ones who weren't there, Willow, I hunted them down. I killed every member of the Cristone Pack. I killed every member of *my* pack that betrayed my parents. There's no one left alive to come after me."

"But there would be children."

"Not anymore."

"Oh my God." She sank onto the tree stump, her fingers shaking as she pushed back her hair. "Everyone?" Her voice was little more than a whisper.

"They took what was most precious to me," I stated emotionlessly. "They wiped out my pack. An eye for an eye, isn't that what your God says? Isn't it what you said?"

"Children?"

"*They* killed children."

"It doesn't make it right!" She fumed at me from her seat. "It doesn't make it better. Did it bring you back your family? Your pack?" Her breathing was ragged as she glared at me. "Did it *quell* your rage?" Her tone was scathing.

I had nothing to say. She would never understand. She hadn't felt the sting of betrayal. She hadn't experienced the loss of an entire pack.

"We're only a few hours from the road," I told her, not looking at her. "I'll take you back down when it's daylight."

"What?"

"You heard me, one more night, and you can go." I turned away, which is why I never saw her grab the water bottle until it bounced off the back of my head. Turning slowly, I looked at her in surprise as she took a step back, a hand over her mouth. "The water flask. Really?"

"You make me furious."

"So you threw a *metal* water bottle at me?"

"You're a shifter, you heal." She still looked shocked at her own actions, so her voice was defensive. "And..."

"And you didn't think you would actually hit me?" I guessed as I stooped down to pick up the bottle. I crossed the space and dropped it on her pack. "See how easily violence made you feel better?"

"It's hardly the same thing," she grumbled, refusing to look at me. "Hitting you with something heavy to knock sense into you is hardly comparable to all the ones you hurt."

"I didn't hurt them," I clarified with a grim smile. "Their deaths were quick. Like my parents'. Only one of them suffered."

"Jonah?"

"Correct."

Willow nodded. Pulling her knees to her chest, she rested her chin on them. "If you killed them all, and there are no survivors to get revenge, then why am I drawing it?"

I shrugged. "I don't know."

"And no one else, your pack authority or whatever you have that polices you, no one held you accountable for your actions?"

"The facts spoke for themselves."

Her look told me she didn't understand, but she didn't ask. Watchful eyes considered me as I stood in front of her. Her eyes narrowed as her mind ticked over. "This is why you won't come back here. You told me earlier that the dead waited for you, but it isn't your pack you fear to go back to. It's the dead of the ones you killed."

My gaze landed back on the peak, even though it was covered by the blanket of night. "It's both." My attention was fixed on the ridge that wasn't visible right now. "I don't fear them. Let them take me if that's what they want."

"Jesus," she groaned softly. "Well, I don't know what I can do for you. I know nothing about ghosts."

"I understand." I pointed at the sleeping bag. "Sleep, I'll take you down in the morning."

"I can't sleep." Willow looked at me as if I were insane. Maybe I was. "You think after all that, I can *sleep*? That's a *lot* of information to process, Caleb." Her fingers drummed against her thigh. "I'm going *up* that mountain tomorrow," she told me with a determined look in her eye, "not down it."

"You want to stay?" Maybe she was the one who was insane.

"I don't quit." Willow picked up the water bottle and unscrewed the cap. "If all your enemies are dead, then that means they're after me, and that makes no sense."

"I'll still protect you."

"By sending me away?"

My back teeth ground together at her stubbornness, and I broke eye contact with her before she saw my anger at her recklessness. The silence between us was thick with tension. "It's not what I want. It's hardly ideal," I finally said. "But I think being away from me is what is safest for you."

"Safe," Willow repeated, her voice dripping with disdain. "I hate that word. And I hate how every time you say you are keeping me safe by staying away, something horrible happens to me."

"You go to the shaman; you tell him to tell Luna to sever the tie."

"That easy?" she scoffed. "Will I order chicken nuggets and fries at the same time?" Seeing my blank expression, she rolled her eyes. "If it was as easy as ordering at a drive-thru, I imagine you would have done it by now."

"That was a shit example."

"Bite me."

We fell back into an uneasy silence. "It's getting colder." I tried to change the subject. "Even if you refuse to sleep, can you just get into the sleeping bag?"

"I want to keep my boots on."

"Um...okay?"

"There could be bugs."

Biting the inside of my cheek, I struggled not to laugh, knowing she wouldn't find it funny, and it was really inappropriate to find anything amusing right now. "I put a spare bag in the side pocket for the boots."

"Oh." She searched for it and found it and, without another word, took off her boots, put them in the bag, securely tying them, and then got in the sleeping bag.

Taking the seat on the stump, I focused on the tree line, waiting for her to fall asleep. She would eventually. Her illness would make her if nothing else did.

"Sending me away doesn't solve anything," she spoke softly, her words muffled by the sleeping bag. "Whatever *this* is, it won't stop if we're apart."

"Willow—"

"No." I heard her move in the bag; no doubt she was glaring at me in the dark. Or glaring at where she thought I was. "If they're all dead, then it's me they're after. You need to stop treating me like a paper doll and accept that I can handle this. I'm not leaving. Not until this is over."

"And if it's never over?"

For a long moment, she said nothing, and then finally she spoke, her voice empty of emotion. "Then we deal with it."

I didn't tell her what I thought of that idea, but then I decided why not? I had nothing left to lose. "So, your idea is we face it together, regardless of everything I told you tonight?"

"Well, I'm not going anywhere, so that's not changed."

Only *everything* had changed, and we both knew it.

TWENTY-FIVE

Willow

I DIDN'T SLEEP RIGHT AWAY. I WAS SURPRISED I SLEPT AT all, given what he had confessed to last night. My mind was still reeling from the revelation. No wonder the shaman and others worried for him. How much hate did it take to kill so many?

The first light of dawn was breaking through the trees, casting a pale, almost ethereal glow over the rough terrain of the mountain. The cold air nipped at my nose, and I remembered waking in the night, shivering, until a large, warm, *furry* body had lain down beside me and shared its body heat. Was I freaked out that the man I had sex with yesterday morning was a wolf when he lay beside me last night? No. Should that feel strange to me? I no longer knew what the definition of the word meant. What I did know was that what Caleb had shared with me the night before, the weight of it still felt heavy in my chest.

I still couldn't digest most of it. Part of me still wished I was in the dark, that there were still unknowns between us. Having it all laid out bare, I had no idea how to process it all. What I did know was that the certainty I had felt between myself and

Caleb was gone. I didn't know what to do with the information, and I was hesitant to ask myself if it made a difference, because I was scared the answer would be no. What that said about me, I wasn't sure.

I didn't have an answer for that either.

Moving my head slightly, I saw him sitting across from me, his gaze fixed on something in the distance, maybe the next trail or maybe, more likely, the memories that he'd finally shared. I did note that he seemed completely at ease. In fact, my eyes narrowed as I observed him. He looked *relaxed*. Had telling me about his past shed the weight that *he* carried?

I wanted to be happy that there was no more mystery between us, but now, knowing the truth, how did I go on like nothing had changed? His past was *so* dark. I understood his need for isolation and solitude. I could never know what it felt like to go through what he did, but would I have reacted the same? I doubted it. Maybe it was the humanity in me that had me stumbling over the damage to his soul. Maybe shifters dealt with it differently *because* they weren't fully human.

But they were. Human with just a little more magic in them.

Ugh, what a mess. I may never understand his actions, but I knew one thing, I was tied to him.

I still didn't know how, or why.

Caleb's head moved slightly, and I knew that he knew I was awake. "It's good that you slept."

"I had a snugglebuddy that kept me cozy." *What the hell was wrong with me?*

"Snugglebuddy?" His voice was tinged with amusement, and I nodded as I sat up. "Still freaking out?"

"I think I will be for a while," I admitted, brushing the hair off my face, feeling like I was lying because I *had* accepted this so quickly, and I didn't know why I did. It felt wrong that I had. "It's...it's a lot."

"I guess it is."

A part of me wondered why I wasn't reacting differently. Was I freaking out? I wasn't sure. I should have been angry, scared, or even overwhelmed by the enormity of what he'd told me, but mostly I felt confused. Confused that I didn't feel any of those things. I wasn't even sure if I felt numb. I still had questions. I needed to know why I was connected to him and what the danger was that we could be facing, but I think it was clear he had even less of a clue than I did.

"It's still you and me," I reminded him softly, a reminder more for myself than him, I thought.

Caleb nodded, his eyes narrowed in focus as he returned his attention to the mountain. "We *will* figure this out. No matter what, Willow."

It was the determination in his voice that I clung to. After everything that happened, the truth was one I couldn't get away from, and that was that I trusted him. I trusted him to protect me. I trusted him to be by my side until this insanity was over.

Caleb stood, looking as fresh and healthy as much as I was sure I looked drained and spent. "You ready?"

Scrambling out of the sleeping bag, I took his hand as he pulled me to my feet. His grip was strong and steady, and I felt something—familiar, grounding. The same connection from the moment we met, but now, with the intimacy of yesterday and the truth laid out between us, it seemed to be more intense. My blood felt like it was humming under my skin.

Caleb's eyes flared, deep chocolate turning almost purple, and I blinked several times, sure I had imagined it.

"Yeah, I'm ready, I just need to go to the little girl's room," I tried to joke.

After I put my boots back on, he pointed me in the direction he wanted me to use, handing me a pack of tissues, and while I went and took care of business, he tidied up my sleeping bag. When I came back, the all-too-familiar bottle of hand sanitizer waited for me, with my refilled bottle of water and a granola bar.

"Breakfast of champions," I murmured as I started to chew. When I was done, I used some of my water to rinse my mouth after brushing my teeth.

"Okay, *now* I'm ready."

We started at a steady pace, and my body felt rested, which was weird, as I'd been scared of the repercussions of yesterday's activities. My mind kept going back to Caleb's fear that he drained me, which maybe he had at one point, but had I become immune to him? To shifters? I never felt drained with Ned or Doc.

"Do you think I got cured of being around shifters?"

Caleb glanced at me, and if he had asked me for more context, I wouldn't have been surprised. But I think he was accustomed to me now.

"I don't get drained like you thought you were doing. My ME has been quite good," I told him as we walked. "In fact, this morning, I feel...energized." When he didn't say anything, I was slightly put out. "Hey! Me and the word *energized* haven't belonged in the same sentence since I was sixteen. This is a big deal for me."

That earned me a smile. "Or it could be you ate well yesterday, you have fresh air in your lungs, and you got a decent night's sleep with no midnight sketches."

Which was also true. My sketchbook had been packed away with no new drawings in it. "Hermit in the mountains? That's my future?" I asked him with a grin, then remembered where we were, why we were here, and the fact he had pretty much lived like a hermit. "Or something," I hastily added.

"Beats murdered in the mountains," he quipped, and when I stopped short, he kept on walking, despite the fact my mouth was hanging open.

"Too soon!" I mumbled as I hurried to catch up with him.

My legs began to burn as the climb got steeper, but I kept my thoughts to myself. The air was thinner now, and I needed the oxygen for my lungs. Caleb was a step ahead of me, his movements sure and confident, but he checked over his shoulder frequently, making sure I was only a step behind him.

When the wind picked up, cold and biting, I was so grateful for my new coat. The world felt a long way away from us, reminding me how far from safety I was, how far from the familiar. But I'd come so far, and I wasn't backing down.

I'd decided to stay with Caleb, and I was sticking to it. Sticking to *him*.

The truth was that whatever our link was, the link knew about his past, even if I did not. I could have run off this mountain after learning what he did, but we would still be connected. No matter what I found at the top of this mountain, I wasn't turning back.

When we reached a small plateau, Caleb came to a halt, beckoning me forward. As I stood beside him, we looked out over the vast expanse of the world below us. The view was breathtaking, bathed in the early afternoon sunlight, making the autumnal colors more vibrant.

"Oh my," I breathed as I took it all in. "It's so beautiful." Looking down, I noted how far we'd come. "We've come so far," I said, and as I spoke, I knew I meant more than physical distance.

"We have," he agreed, his voice low and contemplative, and I wondered if he was thinking of the same things I was.

We stood in silence, both looking out, and I felt the comfortableness between us grow. I didn't want to be the one to break it, and I sensed that neither did he.

Turning away from the view below us, I looked up at the peak, which loomed above us. It was still so vast and imposing, and I wasn't sure how much further I could go. But as I stood there, in the shadow of it, I felt an overwhelming sense of peace. Standing here, knowing how far I had come, I felt like I was back in control. Which was completely contrary to my actual life, as I had zero control over anything that was happening to me, but under the protection of Shadowridge Peak, I felt empowered.

I was choosing to stay. I was choosing to fight. I was choosing to find out why I was tied to Caleb.

When was the last time I had said any of that?

"Whatever waits for me at the top, I'm not scared," I realized, surprising myself with how true that felt.

Caleb turned to look at me, his eyes searching mine, and I

saw the corner of his mouth curl upwards slightly. "You're stronger than you think you are."

Holding his gaze, I believed him. "You've said that to me before."

"And I was right then, too."

"So, tell me, on this peak, are you king of the world?" I teased, trying to push past the ugliness of his words last night. I needed to get back to some form of normal between us, because I had a feeling there was more to come, and I wasn't mentally prepared for *more* right now.

"King?" He seemed to mull it over. "No. Alpha?" His look turned possessive and predatory, his smile wicked. "Fucking right, I am."

My heart rate had picked up, my lady bits had woken up, and my mouth had gone dry. *Holy hotness.*

"I'm not bowing," I blurted, knowing he could see how he affected me, and my brain short-circuited as I admired the magnificent specimen that was him.

Caleb stepped into my space, and I refused to move. Dipping his head, his lips skimmed my ear as he spoke softly. "You sure about that?"

Nervous laughter bubbled out of me. Stepping back, I shook my head as I watched him. "Sly and sneaky!" I protested.

His smile was genuine as he chuckled, turning from the view and dropping my pack to the ground. "All predators know exactly how to catch their prey," he said with a grin.

I could tell it was still kind of forced, but it was lighter than he had been. I needed that, I realized. I needed to see the lightness in him. He was so shrouded by darkness, that I needed to draw him out of its clutches.

Or maybe I was wishful thinking and no amount of trying could wash his hands clean of the blood that stained them.

The heaviness of my thoughts made my own smile fade as I watched Caleb rummage through the pack for food. He moved with a practiced efficiency, every move deliberate like he had done this many times before. When he handed me the food, there seemed to be something more, something subtle and unspoken, as if he was offering me more than simple sustenance.

Was he as keen to keep our connection as I was?

I took the food with a quiet "thanks," sitting down on the flattest rock I could see. The truth was, we were still learning about each other. There was so much about him that I didn't know. So much I was scared to learn after last night's revelation, but I knew I needed to know more. I felt like we had only just scratched the surface. I could feel him watching me out of the corner of his eye, but I didn't call him on it. I wasn't ready to answer questions about how I felt. Emotionally? Mentally? I couldn't answer.

I chewed my piece of beef jerky. I'd protested loudly yesterday about eating it when he bought it, but it beat another granola bar. Between his past, our connection to each other, the danger we were in, or I was in, it all felt like the mountain wasn't the only thing we needed to climb.

"Do you think we'll figure it out?" I asked quietly, more to myself than him.

Caleb had been chewing jerky like it personally offended him, and I wanted to change the subject and remind him that *he* was the one who insisted we buy it. "I do," he told me, his voice low and steady.

Watching him, I wondered what made him so sure. He had answered so calmly, so sure. He wasn't rushing to look for an answer. He seemed to have accepted that it would take time. But time felt like a luxury we didn't have.

Caleb tossed his last bit of jerky aside and packed up my pack once again. "There's a creek," he told me. "It's kind of difficult to get to, so I'll go and get us fresh water."

"Oh, I can try to come?"

His look was one of patience as he shook his head. "I'm going to shift to get partway there. This time of year, the Peak likes to start the game of 'is it stable ground or not?'"

"Your wolf?" I don't know why that surprised me. If anything, I should be surprised he'd stayed human for so long.

"Yes."

"Should I turn my back?"

Caleb frowned at me, unsure of the question. "Why would you turn your back on a known predator?"

"I...I thought you had to take your clothes off," I stammered and was relieved to see him grin.

"I need to go further in first. You can keep your eyes open." Caleb pointed at the rock I'd been on. "Sit back down and try to rest. We have more to go today before we lose the daylight. It doesn't get easier anytime soon."

"Why would it?" I sassed and was rewarded with a wink before he headed into the tree line.

Settling back onto the rock, I decided my butt deserved better, and untying my sleeping bag, I folded it under me.

I was a human woman on a shifter's mountain, while said shifter went and fetched me water. When did this become my life? Seriously? What did I do to be given this hand?

For all my bravado and stubbornness, did I really want to be here? Did I want to dive further into this unknown world that was hidden from other humans? There were so many loose threads between us; did I want to keep on pulling at them?

Turning in my seat, I looked up at the imposing peak. "You are uncomfortable, unnecessarily steep, and freaking cold," I scolded it.

The mountain remained silent, but I grew colder the longer I didn't move, so as any sensible person would do, I crawled into my sleeping bag. Boots and all.

The visions were waiting for me, as if they had been anticipating me being alone, away from the alpha of the Peak. Scene after scene of death and destruction followed. Not just Caleb exacting his revenge, brutal and bloody, but the Cristone Pack delivering their hate. Tears ran down my face as I saw them fall, one by one, until I was no longer sure who belonged to which pack, and all I knew was the devastating loss.

Loss that Luna wept for.

How did I know that? I looked around me, as my awareness floated through the scenes like one of Caleb's wraiths that haunted him.

How could he ever come back from this?

Strong fingers cupped my cheek, and I felt the lightest of pressures against my eyelids.

"Wake up, Willow, it's just a dream."

Opening my eyes, I looked up at Caleb, seeing his concern as he watched me return to the waking world.

"I fell asleep?"

His smile was gentle, his thumb stroking over my cheek. "Yeah, you fell asleep," he confirmed softly.

His touching me like this reminded me of how he touched me in the car. Reminding me that the connection between us was as physical as it was spiritual. I didn't know if that was something I'd already accepted or something I still feared.

"What did you see?" he asked me, and I saw in his eyes that he already knew the answer.

"Death," I confirmed. "So much death."

He looked away, but he didn't stop touching me, and I wasn't sure who was anchoring who.

"Do you think the answers lie in my packlands?" he asked gruffly.

"I don't know. I don't know what waits for us at the top of this mountain, but I know we have to see it through."

"Agreed." Caleb stood, stepping back, giving me room to get out of the bag. "You ready?"

Maybe I was. Or maybe I was going to have to learn how to be. Either way, I was going to face whatever waited for us in his home, and I would get some answers.

TWENTY-SIX

Willow

"I will never get down from here," I told him as I lay half-collapsed against the face of the peak. "The fact you can carry me, the backpack, and yourself up this horrid, inhospitable, evil mountain is beyond me."

"You're being dramatic," Caleb murmured.

"I'm dying."

"You're being very loud for someone dying," he told me, dropping the pack to the ground. It had taken two days to get to the peak. Well, the peak part where we stopped. Even if his packlands were further up, he'd have to cart my dead body there. I wasn't taking one more step *up*.

"Every part of me hurts."

"Mm-hmm. For someone who's been carried for the last day, I don't know how."

Narrowing my eyes on him, I made a face. "You're not human. This mountain is *humanly* impossible to climb. Do not speak," I snapped, breathing in short pants. "Why can't I breathe?"

"Because you're panicking and being completely unreasonable?" Caleb deadpanned.

Wide-eyed with panic, I felt my chest tighten. "Caleb!"

He was in front of me, his hands cupping my cheeks as he tilted my head back slightly. "Hey now, come on, why are you being silly?" he teased softly, dropping a kiss on my nose. It was the first kiss he'd given me since we stepped onto this hellish mountain. "Breathe with me, Willow. You remember how we did it last time? Breathe in," he said soothingly, inhaling with me. "And out." We exhaled together. "Good girl, one more time."

We did it again and again until I was plastered to his chest, our mouths a hairsbreadth from each other. By the time Caleb declared me calm, I was hot and bothered for another reason.

"Better?"

I almost said no, but I was very much aware that I had overreacted and been ridiculous. "The air's so thin up here," I mumbled. I took a breath, the crisp, sharp air filling my lungs. "Sorry about that."

"It's fine. You're not used to it." Caleb stretched and I wanted to wrap my arms around him and not let go.

Because we were up a very steep mountain, and I was scared the whole rock face was ready to slide me right back down to the bottom. Despite my fear that the mountain had sinister intentions towards me, I couldn't deny it was breathtaking.

Literally in places.

We'd stopped late last night, and had I known how narrow the ledge he made me sleep on was, I would have died of fright. However, that particular treat had been what I woke up to.

Caleb had wanted to stop so I could reach his packlands in the morning. I'd been useless since yesterday morning. My legs weren't built for hardcore mountain climbing. No ropes. No tools. Just Caleb and his shifter strength and intimate knowledge of this mountain.

Once or twice, when he'd left me, I'd caught sight of a gray-furred wolf as he went to get water or food. I'd never tried rabbit before it was handed to me on a skewer made from a stick, and I'd been too hungry to refuse.

I lost my sleeping bag after I'd slipped and started skidding down the mountain. Caleb had thrown the bag for me to grab onto, and I'd grabbed the sleeping bag, only for it to snap and both of us career down the way we'd come. He'd caught me, but the bag was gone, and last night, I'd spent the night curled up into his wolf's side. One huge paw had stayed on my thigh, and weirdly, I'd slept like a baby.

But the air was thin here, so it could be that.

"You okay?"

Nodding, I looked over at him, and whatever I had been about to say died on my lips. The sun was resting low in the morning sky, the sky one of burning oranges and purples, casting differing shades of light and shadow over the peak. I felt like I was in a painting. It was so surreal, standing here, this high and breathing.

"Good lord, it's beautiful."

"Yeah." His tone was wistful. "Worth the climb?" I saw his quick smile, and had my limbs not been sore from hanging onto him for almost twenty-four hours, I would have punched him, but I had no energy.

"No. Maybe... Don't talk to me."

At that, Caleb laughed out loud, the sound echoing around us. "Come on, grumpy, it's just over this ridge."

"What is?" I asked stupidly, my gaze still facing east.

"The heart of the packlands." The longing and sorrow in his voice made me turn away from the view and look at the man in front of me.

I crossed gingerly to him, because his offhanded comment the other day about the mountain playing a game of "is it stable or not?" wasn't a joke. Rubble and debris just went from under your feet at any given time. My hands may never recover from the scrapes.

"I'm ready," I told him, looping my arm into his. "Lead on."

Caleb disentangled us, his hand slipping down my arm to lace our fingers together. It was the best we could do with no rope. When he packed for this climb, he must've forgotten how fragile I was. Or maybe he doubted I would ever be this close to his home.

As we walked, I marveled at the scenery, but it wasn't long before I noticed that the beauty of the view wasn't holding Caleb's attention. His dark eyes scanned the horizon, tense and alert, like he was waiting for something to spring from the morning shadows.

A rocky formation that looked completely uninviting loomed ahead of us. "This is it," Caleb declared, and I could hear his reluctance, but he still held his hand out to help me.

Of course this was it. Jagged teeth of a gaping jaw ready to munch me if I fell. "Welcoming," I mumbled as he helped me climb over it. I could feel the tension in him, in the way his muscles coiled as if he was ready to snap at any moment. Even as he helped me, his attention was everywhere else, checking every shadow, tree and rock.

It looked like he didn't trust his surroundings.

"Are you okay?" I asked when he lifted me over the last of the rocks. His unease was infectious, and I could feel it too—the tension in the air, as if the very mountain itself was holding its breath.

"No." He gave me a tight smile. "It's okay, they won't hurt you."

"They?"

"You'll feel them soon enough," he explained, his voice low, gravelly, and for the first time since I met him, uncertain. "This place isn't what it used to be, just remember that."

He stepped aside, and I saw the place he had called home for the first time, for real. Not in a drawing. I'd seen it so many times in my visions that it felt like I was the one coming home. Trees surrounded it, as I knew they did. Tall, towering pines circled the clearing. The ground dipped down, a basin of sorts, shallow, but I could see the bowl of the ground when we approached. In the corner stood the imposing log cabin. I'd seen so much of it when I drew, but I had never appreciated how big it was.

"The hall," Caleb murmured beside me.

"It looks bigger than I thought," I told him, reaching for his hand to steady myself. A light covering of snow lay on the ground, and I told myself I was holding onto him in case I fell.

"The hall was the heart of the pack," he spoke softly, almost robotically. "One of my ancestors thought it would be a good idea to shield it but still have it out in the open." Caleb pointed to the tallest trees. "They shield it from most aircraft, but the authorities know we're here."

"They do?" I asked in surprise. "They know about shifters?"

Caleb was shaking his head. "No, we stay away from humans as much as possible. They think we're some eccentric cult."

Who was to say they were wrong?

"I don't see any houses?" I told him, looking around. "I've never seen any residences," I clarified, "when I drew. It was always this lodge and this circle of ground."

"Some of the homes were lost," he told me, leading me into the trees away from the hall. As we walked, I saw the simple log cabins scattered amongst the trees. They were hidden, blending into their surroundings.

As we walked, I noticed how many were in a state of disrepair, and the more he showed me, the more I realized something.

"You haven't been inside these since the day it happened, have you?"

"Once." His jaw was tight, his eyes haunted with a darkness I could never imagine. "The day I picked up pieces of my pack and burned them."

"I'm so sorry." It didn't feel like it was enough, and I knew it could never *be* enough. "I'm sorry that you had to do that alone."

"I'm just pleased there was someone left to do it."

"They all died?" It was the first time that I'd asked for clarification of what he'd told me before.

Caleb looked away, his eyes back screening the trees. "Not

all."

"So you still have a pack?" I asked him excitedly.

The look he gave me was full of scorn. "Shadowridge Peak died the day my father did."

"But the others?"

"You think they wanted to stay on this peak? You think they wanted to sleep in their beds, knowing it's where the rest of their kin were murdered?" Caleb scowled at the homes that lay empty and neglected. "You think that *I* was fit to lead them?" His voice dripped with acid as he spoke. "My pack needed time to grieve, and they wouldn't get that with me."

"You made them leave?" I asked in disbelief. Surely then was the very time he needed his pack around him? Surely *they* needed him, their alpha? "When they needed you?" I couldn't hide my shock from my voice, or my face it seemed, as Caleb's scowl grew darker when he looked down at me.

"You think we should have gathered around the fire and toasted to the dead?" he asked disdainfully.

"*Yes!*"

He stepped away from me, arms folding across his chest. "My parents were betrayed." The pain radiated through every word he spoke. "You think I had any *trust* left? You think, after I killed all those shifters, that my pack *wanted* me to lead? Trust is earned, Willow. Every single one of them was in doubt. How could I know they were loyal? How did they know I wouldn't kill them? My pack was weakened. We were ripe for attack. Had they stayed, they would have died."

"You don't know that." My voice sounded as fragile as his control when I spoke.

"I wasn't willing to test it," he snapped angrily.

"You *left* them?" My voice was incredulous. "After all that, you walked away?"

"My presence here would have brought more harm than good. I went to the Pack Council and I disbanded my pack, as I had *failed* them. I had failed to protect them and my family." His head was held high. "I told them of my revenge, and they gave me their punishment."

"You didn't *fail* them!" I was almost shouting. "You weren't *here*!"

Caleb moved so quickly I stepped back when he towered over me. "*Exactly*! I *wasn't* here, Willow. I *failed* them."

"Oh my God, that's not how it works, Caleb!"

"I don't give a fuck how it works in your world. *This* is how it works in mine!"

"You complete idiot." I was seething. "I can't believe you walked away and left them. They were hurting. They needed to heal, just like you did!"

"They healed in their new packs. They flourished elsewhere."

He didn't sound like he believed it, and I didn't either. "You mentioned punishment. What happened to you?"

Caleb didn't look at me as he spoke. "I walked away from my pack. I wasn't fit to lead, but the Pack Council are cruel bastards. They would not let me give up the mountain. Shadowridge Peak is still the home of the Shadowridge Peak Pack." He looked at me, eyes full of self-loathing. "Pack members: one."

I wanted to cry. I wanted to scream at him. I wanted to hold him and never let go. "You are the most stubborn, unreasonable man I have ever met." Pushing my hood back, not caring that it was snowing, I clutched my hands in my hair. "No wonder this place haunts you. You left the living *and* the dead on it."

Caleb huffed out a breath that sounded suspiciously like a laugh. What the hell did he have to laugh about?

"You're laughing?" I asked incredulously.

"Don't you see, the joke's on them!" When he saw that I didn't know, he carried on. "You want to know why we're here? The Pack Council! They asked a shaman to decree what our Goddess Luna wanted from such a dangerous alpha." An ugly sneer twisted his features as he spoke, his eyes housing a darkness I hadn't seen before. "To be a packless pack," he spat out. "But a pack has to have a home," he continued furiously. "And this peak is my pack's home. No other can claim this peak while I still live." He leaned forward, madness in his eyes. "*That's* what they want from me. They want my mountain."

"Wha-what?"

He turned to look back towards the main hall. "When I left, I thought that was it, an alpha with no pack. It's what I asked for. I thought, if I stayed away, the dead would rest. But they've done something. They've worked some magic and linked you to me. They weren't ready to lose this mountain. They want it, they've always wanted it."

He was insane. He was definitely talking like a madman. "Why would they want it?"

Caleb blinked as if he didn't understand the question. "Why? Isn't it obvious?" When he saw that I didn't think it was, he threw his hands up in exasperation. "Look at its position! Shadowridge Peak sits in a strategic position to Blackridge Peak. The cliff face, the ascent, the way the packlands are positioned for the best vantage points? If you have Shadowridge in your control, then you have a strategic advantage."

I felt a cold chill creep up my spine. "That makes no sense, Caleb."

He gave me a look of pity. "It's not the mountain itself," he explained, reining in his anger. "It's the *control*—the power. You look at us and you see what? Superhumans? We think we've evolved, that we're civilized..." He grunted. "But the truth is, Luna graced us with the essence of the wolf, and we've never evolved from a pack mentality. It doesn't go away. Our shes go into heat. Our males fight the aggression that comes with maturity. An alpha needs a mate. We fight for territory and dominance. And it's the same old story."

I was almost too scared to ask. "What's the same old story?"

He blew out a breath, his hands slipping into his pockets. "Whoever controls the packlands controls the region."

He looked at me then, his gaze sharp and piercing. "When I left, while I *grieved*, they saw weakness. They saw an opportunity to take what is *mine*. And now I'm back..."

"You think they want to take it from you?" My mind was racing. "But...if they wanted to take it from you, wouldn't they have done so ten years ago?"

"Too obvious."

Right. "And how do I fit in?" I was genuinely curious. I mean, obviously, the altitude had gone to his head, or he was completely mad, and I refused to accept the latter.

His jaw was clenching, and he spoke through gritted teeth. "They'll do whatever it takes to make sure I don't stand in their way."

The weight of his words settled between us. Did he hear

himself? This wasn't just about the packlands or the mountain, it was about *him*. They'd told me if he was alone too much, he would let the madness in. Was this what this was? The reason he didn't trust his own kind? I knew why he'd become a loner, isolating himself; he was grieving. But this...I didn't have an answer for this.

"I'm human," I reminded him gently. "Your Council can't do anything to me, Caleb. There's no reason for them to know about me. I'm just a human."

"I know," he admitted. "But it doesn't make sense, Willow. This." He grabbed my hand. "Can you feel it? It's every day. Every waking moment, I'm aware of you, where you are, the need to touch you. It's not natural."

Wow. "Not pulling the punches this morning on the crazy train, huh?"

He ignored me. "And when I'm here. I can feel it—like eyes on my back. Waiting. Watching. They want me to leave."

"The mountain wants you to leave?"

"No. The mountain wants me here. *They* want me gone. They're not getting my mountain."

His paranoia wasn't completely unfounded—it had to be rooted in something deeper. Something I didn't understand. Not yet. But watching him become this unhinged *thing*, I could see what the shaman, and Cannon, and the others had been warning me about. The isolation. It had worn him down. The constant vigilance of thinking someone was coming for his mountain. He was tense and suspicious of everyone and everything. Did it include me?

"What about me?" I asked him, already dreading the answer. "Am I trusted?"

Caleb paused for a moment, and I thought I saw softness for just a second before the hardness fell over his eyes again. "I'm trying," he told me quietly. "You're so pure and innocent. I don't know how they got to you, but we'll figure it out. You're linked to me. I don't understand it, but we can't ignore it. It may be the only lead we have."

It was scary to see how far he'd gone off the deep end.

I nodded, even though I wanted to scream. I tried to understand the weight of his words, and I tried to convince myself that he was just trying to protect me, but it was more likely that he was protecting himself. His past was dark and horrifying, and he'd committed atrocities that I still hadn't accepted, but the uncertainty of broken trust and betrayal had bedded deep down in his soul, and I feared returning here, to this mountain, had been his undoing.

I didn't know what to do. Leaving him here wasn't an option. He would never leave me, and I refused to leave him.

Standing in this clearing had brought a change over him, one so sudden that I wasn't sure how to proceed.

"Caleb," I spoke softly, gently. Holding out my hand, I stepped closer to him. "We're in this together. I'm not going anywhere. We can figure this out, *together*."

He looked at me with a wariness that tore at my heart, and as I watched him, I saw them. The shadows that surrounded him. Here, in this place, they manifested into something almost corporeal.

"I won't lose this place," he whispered, his eyes flicking away, settling on a cluster of shadows that I was sure was moving.

"You won't." My eyes focused on the darkness, and I spoke

directly to them. "I'm right here, by your side. You are not alone. Not this time."

He nodded, his eyes still searching the trees. "I'll protect you," he told me. "We'll sever this link, and you can be free."

Tears welled in my eyes as we stood there, and I listened to his ramblings as he told me how he thought they were trying to trick him.

He'd been fine. He'd been good.

Confessions of mass murder aside, he had been *normal*. Until he'd stepped over those rocks onto this land, and it was like a switch had been flipped.

There were no answers for us on this mountain, I realized. All there was, was Caleb's madness and my desire to set him free.

I just didn't know how I was going to do it.

TWENTY-SEVEN

Willow

Standing in the shadow of the hall was intimidating. We'd climbed Shadowridge Peak, and while I thought I would get answers here, I just had more questions.

It was so cold the air felt frigid against my cheeks. I knew I had no sleeping bag, and I was reluctant to ask Caleb where he thought he was going to put me that didn't end up with me freezing to death. While I stood in the recess of the hall, I knew with absolute certainty I wasn't stepping in there.

I knew it was where he killed all those people, and while I would never describe myself as overly sensitive, willingly walking into a place that had seen so much death, I didn't think I dared to do it.

I watched Caleb carefully, each movement he made, each flicker of emotion that crossed his face. He was normally so stoic, but here, with those shadows lingering, I wondered if he knew how he looked. He was at the edge of the clearing, near the jagged entrance, his posture rigid as he stared out at... nothing.

What was there to see? The view was beautiful—I couldn't deny that—but there was nothing that he needed to stand guard against.

The night was falling and so was the temperature, and as the shadows crept along the ground, I was no longer sure what was the effect of the dying light and what was the spirits that lay around him like a cloak.

Despite everything that had happened in the last few months, I wouldn't have called myself psychic, but it was so very hard to deny that there was *something* otherworldly clinging to him. Something was so wrong here. *He* was so wrong here. Edgy. Paranoid. I could see it in the way he moved, in the way he barely seemed to remember that I was here.

And I was beginning to doubt that my being here mattered. Between his confession, his erratic behavior, and the madness that seemed to have enveloped him, Caleb was unraveling at the edges. It kind of made sense, but it was also so baffling that I was lost.

And still, I felt that there was more. Something even deeper. Was it only the spirits that crept around the edges of my awareness, shadows in the night that didn't belong? Or was there someone—something—influencing him? Something that twisted his thoughts and was pushing him to the brink of something dangerous?

He told me he was strong. They'd explained Will to me. But to hold people still in a room, many, many people, to hold them and one by one kill them, that was more than strong. An alpha had Will; could Cannon match his strength? I had no idea. And I wasn't sure if we'd need to find out, because right now, to me, an outsider, it looked like Caleb was being manipulated.

I just didn't know by who or why.

But we needed to know. I had to find a way to reach him, to make him realize that his actions were so out of character for him, before whatever pulled at him also dragged him under.

A blast of wind caught my hood, blowing it over my face, and when I pushed it back enough to see, he was gone.

"Caleb?" My voice sounded so small in the clearing.

Movement caught my eye, and I saw the wolf coming out of the trees. I'd felt it beside me while I slept, and last night, I'd been awake when he settled down beside me. This was the first time that I was seeing the gray wolf properly.

I knew little of wolves, but I was pretty sure they weren't supposed to be so big. Not stupidly big—they weren't pony-sized—but he definitely wasn't *normal*. The gray was dark but not dark enough to be mistaken for black. Had I been painting, I would have called it dark slate, not quite charcoal, but close. His fur was short. He had no other color on his coat, but it was his eyes that held my attention. They were a deep and beautiful blue.

Why I was so hung up on the fact his eye color changed when *he* had changed from a man to a wolf was probably stupid, but one of Caleb's best features that I loved about him was his deep chocolate brown eyes, and for them to change when he "changed" threw me for a loop.

The wolf approached me. *Caleb* approached me. Its head was held high with a majesty I had never experienced before. His gaze was so sure, so steady, and I met its highly intelligent look with my own, knowing how unsure I was.

I had no idea how to act. What if the wolf was more primal and it bit me? Ate me? Is that why he didn't care if I had a sleeping bag? He was going to munch on my bones for dinner.

Will you get a grip? My inner voice sounded exasperated with my out-of-control panicking spiral.

"Caleb?"

The wolf watched me, and then, with a jerk of its head, it started to walk away. I had no choice but to follow it. He paused, moving around me, shielding me from the wind with his body. I appreciated the gesture, but still, the courtesy didn't make me feel any less tense.

"Some warning that you're going to turn into a wolf would be nice." If he heard me, he ignored me. "Coming out of the trees as a giant wolf is kind of freaky, you know. You should warn a girl."

A blue eye fixed on me, and I decided it would be best if I stopped talking.

I hadn't been paying attention to where he was leading me until I was at a small, compact cabin. This one didn't look as desolate as the others, and when Caleb pushed at the door, it swung open with no resistance. He stepped back and looked at me, and I looked between him and the half-open door.

"You want me to go in there?" The wolf's head dipped. "But you're not coming in?" The wolf took a step back. "Right." I looked at the open door again. "Why can't you ask me to go in there as a man? Why change to the wolf?"

The wolf not so subtly stepped behind me and nudged me through the door, careful not to enter.

When I turned to protest, he was already trotting back the

way we had come. That was it? I was to go into this creepy abandoned cabin and what? Wait?

It wasn't warm, but it was better than being outside. Slowly, I took a few more steps inside, crying out with alarm when the lights came on. They were dim, but they brightened up the place. Looking around, the open-plan living space with the kitchen in the corner was pretty. Comfy even. One door to the back led to a small bedroom, and the other led to the bathroom.

My gaze rested on the shower for too long. Was it possible? Was there hot water? Coming back into the living space, I saw him outside the window. In his jeans and nothing else.

Hurrying to the door, I stepped out onto the small wooden porch. "You're going to freeze."

"Nah." He didn't look at me, placing my backpack on the porch. "The generator's on. It'll take a while to get everything running again. I'm feeding the supply to this cabin, but heat and hot water shouldn't be too far away."

"Why change form?"

"Going hunting, I'm a better hunter on four legs than two." He still didn't make eye contact.

"You're not going to come in, are you?"

He shook his head. "No."

"Whose home was this?" I didn't know why I asked. It wouldn't make a difference to me, and I wouldn't know if he lied.

"Nell's. Never liked me much. Said I was pampered." His eyes were back on the tree line. "Never really cared for her either, if I'm honest. Old age got her before Cristone Pack did, so this one is safe."

Safe.

I stepped closer to him, my heart pounding. "Caleb, you need to listen to me." He never turned his head to look at me, but I kept on going. "Something's happening to you, something I don't think you are aware of."

His silence was unnerving, but finally, he turned to me. The look in his eyes sent a chill through me that had nothing to do with the cold. "What are you talking about?"

The way he was looking at me but not really seeing me made me want to reach out to him. "Caleb." I took another step closer, careful, measured. "You know what I'm talking about. Being here, the darkness that follows you, you're not yourself, Caleb."

"I'm going to get dinner," he told me, his voice low, rough, and irritated. "Try to get warm. Run the water for a few minutes, clear the pipes. Shouldn't be too bad."

It'd been ten years, maybe longer since those pipes had been run, was he serious? "Are you listening to me?"

"Yeah. I don't know what you're trying to say to me, Willow. I'm fine."

"No, you're not." I tried to make my voice gentle and careful. "You've been different since we got here."

"Have I?" I heard the defensive tone, and I made my own voice firmer.

"You've been erratic, paranoid…angry."

"You got this from me turning on the generator?" His arms crossed his chest, snowflakes melting on his bare skin.

"Don't do that," I warned him. "I'm not fighting with you." Taking a deep breath, I stepped off the porch. "I'm not trying to hurt you." Reaching for him, I let my hand fall when he stepped back, trying to hide the pain of his action as I carried on. "You told me yourself, there are...*things* here, and I think they are influencing you, Caleb. You're not being rational."

His eyes flashed with something. That murky purple color was back, and I was worried I'd pushed too far. But I had to make him see it, I had to make him realize.

"You think I'm losing my mind?" His hands were clenched at his sides.

"Are you?" Swallowing hard, I held his gaze. "Ignoring the fact that you're in jeans, barefoot, and shirtless in the freezing *snow* like it's perfectly fucking normal, you've got all this darkness around you."

"I'm a shifter, we run hot."

"You don't run with anti-freeze, though, do you?" My anger was rising. "You're listening to the shadows that surround you! Whose voices are you listening to? You told me the dead lived here; are you so eager to join them?"

Caleb watched me, remaining quiet, and I could feel the weight of his struggle as he tried to hold onto his temper. He didn't want to hear this, I knew that, but I wouldn't remain quiet until he *believed* me.

I refused to back down. "Please, take a moment. Come inside before *my* toes fall off just by looking at yours." My breath was shaky. "Come inside. Nothing bad happened here, you told me yourself. Come in, think about it. Talk to me, we can brainstorm."

"Brainstorm?"

"Caleb." My voice held a note of rebuke to it. "We're here *for* this. I've been drawing it. I never knew you were *listening* to it. I know you've felt it. I've felt it. I'm seeing it right now, the way your thoughts shift. The way you're constantly on edge—"

"Because someone is trying to hurt you!"

"And you're supposed to be *helping* me figure out who that is. Not whispering to the dead like a crazy person!"

I knew I lost him the moment my temper slipped out. He took another step back, the shadows forming around him, and I hated it. It was scary and it was so far out of my control all I wanted to do was weep.

"They told me that a shifter heals," I spoke quietly, to him, to them, I no longer knew. "They told me that you shift into your wolf, and your aches and pains go away. That you heal." Licking my bottom lip, I watched him, knowing my eyes were filled with tears. "Why aren't you healing when you shift? Why are you not letting the shift heal your mind?"

"You know nothing," he seethed, his voice barely more than a growl.

"Maybe," I answered sadly. "Can you tell me you know any more than I do?" I went back to the front door. "Go and hunt, lose yourself. Let them win, Caleb. Let them beat you."

I closed the door on him, hearing the snarl of rage and wondering for a moment if he was going to barge through the front door, but nothing happened.

I was almost disappointed.

Looking around, I wondered what the heck to do now. Carefully, I opened the door, seeing the jeans discarded on the ground, and picking them up, I took my backpack inside. Latching the door, I dropped both items and went looking for the source of heat. There was a fireplace, but it was cleared and empty. I didn't fancy going to look for firewood, and what the hell would I light it with? Caleb had cooked us a rabbit, but the source of the fire might as well have been magicked from his ass for all I knew.

The furniture was covered in sheets, and after removing them, I found a radiator. Testing it, I turned it on, and then bundled under the dust sheets, I sat on the couch and prayed for the generator to work and the heating to come on.

I WOKE UP TO THE SMELL OF COOKING. I WAS IN A BED AND so confused and disoriented I was sure I was dreaming. This was not my room, and this was not my home.

Carefully, I got out of bed and tiptoed to the bedroom door. Opening it, I was disappointed and relieved to see a familiar face.

"Doc?"

He turned from the stove and grinned in greeting. "You look like shit."

"It's so good to see you!" I almost tripped over my blankets, hurrying into the room. "You got the heating working? Why are you here? Does Caleb know? Oh my God, is that bacon?"

Doc laughed at me. "You need to eat," he told me, plating up bacon and eggs. "This mountain is stunning, but the store options are lacking," he said with a wink. "I brought what I could, but it's a hard hike. Glad I had three full shifters with me."

"Who?" Sitting down, I happily took the plate from him. "Who came with you?" I started eating, not even waiting. "Does Caleb know?"

"He knows. The shaman said he'd have felt it the moment

we stepped onto the packlands." He answered my unspoken question, "We haven't seen him."

"He's staying away?" I chewed my bacon even though I was no longer hungry.

"Seems to be."

"What do we do?"

Doc shrugged. "Caleb's a problem for Luna and the shaman." He sat down across from me. "You, on the other hand, are my problem."

"I am?"

"As your physician, I'd say so, wouldn't you?" He poured me a cup of tea, and I took it enthusiastically. "You climbed this mountain? Are you crazy?"

"I had Caleb with me."

"And I'll ask again, are you crazy?"

"He wouldn't let anything happen to me," I argued defensively. "He carried me most of the way."

"And left you to freeze in an abandoned house."

"He'd have come back."

"To bury you?"

Sitting back, I gave him a look full of reproach. "He didn't get worse until he was here."

"So...it's true?" Doc asked, leaning forward. "He's losing himself?"

"I don't know. He's not himself."

"You've seen it?" Doc was watching me carefully, and when I nodded, he let out a sigh. "I was hoping you would anchor him."

"Me?"

His eye roll was almost insulting. "He cares for you, a *lot*.

We thought if anyone would get through to him, it would be you."

A wild idea popped into my head, and I placed my fork down. "You're not the reason why my places were broken into, or I was in a car crash?"

"No!" He thought about it. "Well, I *am* the reason the truck rolled, but I didn't *plan* it, if that's what you're asking."

"You knew we were here though?"

"The shaman did. Luna sent a sign that he needed to be here on Shadowridge Peak. He turned up at our main hall and commandeered me, Cannon, and Royce to take him here."

"Oh." I resumed eating. "Caleb thinks your pack authority wants him to relinquish his claim on the Peak."

Doc nodded thoughtfully. "I think it's safe to say Caleb isn't himself. His pack was one of the longest, oldest packs in these parts. Luna will want that bloodline continued. The shaman thinks that's why she was sending visions of him to you."

"But I'm not a shifter."

"I know," Doc agreed. "Still haven't figured that part out yet."

"I'm not following," I admitted. "Who is after me?"

Doc looked at me, a speculative gleam in his eye. "Did he tell you?"

"About the attack and his revenge?" When his head dipped, I nodded. "Yeah, not the bedtime story I needed to hear."

"There are some of his pack left. It's very unlikely that any of them would want to harm him, but Cannon is looking into it."

Finishing my food, I looked around. "So you're coming to take me home?" I guessed.

"I came to check on you, make sure your ME wasn't kicking your ass all over this mountain." He saw my look and grinned. "And the shaman believes you are pivotal to healing Caleb."

"Ah, the ulterior motive."

"Do you think he's rogue?" The question shouldn't have surprised me as much as it did.

"I think he's lost," I answered carefully. "From what I've seen, I think he's worse when he's here. I know why he left this peak, and selfishly, part of me wished he had never returned."

Doc rubbed his eyes. "The whole mountain needs purged," he said with a grim look. "All that death in one place, no wonder he's losing it."

"Can the shaman help? Can Cannon?"

Doc sighed, getting to his feet and taking my empty plate. "Caleb needs to want to be helped," he answered. "According to the shaman, it only works if Caleb wants it to."

"And how do we convince him he wants to?" I asked skeptically.

Doc turned to me. "I believe that's where you come in."

TWENTY-EIGHT

Caleb

THE COLD, CRISP AIR FELT ALMOST SHARP IN MY LUNGS AS I crouched in the bushes, senses heightened, trying to push everything from my mind as I hunted. I had left her behind, alone, in an abandoned cabin that I hoped would heat up for her. That generator hadn't been on for so long I wondered if it would last. Knowing that I hadn't waited to see bothered me, but I needed to get away from her.

The truth was, I was hunting as much for clarity as I was for dinner.

The ground felt uneven here. Despite all my years away, this place was still familiar. The feeling that something was wrong, which I had been feeling for so long, was stronger now, gnawing at my gut for days. I thought it would be better here on the Peak. This was my mountain. My home—the one constant in my life, the one thing I thought I could control—but the control felt like it was slipping through my fingers.

Why did nothing feel right anymore?

The sounds of Shadowridge Peak, the taste of the air, the energy that surrounded me, *nothing* felt right.

And Willow? I wanted to bury myself inside of her, taste her, take my time fucking her, not the quick fumble at the side of the road, in a cramped car, but stretch her out on a bed and really spend the time learning every single inch of her. I'd had a brief taste...but, fuck, I wanted more. I wanted all of her.

But I couldn't.

I saw the way she looked at me here. I saw the mistrust in her eyes. I thought her being here would make it better, but what did I expect? I told her about the many that I killed, and she judged me for it. She would never let me near her again.

I knew that now. I knew it the moment she stepped away from me.

Closing my eyes, I inhaled deeply, filling my lungs again with the fresh air, trying to ignore that it tasted tainted. Snapping my eyes open, I growled low in my throat. I felt restless, irritated by everything that was around me. The hunt wasn't going well either. No matter how hard I pushed forward, I couldn't shake the distraction of Willow's presence on the mountain.

I kept hearing her words echoing in my head.

"The darkness that follows you, you're not yourself, Caleb."

As if she knew me well enough to be able to judge that. As if she hadn't burst into my life, ripped everything apart, and had no idea what she was doing. I let out another low growl as I recalled the sight of her after I told her what I did, looking at me with those wide eyes of hers, staring at me like she was seeing something *broken*. Seeing a side of me she never thought existed.

Maybe the worst part of it all was the feeling that she wasn't entirely wrong.

A flash of movement caught my eye, pulling me back to the hunt. A deer, walking carefully through the underbrush, the snow and cold not bothering it too much. This mountain had been abandoned for too long. Prey forgot what it was to be hunted. To be prey. My body tensed, muscles coiling as I prepared to give chase, but I didn't move.

Something held me back.

I watched the deer disappear into the thick trees, my instincts gone, my drive lost.

What was happening to me?

Everything just felt...wrong.

This was Willow's fault.

Those words she said, the accusation in her tone, they cut deeper than I wanted to admit. I resented the way she made me feel.

Unstable.

Off-balance.

A constant reminder that the ground beneath my feet was unsteady.

I hated her for it. I knew I shouldn't, but...I did.

Willow was not my enemy, but who the fuck did she think she was to accuse me of losing myself? I couldn't control the feeling of rage at her words. How could she understand the weight of what I had been through? No one could. Not her. Not any pack. No one.

Not even me.

They thought they knew me, but they knew *nothing* about me. They thought they understood the "tragic loss"—they understood *nothing*. They would never know what it felt like to know that feeling of betrayal. That loss of trust and family.

She said I was paranoid. Didn't she understand that I'd be a fool not to be?

They all expected me to trust them. *Trust*. I'd trusted before and I'd paid the price for it. My *pack* paid the price for it. I didn't trust anyone. Not anymore.

My head turned south as I felt them step onto the mountain. Turning, I focused on my senses, tuning into the intruders who dared walk over my lands. The wind shifted, carrying their scent to me. My growl was low as my anger rose. The scent of another caught the breeze—a familiar one, human.

Willow.

Even when I tried to focus on something else, I was never free of her. She was all I could think about.

Had the generator come on? Was she warm? Was she worried about me, thinking that I was out here, losing myself, spiraling out of control while she froze in an abandoned cabin? I could almost hear her worrying about me.

I shouldn't have left her.

Shaking my head, I tried to clear the heaviness of self-doubt. She would be fine. She was safe. I was in control. I was in charge of this, and she would be fine.

But there were shifters after her. What if they were on the mountain? What if they got to her? What if I lost her? I'd already lost so much. I *wouldn't* lose Willow. I started to turn back, return to her and ensure she was okay, my wolf anxious to be by her side.

Shadows moved around me, and I shook my head as the wind through the trees started to sound like whispers.

But what if that's what they wanted? I felt the others on my mountain. I would know if there were more than Blackridge Peak wolves on my land. Willow was safe where she was.

I had to stop being consumed by her. It seemed that ever since she came into my life, ever since I had gone looking for her, something had shifted within me. My instincts, the very ones that kept me sharp and alive, felt like they had dulled. She was an intruder in my mind as much as in my life. Would I even be back here if she hadn't forced my hand?

I stayed far from here for ten years. How had she made it that I returned?

We were here to figure out what the hell was going on with us, what was the link we shared, but how had she convinced me that this was for the best? And now that I was here? She wanted me off it? What the fuck was her plan?

I thought we were here to figure out what *bound* us. But since I got here with her, I felt like I was walking through someone else's territory, but this was *mine*.

Another scent reached me, this time a rabbit. But I didn't move. I had no appetite. Not when my thoughts were so confused, filled with doubt and frustration.

She had done this. She had made me this way.

No matter how far I got away from her, she was always there, at the back of my mind, lingering. Tugging at something inside me, something that I didn't understand. I hated how much it unnerved me. I hated how being linked to her allowed her to see into my past.

Unnerving me.

"You've been erratic, paranoid...angry."

I hated the thought that she might be right. She'd said it so calmly. So clearly. There had been no doubt in her mind that she was right, like she could see me unraveling in front of her. *Had* she seen something I hadn't?

What had she drawn?

Suddenly, I wanted to return to her and demand she show me her sketchbook. The very thought of her seeing something had me so on edge that I felt my hackles rise. My wolf paced, furious, resenting her thinking she knew me.

Thinking *she* knew Shadowridge Peak.

I knew this mountain better than anyone.

She wanted me to leave. After all that time they took to get me to come here, now she didn't like the truth of what she saw. The betrayal and death weighed heavy on my soul, the taint of it so strong she would never understand. She may paint my past, but she would never understand the history here. She would never know the sense of betrayal when someone you loved sliced through your heart with their actions.

That's why I resented her.

Willow thought I had to listen to her. That she could *fix* me. She had never been here. She hadn't lived through the whispers of the trees, the feeling of eyes that were always watching from the shadows, or the way this mountain would turn on you if you weren't careful.

No...I wasn't losing it.

Willow was losing her *control* over me. Here on Shadowridge Peak, I knew myself again. I was strong. So much stronger than they thought. *That's* what they were afraid of. They didn't want me strong and in control; they wanted to keep me weak.

That's how they would take my mountain. *That's* how they thought they could beat me.

Fury coursed through me. I felt the intruders cross onto packlands, and I hesitated, torn between confronting them or confronting *her*. I could already imagine the look on her face, those concerned eyes, probably wondering how she could *help* me, how she could heal something that *wasn't even broken*.

Or was I?

No!

I would not let them make me believe their lies. I'd been through too much, fought too hard to let someone like Willow *fucking* Harper come into my life and tell me I was damaged.

She'd turned my life upside down enough. No more.

Picking up my pace, I ignored the tiny whisper of doubt in my mind as I moved through the trees, preparing myself to face them. All of them.

Face them here, where it all began.

I knew where they were when I got back to the cabins. The sight of Willow waiting for me was almost a relief, but seeing the others surrounding her had my blood boiling. She looked up from where she was sitting near a fire, her face shadowed, her eyes already checking me over to ensure I was unharmed.

Even looking at me as my wolf, she didn't flinch. She watched me, unafraid of *what* I was, only ever concerned *for* me.

She didn't speak, but I could hear her unspoken questions. The unspoken worry. The same damn hovering that made me want to scream.

"Caleb," she greeted me softly, her tone cautious. "Do you mind the fire?" She gestured to the small, compact campfire, and I had half a mind to walk over to it, piss on it, and kick it in their faces. But I wouldn't. Not in front of Willow. I heard Cannon huff with contempt, and I was pretty sure my thoughts had been portrayed clearly to the other alpha in the group.

"There's clothes for you in the cabin," Royce said flatly, matter-of-factly, but I heard how guarded he was. Wary.

"I'll get them." Willow was on her feet. "He doesn't need to go in." She hurried inside before I could stop her. She returned so quickly that they must have been on the floor by the door. Walking quickly around the side of the cabin, she took the bundle of clothes. Following her, I noticed she had her back to me as she held out the bundle, careful to keep them off the wet ground.

"They brought food," she told me, her voice barely a whisper. "I don't know if you've eaten. The generator worked."

Shifting, I stood behind her, my body instantly missing my wolf's natural fur coat.

"Did you bring them here?"

I saw her back stiffen in surprise, and I wished I'd asked her that when she was facing me. She was a shit liar.

"No, I did not." Her tone was cold and clipped, meaning I'd pissed her off. Good. Now she knew how I felt.

Coming to stand behind her, I saw her tense even more. I was naked and she was fully wrapped up, but she may as well have been as naked as I was from the way her heartbeat picked up.

Skimming my hands over her shoulders and down over the fabric of her coat, I pulled her into me, knowing she knew I was bare behind her. Pushing my way into the crook of her neck, hampered by the heavy winter coat and all her hair, I just wanted to scent her. Mark her as mine.

"Caleb?" Willow's voice was less certain, shakier, confusion oozing from her, but I could scent something else, something I bet she wished I didn't know. She was aroused.

"I could fuck you right here," I whispered into her ear. "Rip these clothes off you, pin you to the wall, and fuck you long and deep." She didn't say a word, but I could feel her trembling, her pulse racing, and moving her hair away, I exposed her neck, my tongue tracing her vein. "You'd like that, wouldn't you? You want me filling you up, stuffing you full."

"I don't think..." She cleared her throat, trying to step out of my hold. "I don't think that this is appropriate." Turning, she tried to glare at me, but I was naked, and she wasn't used to the fact that shifters are very comfortable in their own skin. Her eyes dropped down my body, fixating on my cock, seeing it swell with need. "Oh, shit..." Hastily, Willow turned away, but not before she threw the bundle of clothes at me. "Get dressed!" Her hands were on her cheeks and, even turned away from me, I knew her eyes would be closed. "We're not alone!" she reminded me sharply.

Smirking at her reaction, I looked at the clothes. Taking the jeans and long-sleeved T-shirt, I dropped the rest to the ground. When I pulled my head free of the T-shirt, I noticed that she was facing me again.

"You were gone all night."

"Needed to clear my head."

Her eyes softened. I could tell she wanted to say more, snap at me, but she held back. Which was smart of her. I wasn't in the mood for a lecture about losing control; I was more interested in the shifters on my mountain.

The silence stretched between us, heavy and full of things we weren't saying, and as I watched her, I saw the worry she had for me in her eyes. Which did nothing except piss me off even more.

"Why are they here?"

She licked her lips, looking away from me. "They're concerned."

"They don't know me."

"Then let them get the chance!" she hissed in temper. Pushing past me, she walked around the side of the cabin.

I didn't like her walking away.

Following, I narrowly missed the boot that was flung at me. "And put boots on. You make me even colder seeing your toes freezing in the snow like that."

Doc jerked his head away from my line of sight, and I knew he was fighting a laugh, but my attention was on Cannon.

Ignoring the boots, I looked at the only threat to me on this mountain. "What do you want?"

Cannon's eyes narrowed slightly, but he didn't look away. "What we all want. To understand what's happening to you. To Willow."

The reminder that it wasn't just me jolted through me. I glanced at her, seeing her cheeks flushed with cold, bundled into a jacket, and still freezing, but still here.

Why?

"The shadows grow darker around you." The shaman spoke for the first time, and the manners my mother instilled in me as a young pup made me bow my head in respect for the old shifter, the one who had a direct link to the Goddess.

"You can see them too?" Willow asked him, making everyone's attention turn to her.

"I can, child. They pull at him."

"*Nothing* is pulling at me," I snapped irritably.

"They wrap themselves around him," Willow continued as if I hadn't spoken. "It's been worse since we got here."

"Have you drawn it?" Doc asked, and I heard the curiosity, not just in general but the scientist behind it.

"No, I'm afraid to put it on paper." Her head was down, and that only angered me more.

"Why?" I demanded, stepping closer to her.

"Because it scares me." She looked up. "*You're* scaring me."

TWENTY-NINE

Willow

I REALIZED WHAT I HAD SAID AND CURSED MY FOOL tongue when I saw Caleb react to my careless words.

"I scare you?"

"No!" I blurted. "I'm scared for you."

"That's not what you said." He looked at me, suspicion and hurt written all over his face. "I never scared you before. What changed?"

How could he even ask me that? "*You* changed!" I could feel my frustration bubbling over. "You became a completely different person once you got here. You're not yourself, and all these shadowy things around you, it's not right."

"You're overreacting."

"No, I'm *not*. You're in denial! Cannon and the shaman are here. Let them *help* you."

I saw him look over at them, his lip curling upwards in a sneer. "Help me? Where was your help, old one, when they slaughtered my family?" I watched him as he ran a hand over his hair, his hand trembling as he fought to stay in control. "Where was the justice for my pack after their murder?"

"You carried out the justice you deemed fit," the shaman replied to him, not cowed by the level of anger directed at him. "You acted before anyone else could."

"I didn't get here until *three* days later."

"And how was anyone to know what happened in so short a time?" the shaman asked him reasonably. "You knew. You had three days to alert the Pack Council, but in your hate, you came here, you acted, and your enemies' blood is on your hands."

"My father's blood was on theirs!" Caleb roared at him. I saw his eyes become that murky purple, and so did Cannon, who took a step towards Caleb.

"Your wolf is too close," Cannon warned him, his voice calm and steady. "We're not all shifters here."

Glancing at Doc, I saw he had taken a step back, and the rational part of me knew I should do the same, but I had already hurt Caleb with my thoughtless words, and the guilt was already gnawing at me. The sting of seeing his expression when I spoke was enough to take every word back. But I couldn't.

Quickly, I looked at all of them. Royce stood straight and solid. He looked like he was ready to pounce at any given moment. Doc had stepped back, closer to the porch of the cabin. *He* looked ready to duck into the house at any moment. The shaman, the smallest of them, stood in the middle, serene and composed, and I envied him the grace. Cannon was tall. Imposing. His stare hard. Like Royce, he looked ready to react. Only from Cannon, the intent was far more lethal looking.

And Caleb looked...agitated.

He was standing still, but I could see how restless he was. His eyes prowled over the three of them, Doc not worthy of his attention. He was barely looking at me, his attention fixed between the shifters in front of him. Tension radiated from him, from the tightness of his jaw to the closed fists at his side, and all around him, the shadows swirled.

My heart squeezed painfully as I watched him. He'd been so strong for so long, but whatever it was that surrounded him here, the dead or otherwise, it was pulling him deeper than I realized. It was dangerous. I could feel that now, and from a glance at the shaman, I could see he saw it too.

I'd told him I was scared of him when he was already teetering on the edge; I may as well have just pushed him right over.

And *that* was why I would not step away from him.

No matter how much my brain was screaming at me to get back, to run down this mountain and never look back, I knew I would not move. No matter how much my instincts told me to go home, back to Whispering Pines, to safety, I would not turn my back on him.

He'd been alone too long. He needed me. Whether he wanted me or not, I was staying right where I was.

Looking at him now, I could see what isolation had done to him. Causing him to doubt everyone, even himself.

His paranoia was blinding him. What could I say without making it worse?

His eyes were more purple than brown now. I wasn't even sure that was possible, but I heard Cannon's low warning once more to get his wolf under control.

Letting out a shaky breath, I wrapped my arms around

myself, feeling the chill in the air despite the fire. Caleb's eyes burned brighter, the shadows thickening, making him appear a blur of darkness and muscle.

"They hold too much power over him," the shaman said softly, the sadness heavy in his voice. "Cannon, it may be time."

Time?

"Time for what?" Scared, I stepped forward, towards Caleb. "What do you mean it may be time?" Looking between them, I took another step. "*Answer* me."

Caleb's laughter caused me to spin around and almost fall backwards, as I realized how close he was to me.

His eyes glowed with a power I would never comprehend. Dark lavender, they shone with malice. There was a wildness to him, something dangerous and entirely unpredictable.

"Willow, get away from him," Cannon warned me, his voice tight with control.

Fear glued me to the spot, and something else. Something deeper. Images flashed through my mind, again and again, seeing his family killed, seeing their corpses, hearing his howl of pain. Witnessing his revenge as if I were there.

The need to stay by his side was almost crippling. I knew he needed someone to stay with him. *Believe* in him. He needed someone to let him know he wasn't alone. He needed me to stay.

I hoped I was enough.

Stepping forward, into his space, facing him as he stared down at me with the eyes of a stranger, I reached up, my hands gripping onto his shoulders, and I jerked him roughly down to my height. Before he could react, I surged upwards on my toes, and I kissed him full on the mouth.

I wasn't sure when it happened, but somewhere in all the crazy, I'd stopped seeing him as the man who'd pulled me into this world of shifters and danger. Somewhere between then and now, I'd fallen for him. Completely, and that maybe scared me more than anything else.

But it still wouldn't make me leave him.

His lips remained unmoving under mine, probably as stunned as I was at my foolishness, but I no longer cared. Pressing harder, I willed him to respond, to break through whatever walls were holding him back. Just when I thought he wouldn't, I felt his resistance crumble.

Caleb's arms swept around me, pulling me into him with a force that took my breath away. His grip was firm and possessive, and the air between us was charged with something electric. His fingers dug into my hair, tilting my head exactly where he wanted it, as his lips pressed against mine, demanding. *Fierce.* There was nothing hesitant or uncertain now.

His tongue swept into my mouth, igniting a fire deep in my core as I melted against him. This wasn't just a kiss; it was a battle of wills. My hands tangled in his hair, pulling him down closer, if that was even possible. His body was hot, solid, and I could feel the power of him in the way that he held me, like he was restraining himself from holding me too tight.

I didn't want him to hold back. I wanted all of him. The good, the bad, the chaotic, and everything in between.

I think he sensed my need, because the kiss deepened and grew hungrier, causing me to moan against his mouth as my body naturally arched into his. I was on fire, the world around us—the mountain, the cold, the others, the tension—disappeared as I clung to him. There was only Caleb, his mouth on mine, his hands holding me tighter, his breath mingling with mine.

Time seemed to stretch, every second filled with the intensity of the moment, of him.

Abruptly, Caleb pulled back, his breath coming out in rough, uneven bursts. His forehead rested briefly against mine. His eyes, dark once more, searched mine, like he was trying to figure out what just happened.

We stayed like that, our breathing heavy between us as we searched each other's eyes for some understanding, wondering if he also felt that something fundamental had shifted between us. Something deeper than words or actions could describe.

This was way more than lust or attraction. This was about *us*, and I had no idea what that even meant now.

"Glad to see you remembered you weren't alone." Cannon's dry voice made me jerk back. Too late, I saw Caleb's look become guarded.

I took a step back as I saw his arms drop, his hands at his side forming into fists. The cool mountain air bit at my skin as I saw his look of confusion morph into one of distrust.

"Caleb?" My voice sounded wary and hesitant, and I wished I sounded stronger. "Whatever you're thinking, you're wrong," I warned him, watching him take another step back.

"What's happening?" Royce asked cautiously.

"You tricked me?" Caleb's voice was low, but his tone held a note of accusation that hurt more than he knew.

"No!"

My heart was pounding, my body tense, as I saw him look between Cannon and me and come to a wild conclusion.

"They're using you?" he said with an understanding that

was devastating, as I knew he believed it. "To get to me, they're using you."

"You're really going to regret saying that," I warned him, stepping closer, hating that he stepped back. I'd had him, I knew I had, and now I had lost him again. Lost him inside his own head, too far gone to listen to me. "I'm standing right here, Caleb, *for* you. I'm fighting beside you, willing you to come back to us."

"There is no us."

Motherfucker. He did not *get to say that to me.* Not after that kiss. No way.

"You should stop talking, Caleb," Cannon said abruptly, stopping me from what I had been about to say. "You'll thank me if you come back from this."

"When did they get to you?" Caleb asked me, his eyes hard and cold. "After I left Blackridge Peak or before I even met you?"

"Get to me? No one *got* to me, you idiot." I moved towards him, anger making me reckless. "I kissed you because I've fallen for you! Because I *care* about you, you complete asshole."

"Or they want you to make me believe that!"

"Or your fucking demons want you to think that so you can go batshit crazy!"

In the blink of an eye, he changed. He went from Caleb the man to Caleb the wolf, causing me to stumble back in shock.

With a low warning growl, he lowered his head, his snarl vicious, and out of the corner of my eye, I saw a bigger black wolf circle the fire.

Holy shit, this was bad.

Strong hands caught me and pulled me backwards, half lifting me off the ground.

"Stay close," Royce warned, his attention on the two alphas.

"He can't attack him," I whispered fearfully. "We'll never get him back."

"Think that boat sailed, girlie," Doc spoke from behind me.

No. I refused to let it. "Caleb!" I saw the wolf's head snap in my direction before returning to fix on Cannon. "Caleb, don't fight him!" I pleaded, ignoring the hushed warnings of Royce and Doc. "Go. Go now!"

Caleb's head lifted slightly, and I could almost feel his indecision.

Stepping away from the men behind me, I inched forward. "Please, Caleb. Go. Don't do this."

The wolf straightened, his attention shifting between me and the alpha in front of him.

"*Go, Caleb!*" The voice didn't sound like my own as I screamed the desperate plea. Caleb jumped backward. I felt the attention of them all on me as I screamed across the clearing. "Just go!"

He turned and ran, and I felt my racing heart, pounding in my ears, finally slow down. Cannon changed form, and I averted my eyes as the broad alpha stood naked in the snow.

"What was that?" Doc asked me, coming to stand beside me as Royce handed his alpha a pair of sweatpants.

"Luna," the shaman spoke from behind me. "The power of the Goddess was in your voice, child."

"The power of desperation was in my voice, sir." I hung my head tiredly. "That's all it was."

"Now what?" Royce asked gruffly.

"We leave," Cannon said to the shaman, who nodded.

"Leave him to his madness?" Doc asked skeptically.

"He isn't mad," I protested, but I wasn't even convincing myself.

"Pack up, child," the shaman said quietly. "We're leaving now."

My feet refused to move. One by one, I felt them turn their attention to me.

"Willow?" Doc spoke, his voice low and gentle. "You can't save him."

Yes, you can.

My gaze flicked to the shaman before returning to look at the spot in the trees where Caleb had vanished. "Yes, I can." My voice was strong and steady. "I've got to."

It didn't matter what Doc argued or Royce added reasonably, I wasn't leaving this mountain. Not without Caleb. Cannon said nothing, just went into the cabin, and when the others realized he had unpacked all the food Doc had brought into the kitchen cupboards and fridge, the others said nothing.

"Left a phone on the counter," Cannon told me, his voice gruff, his face unreadable. "You have one week. There's enough food to get you by. After a week, if he's not back and willing to listen, I will remove you myself."

"He'll come back."

I could see not one of them believed me. Turning my attention to the shaman, I didn't know what to say.

"You said I sounded like Luna. Why would I sound like a Goddess?"

The old man had his head tilted to the side as he considered the question. "You are a mystery to me, child. You see things you should not, you speak with a power you do not hold. I do not have an answer."

"Well, that's comforting," I grumbled.

All too soon, they were gone, leaving me in a cabin, in a place where only the dead had walked for ten years.

I'd made this decision. I knew it was the right one. I knew he would come back to me when he knew they were gone.

I knew it.

I would wait for him. Even if it meant standing on this godforsaken mountain, standing *with* him, surrounded by his demons, and together, we would wait for the storm to pass.

THIRTY

Caleb

I felt them leave. I was angry at myself.

I had run.

Like a coward.

Like a lowly cur who was too chickenshit to fight.

I disgusted myself.

It had been a few days since I left, but she was in the cabin. The lights were low, but she was still awake. I could hear her moving around. She'd left my jeans on the porch, wrapped in a blanket, I assumed so they wouldn't get wet from the snow that was falling.

She had stayed.

Another trick?

I remembered her telling me that she cared. That she'd fallen for me. It's how I knew it was a trick. Humans weren't allowed in my world.

She wasn't allowed in my world. Her and me? A shifter and a human? It would never happen. My laws forbade it. Why hadn't I seen that sooner? Had I been gone so long that I forgot simple pack reality?

Had she been so good at seduction that I forgot who I was?

I thought she was pure. Innocent. She was probably a cheap whore they found somewhere.

My wolf growled in warning, hating the way I'd spoken about her, and I hung my head, shame coursing through me. I knew that wasn't true. Willow *was* innocent; she was everything I was not.

I heard the door creak open, and turning my head, I saw her standing in the doorway, a blanket wrapped around her.

"Hey."

I walked forward as my wolf. I watched her as she took a step back into the cabin.

"I have soup on the stove," she told me. "I'll get you a bowl." As she turned away, I knew that was her way of letting me change form.

Pulling on the jeans, I stepped onto the porch, but even a Will as strong as mine couldn't make me walk inside that cabin.

She must have anticipated my reluctance, because she returned with a tray and two bowls of soup. We didn't speak as we ate a simple meal, Willow cocooned in her blanket, avoiding looking at my bare feet on the wooden porch.

"You scared me the other day." Placing her bowl on the tray, Willow looked at me. "Do you really think I'm here to manipulate you?"

"I don't know why else you would be here."

Her eyes flashed with pain, but she turned away quickly. "I'm truly sorry you think that, Caleb."

"When are they coming back?" I placed my own bowl on the tray. The soup had been nice, warm.

"A week." She refused to look at me. "They're not coming back for you," she added. "They're coming for me." She looked back at me. "But that will only fuel your conspiracy theory, right?"

"You're feeling feisty."

"Am I?" Her eyes narrowed in anger. "I told you that I care about you! I kissed you, letting you in, letting you feel *everything* I feel for you, and you accused me of being a...a *spy*."

"It doesn't make sense."

"That I'm a *spy*? No shit!" She was angry, her cheeks flushed with temper. Seeing I wasn't to be moved, she let out a loud sigh. "Fine. What doesn't make sense?" Her eyes were hard, her face a mask of hurt. "That I could love you?"

Love?

Standing, I shook my head, enough was enough. "You don't love me," I told her angrily. "Goddess, you have no shame at all, do you?"

"How dare you." Willow was seething. Standing quickly, she tightened her hold on the blanket. "You know what, fuck you, Caleb." Storming inside, she slammed the door shut behind her.

Fuck me? *Fuck me?* Furious, I stormed into the cabin. "You tell me that and think I'll just believe you?"

Throwing her hands in the air, she shouted at me in exasperation. "Why would I lie?" Her hands fell to her hips. "Because I'm a spy?" Her tone was mocking, her face twisted into a grimace of hurt and disgust.

Shaking my head, I turned away. "You should go." I heard

her fall still behind me. "You don't need to stay any longer. Go now. I'll take you down myself."

"To make sure I leave, right?"

"Willow..."

"No. You don't get to *Willow* me." She glared at me, anger simmering just below boiling. "You spent ten years hiding from this mountain, and now you think I'm going to leave you and your whispering shadows on it? Are you crazy?" She half laughed. "Yes, you *are* crazy. That's what they've been trying to tell me."

My anger was too close to the surface. I could feel my control slipping, the darkness that she so openly mocked wrapping around me, offering me their comfort.

She must have sensed the change. I saw her face become wary, and her scent changed to one of fear. "Caleb?"

"You need to *go*." My head was down, and I felt them pulling at me, urging me to lose control. Urging me to lash out at her, make her feel how betrayed I felt when she lied to me.

How could she love me? I was a murderer. She didn't love me. They made her say that. To manipulate me. To force *me* to leave.

"Caleb, what's happening? You're scaring me, your eyes are purple again..." She reached out to me, her voice calm but shaking slightly. "You're not yourself, Caleb...this isn't you."

"Get *out*."

She didn't need to be told twice. With one fearful look, she ran past me, out into the snow. Out into the black merciless night.

Panting, I tried to wrestle for control. Looking around, I saw the familiar cabin of Nell's. I shouldn't be in here.

She made me come in here when she knew I didn't want to. *That bitch.*

With a snarl, I ran after her.

I reached her easily. Grabbing her, I pulled her towards me with a growl that sounded loud in the quiet of the night. My strength easily overpowered hers, and I saw her fear as I looked down at her.

"Caleb, you don't want to hurt me, I know you don't," she whispered quickly. "Let me go."

I felt them pulling, tugging me under, whispers getting louder in the night.

Screams sounded all around me.

Screams of my pack as they were killed in their beds because of a *traitor*.

I remembered the fear. Knowing I would never reach them in time. That I would never stop the massacre of that night.

Knowing that I was responsible for the slaughter that followed.

I slashed out at the memories. Purging them from my mind so I never had to see it again.

Willow gasped, her sudden sharp inhale catching my attention.

Looking down, I saw the blood. Deep scratches torn through her clothes, across her skin.

My hands were claws.

Claws painted in blood.

Her blood.

The whispered screams turned to taunting laughter. Filling my head. Echoing all around me. Twisting and turning, I tried to clear my head of the sound.

"Caleb?"

The laughter stopped abruptly as the fog lifted from my mind, as I stared in horror at her as she bled in my arms.

"No...*No! Willow!*"

Her legs buckled and I followed her down to the ground, my hand pressing against the wounds. "Willow, no, I didn't—" My voice cracked as the magnitude of what I'd done overwhelmed me. "Willow, I didn't mean..."

Her hand cupped the side of my face, her eyes full of pain, but she touched me so softly. "You didn't do this," she whispered, her voice faint. "This wasn't you, Caleb. I know that. I don't blame you."

I felt nothing but sudden clarity. My mind felt clear for the first time in what felt like years.

But it was too late.

I'd hurt her. *I* was the one who made her bleed.

Tilting my head back, I screamed into the night. "*Goddess!* Help me!"

The mountain was still, broken only by Willow's ragged breathing. Bending down, I kissed her forehead. "I'm going to fix this."

"It's okay, you're going to be okay." She smiled up at me as I cradled her in my arms. "I can see you." Her voice was little more than a whisper. "Your eyes are clear of the shadows. Don't let them come for you." Her voice was so faint. "I would have loved you. If we had more time. I'm sorry."

Her eyes closed and I felt her life spilling out over my hands, not as fast as before.

"No."

Looking towards the sky, I saw the sliver of the silver moon as it appeared slowly from behind the cloud cover.

"*No.*" Getting to my feet, I lifted her in my arms as I headed to the cabin. "No, Luna, you don't get to take her too."

Laying her down on the bed, I stepped back. Her chest barely moved as I made my decision. Biting into my wrist, I stepped forward. I heard the creak of a floorboard behind me.

With my wrist over her mouth, I turned and faced the door to see who dared enter here.

"*Stop.*"

Acknowledgments

As I wrap up this second installment of Willow and Caleb's journey, I am incredibly grateful for the support of everyone who has helped to make this story a reality. I love writing, but the support of my community is what makes it almost...magical.

To my beloved Mr. M: your love, support, and encouragement give me strength, particularly on challenging days.

To my editor: Your insights, feedback, and sharp eyes have elevated this story to something I'm proud of. Thank you for your honesty and patience and for helping me bring this world to life.

I'm so grateful for my family and friends, who always understand when I disappear into my writing, who cheer me on, and who remind me to take care of myself. I'm so grateful for your love and support; it means the world to me.

For the creators, dreamers, and storytellers who have inspired me: Thank you for showing me the way and proving that stories, particularly those filled with love, danger, and magic, can touch hearts and change lives.

To every reader who has held this book, thank you for being a part of this world, for turning the pages, and for coming along on this journey with me. I hope you enjoyed reading this second book as much as I enjoyed writing it.

With love and hugs,
    Eve 🤍

About the Author

Eve L. Mitchell is a USA Today Bestselling author of Contemporary Romance, New Adult Romance, and also enjoys writing Paranormal Romance. If you're a fan of morally grey alpha-holes, chances are Eve has your next book boyfriend waiting to be claimed.

As an avid reader since childhood, Eve still considers herself a reader first. She believes there's nothing quite like the thrill of getting a new book, whether on her e-reader or in her hands. The thought of sharing that excitement with fellow readers fills her with wonder. Writing under a pen name helps keep her "Secret Agent" status intact.

Eve resides in the North East of Scotland with her three coffee machines and her significant other, Mr. M. When she's not writing, she enjoys NFL football, playing music loudly, and having long conversations with the voices in her head that often turn into the stories she creates.

THE BLACKRIDGE PEAK SERIES

The Blackridge Peak Series is a wolf shifter series about rival packs, hidden secrets, a little bit of magic, and a girl who's trying to find her way amongst a pack that doesn't want her. Kezia is an outsider, and when given the chance she leaves the pack that never truly accepted her. But trouble follows Kezia and she soon learns that only an alpha can protect her.
An alpha who may be her mate.
The series includes **Wolf's Gambit, Wolf's Betrayal, and Wolf's Endgame.**

THE WATCHER SERIES

The Watcher Series is a paranormal romance trilogy that will take you on a journey where you will get lost in a world that will hold you in its depths. With a blend of steam, humour and angst, be ready to buckle up for the ride.

With demons, devils and one sassy, clueless witch, what more could you ask for? Join Star as she gets a crash course in what not to do when you get involved with the Watchers.

An enemies-to-lovers story that has all the emotions packed between the pages as the heroine deals with love, betrayal, loss and so much more.

This series is a trilogy and must be read in order. If you love cliffhangers, this series is for you. If you hate cliffhangers, don't worry, the next book's already written.

The series includes **A Glow of Stars & Dust**, **A Flame of Stars & Midnight** and **A Blaze of Stars & Dawn**.

GET THE SERIES

THE AKRHYN SERIES

Creatures of evil roam the shadows - the Drakhyn. They may look like humans, but their taloned hands and razor-sharp teeth serve one purpose only; killing.

A Sentinel's purpose is to patrol and protect. They are highly trained soldiers with superior skills and abilities. Whether they be Vampyres, Lycan, Castors or gifted Akrhyn, their purpose is the same; hunt the Drakhyn and rid the world of their evil presence.

This fantasy trilogy covers tropes of chosen one, fated mates, good vs evil.

The series includes **Into Darkness**, **Lost in Darkness** and **From the Darkness**.

THE BOULDER SERIES

The Boulder Series is an interconnected series that explores the relationships between friends, family, and the family you choose...with some love, heat, and underground fighting along the way!

The series covers tropes of forbidden romance (ex-boyfriend's older brother), enemies-to-lovers, friends to lovers, opposites attract and second-chance love.

The Boulder Series will take you on a rollercoaster of emotions. You will laugh, scream, feel the characters' excitement, and it's possible you may throw your e-reader (just make sure it lands somewhere soft).

A complete four-book series that has all the feels. What's stopping you from jumping into Boulder?

The series includes **Unbroken Devotion**, **Dark Heart**, **Unbroken Bonds** and **Dark Soul**.

GET THE SERIES
WWW.EVELMITCHELL.COM

THE DENVER SERIES

The Denver Series is a three-book mafia romance shared world series. Each book is a standalone, featuring cameos from the other books. Although it is recommended that the books be read in order, it is not necessary to do so.

The series covers tropes of opposites attract, enemies-to-lovers, and forbidden romance (stepcousins).

The Denver Series is a steamy contemporary romance series that dabbles in the mafia romance genre, with book one hinting at it and the other two exploring the darker side of this much-loved genre.

A complete three-book series where sassy heroines meet and fall for their dark alphahole heroes.

The series includes **Her Greatest Mistake**, **Beautifully Broken** and **Keeping Harmony**.

GET THE SERIES

THE RUTHLESS DEVILS SERIES

A college sports romance series following twin brothers and their cousin. Three football stars who have it all: looks, money, talent and the world at their feet. No one messes with the Devils. Each book deals with a different Devil and their love interest who will either make them or break them.

The series covers tropes of enemies-to-lovers, second-chance romance and forced proximity.

This is interconnected three-book series with an underlying story arc that carries through from book one to book three, and therefore the series must be read in order. The series deals with some elements that sensitive readers may find triggering.

This series includes **Ruthless Heart**, **Ruthless Desire** and **Ruthless Charm**.

GET THE SERIES
WWW.EVELMITCHELL.COM

The Torn & Broken duet is a duet with a twist. You can read either book as a standalone. *Torn by Grace* was written first and one of the female side characters in that book is the main character in *Broken by Faith*, however, you don't need to know what happened in *Torn by Grace* to enjoy *Broken by Faith*. There is a little bit of crossover, but no spoilers.

Torn by Grace is a second chance, enemies-to-lovers, brothers-best-friend romance.
Broken by Faith is an enemies-to-lovers, forced proximity, fake relationship romance.
The series includes **Torn by Grace and Broken by Faith.**

THE ORDER OF THE RAVENS SERIES
written as Ava Speirs

The Order of the Ravens Series is a traditional epic fantasy series where the focus is on action and adventure.

Bastian dal'Leif is a Knight of the Order, an Order that has fallen into distrust. The Order of the Conclave which were once seen as warriors of the Gods and a beacon of hope, are now cast in shadow.

Bastian and his men remain true to their Order but are forced to become mercenaries, selling their swords for coin.

In the halls of his Order, Bastian is entrusted with a mission. A mission he is reluctant to accept.

The mission is so dangerous and deadly only a fool would take it...and only a coward would reject it.

The series includes **Knight of Sword & Shadow, Knight of Sacrifice & Shade, Knight of Dagger & Darkness, and Knight of Trials and Twilight.**

GET THE SERIES

www.ingramcontent.com/pod-product-compliance
Lightning Source LLC
Chambersburg PA
CBHW030553170726
48283CB00002B/299